THE CURSE
OF MONTEZUMA

THE CURSE
OF MONTEZUMA

A Western Trio

LES SAVAGE, JR.

SAGEBRUSH
Large Print Westerns

First published in Great Britain by ISIS Publishing Ltd
.First published in the United States by Five Star

Published in Large Print 2009 by ISIS Publishing Ltd.,
7 Centremead, Osney Mead, Oxford OX2 0ES
by arrangement with
Golden West Literary Agency

British Library Cataloguing in Publication Data
Savage, Les.
   The curse of Montezuma
   1. Western stories, American.
   2. Large type books.
   I. Title II. Savage, Les. Comanche legend.
   III. Savage, Les. Legend of Yellow Hole.
   813.5'4–dc22

ISBN 978–0–7531–8261–1 (hb)

Printed and bound in Great Britain by
T. J. International Ltd., Padstow, Cornwall

TABLE OF CONTENTS

Comanche Legend 3

The Legend of Yallow Hole 73

The Curse of Montezuma 175

COMANCHE LEGEND

"Comanche Legend" was Les Savage, Jr.'s title for this short novel when it was submitted to Fiction House. It was purchased on June 18, 1946 and the author was paid $370. The title was changed to "Brand of the Mustang-Queen" prior to publication in *Lariat Story Magazine* (1/47).

CHAPTER
ONE

Caddo Adair found the horse trap about three in the afternoon. Caddo pulled his sorrel into the shade of the yellow autumn aspen and stepped off, a square, well-built man in his faded Levi's and flannel shirt. He was about to hunker down when the pair of riders appeared at the open end of the draw. He straightened out his legs and allowed his hand to drop on the butt of his big Spiller & Burr.

Tripp Garretson walked his black purposefully on up the coulée till he was directly opposite Caddo, in the sand below, and stopped it. His seat in the saddle contained as much swagger as his walk. His long body held the same lean bitterness as his face, and his eyes looked feline, somehow, the whites of them tinged with yellow behind thick blue lids. There was a studied casualness to the way his wooden-handled Colt hung against his negligible hips.

"Hunting for Irish Nyles, Caddo?"

"Your business?" said Caddo.

Dana Border had come up with Garretson. He was a man more Caddo's age, about thirty. He wore an ancient horse-thief hat with the brim pinned up in front to keep it from flopping in his eyes. He had been almost frozen to death up in the Big Horns in his youth and it had left him with an obsession about cold. He huddled deeper into the immense, hairy buffalo coat as he spoke.

"Man named Pegoes Oporto come up from Brazil to buy the Hart Farms, I hear. Something about Comanche, too. I haven't been in the territory long, Caddo. What's the straight dope on that danged horse?"

Caddo studied them narrowly. "You know."

"Only in a vague sort of way," said Dana Border. "You hear all kinds of stories on something like that. What's the real one?"

"Comanche was Captain Keogh's horse," said Caddo. "A purebred Arabian from the Huntington stud farms in England. When Custer was wiped out by the Sioux, Comanche was the only horse out of the Seventh Cavalry left standing on Custer Hill. It was so badly wounded the Indians didn't bother running it off. When the Army found the massacre, they took Comanche back to Fort Lincoln and kept him in a sling a year till he was healed. He broke loose somehow. Next heard of he'd been sighted between the Little Horn and the Rosebud. They figure he was hunting Keogh. Since that time a lot of attempts have been made to capture him, unsuccessfully. He's become a killer, and about the cleverest beast this side of hell. Two horse-runners have already been trampled to death trying to snare him. He's turned into sort of a legend."

4

"A valuable legend, I'd say," said Garretson. "I hear he's servicing Tommy Hart's Arabians."

"Hart tried for a long time to capture Comanche," said Caddo. "He knew what a valuable animal any colt out of that horse would be. When he couldn't get Comanche, he did the next best thing. Every year in season he turns a selected group of mares into a box end of Little Horn Cañon. Comanche's come to know they'll be there. It's as regular and sure as if Hart had Comanche standing at stud in his own barns."

Tripp took out the makings and began deliberately rolling himself a smoke. "This Oporto. I understand he won't close the deal to buy Hart Farms till Comanche is caught and brought in. Offered five thousand to the man who could do it. I should think you'd try for that kind of money, Caddo."

There was a certain bitter resignation in Caddo Adair's voice. "Think I haven't?"

Tripp drew his lips in against his teeth and thrust the tip of his tongue between them to lick his cigarette paper. "Being foreman of the Hart Farms doesn't exactly give you much time for wild horse chasing, does it?" He took the Bull Durham tag between his teeth to pull the bag shut again, stuffing it back in his pocket. "This Irish Nyles. Think maybe he could snare Comanche?"

"I never saw him myself," said Caddo. "He's sort of a wild kid. About as hard to get hold of as Comanche. It's the consensus around Sheridan that, if anybody can trap Comanche, it's him. He's about the last bet."

"I know him a mite," said Garretson, taking a deep drag on the cigarette. "He's wild all right. Ran away from home. Lived with the Indians. Like an animal. You can hardly get near him. I don't think you want to get near him, Caddo. I don't think you want to find him."

A furrow had been growing beneath Caddo's eyes. "What are you driving at, Tripp?"

Garretson stared enigmatically at Caddo through the twin streamers of smoke he emitted from pinched, fluttering nostrils. "You always were the best horse handler in Wyoming Territory, Caddo. Let's hope you keep on being the best, for a long time to come."

Caddo's words came out on an angry, gusty breath: "You always liked to sit back and smell the stew before you tasted it, didn't you?"

"All right." Tripp Garretson took another drag. "I'll come to the point. You will keep on being the best horse handler in the Territories if you see to it that you don't find Irish Nyles."

"What's Irish Nyles got to do with it?"

"That ain't important. Why don't you get on your sorrel and trail back to the Hart Farms and forget you ever found this horse trap?"

Caddo's eyes were squinted almost shut now. "Somebody doesn't want Comanche caught?" Garretson took another pull on the smoke without answering. Dana Border's buckskin shifted nervously. Caddo bent forward slightly. "I might have known it wasn't anything honest brought you here. Who you working for, Tripp?"

"You know I was always the personification of independence," said Garretson. He waited a moment, studying his cigarette. Finally, with the fag, he indicated Caddo's sorrel. "If you're stepping on, we'll ride back a piece with you."

"I'm not stepping on," said Caddo.

Garretson closed his thumb and forefinger on the tip of his cigarette in a quick pinch, dropped the butt to the ground. Caddo saw the man's heel touch the black, but could not move out of the way soon enough. He found himself pinned against his own sorrel by Garretson's horse sidling into him. The yellowish color of Garretson's eyes seemed to have deepened as he bent down from the saddle to grab Caddo's shirt front in his fist, pulling Caddo up onto his toes.

"I'm not a man to make threats, Adair. I don't have to. You're just not going to find Irish Nyles, that's all, understand? You're just not going to find . . ."

It ended in a shout as Garretson grabbed wildly for his saddle horn, trying to keep from going off his horse. But Caddo had grabbed his boot and heaved upward hard, thrusting his shoulder against the black at the same time. Garretson went off the horse as it was thrown off balance, forced to take a step aside. Dana Border had torn his buffalo coat away from the gun stuck nakedly through the center of his belt, and had it pulled halfway clear before he stopped, staring blankly at Caddo.

"Go ahead," said Caddo, free of the horse now and holding his own gun in his hand. "If you want to."

A dusky grouse was sitting on a branch up in higher timber, filling his neck pouches with air till they looked

7

ready to burst, and then pumping his head up and down to deflate them and send his hollow *hoot* through the draw. It was a mournful sound to Caddo Adair, hunkered in the dusk filling the aspens. Garretson and Dana Border had left hours ago, Tripp so enraged he could not speak as he remounted his black. Caddo had waited here all afternoon, and the evening chill was beginning to enter his bones.

At first, it was not definable, over the lament of the grouse. Then the ground began to tremble and Caddo's head raised. They came running up from the lower end of the draw, half a dozen dim shaggy beasts in the gloom, lather gleaming faintly across their chests and shoulders, eyes momentarily flashing brightly. As they drew nearer in their dead run, Caddo could make out the big blue roan in the lead already growing his winter coat. The animal spotted an opening by the chokecherry and wheeled toward it. His eye caught the flutter of a handkerchief where it was tied to the brush, and it turned him back. He tried again in another direction at the next open patch, turning up the other slope, but a cardboard carton turned him back from there. In this stage of excitement, the slightest thing would do to spook these wild mustangs. Caddo was standing tensely now, unable to deny the exhilaration that was in him. Then he saw the rider behind them.

He was no more than a lean supple rail of a kid with shoulders already too big for his narrow hips, forking a bare buckskin bronco in a wild swaying Indian seat with no more than a dirty hemp war bridle on the animal's jaw for control. His matted thatch of yellow hair gleamed vagrantly in the twilight. The boy came in a crazy shouting dead run that only wild youth would inspire.

It usually took two men to drive a wild bunch into a wing trap that way, but the boy was right on their tail now, and, as they saw the wings and tried to wheel out to the right, he quartered in on them from that angle in a wild wheeling turn, forcing them headlong down the narrowing funnel formed by the cedar-post wings. The blue roan went straight into the pen, running so fast he was unable to turn in time to keep from smashing into the back fence. The whole pen shuddered, and the rest of the horses jammed in on him, whinnying and kicking and pulling up so much dust Caddo couldn't see anything for a moment. When it had settled, the boy had the gate thrown across the opening of the trap, and was already back on his buckskin.

Caddo stepped from the aspens. "Irish?"

The boy wheeled his buckskin, gaping at the man, the look of a startled animal twisting his gaunt face. Then, in one frightened movement, he wheeled the buckskin and thumped moccasined heels into its scarred flanks. The animal grunted and burst into a run back down the draw.

With a curse, Caddo whirled and leaped for his sorrel, both feet off the ground before he reached the animal, his left toe going into the stirrup and his right leg lifted to slap across the saddle. The animal was already wheeling, and the motion forced a centrifugal force that threw Caddo into the saddle. He tore the reins off the horn and touched the sorrel's flanks with his rowels. The horse leaped into its gallop after that buckskin.

"Irish," shouted Caddo, "come back here! I'm not going to hurt you! I just want to talk. Oh, damn you, I've been hunting a week for this and you're not getting away now!"

He saw his sorrel could never catch the buckskin. The ridges on either side of the draw narrowed and lowered until they swept into flats beyond. Clear Creek crossed the flats 100 yards past the end of the ridges, too deep to ford at that point, and this would force the boy to turn either right or left. Caddo took the fifty-fifty gamble and wheeled his sorrel up onto the right slope, forcing the animal to the crest. The sorrel was heaving by the time they had reached the top, but Caddo had not seen the boy look back. He dropped down the opposite slope and was almost at the bottom when the buckskin came clattering around the end of the ridge on rough shale and broke through a cherry thicket into the open. It put Caddo in the position of breaking from timber onto the boy's flank, and for those few moments, while the buckskin was crossing in front of him, he had his chance. He already had his dally rope out with a loop built and was ready when the buckskin crossed his range. He did not let the boy see him whirling. It was a hooley-ann, coming in one sweeping throw down from his hip, his hand turning over in the last moment to send the small loop out in a horizontal plane that dropped onto the boy from just above. Nyles saw it and tried to slide out from under, but the loop caught his upthrust arm and slid down.

Caddo shoved his reins against the sorrel's neck and the animal whirled away and the rope jerked taut. The buckskin was suddenly bare, running off into the cherry bushes, and Caddo was out of the saddle before Nyles had struck the ground. The sorrel reared back, stiff-legged, to keep the rope taut, maneuvering from side to side to keep Nyles tightly in that noose no matter how much the boy struggled. Caddo reached him and touched the rope. The sorrel gave him slack enough to throw another loop around the boy's feet, drawing it up tightly. Then he stood there, holding the hemp and staring down at the wild animal he had caught.

Irish Nyles must have stood six feet in the tattered Ute moccasins he wore, with a frame that indicated magnificent possibilities if he had weighed fifty pounds more. He was like a hunted lobo, with all the weight run off him till the gaunt refinement of his body held a driven, almost painful look. His dirty, torn Levi's were belted by a rope about a middle so spare Caddo could have spanned it with two hands. He wore a greasy buckskin vest over his bare, scarred torso, and his dirty, cockle-burred yellow hair hung down his skinny, corded neck like a horse's mane. His eyes were a startling deep blue, and filled with the bitter intensity of animal rage as he writhed from side to side, fighting the rope, his thin, bloodless lips twisted, his nostrils fluttering.

Caddo gave another hard tug to the rope. "I heard you was a wild one," he said, "but I never bargained for anything like this. Take it easy now, sonny. I got you hog-tied for fair and you might as well listen to what I say. I'm not going to barbecue you. I got a job you might be interested in."

Nyles's struggles abated, and his voice came out harsh on his heavy breathing. "Job?"

"Ever hear of Comanche?"

The boy had quit fighting completely now, and he stared sullenly up at Caddo. "I don't want the job."

"Afraid maybe you can't do it," said Caddo, wiping dust off his face with a grimace. "I heard there wasn't a wild one you couldn't catch."

"Not Comanche." The boy made an abortive struggle to get free, but Caddo jerked him up short. Nyles lay quiescently for a moment, his breathing subsiding. "That's the Crow Reservation," he said finally.

"Tommy Hart has a territorial franchise on the section," Caddo told him. "He had to get that so he could pen his mares there for Comanche in season. We won't have any trouble with the government."

The boy shook his yellow head angrily. "No."

Caddo squatted down beside him suddenly, those eyes squinting at the boy. "What's the matter, sonny? You afraid of something?"

CHAPTER
TWO

Major Ellis Hart had retired from the service to establish his breeding farms outside of Sheridan, but the wounds received in the Indian wars and a predilection acquired in the Army for certain potables brought about an untimely demise that left the younger Hart in charge of the farms. The idea of the Arabian horse was too new in this raw, wild cattle country for the farms to prosper, until the legend of Comanche began to grow. Now, with that fabulous story known over the world, the Hart Farms had grown with it, becoming the largest and most famous horse farms in the Northwest.

Caddo Adair dropped down the wagon road from Crazy Dog Hills toward the large hip-roofed barns and solid pack-pole corrals. Bob Ligget was gaiting a gelding in the first pen they reached, and he halted the horse abruptly to stare at the wild figure riding beside Caddo. Caddo passed through the corrals that flanked the road and rounded the last barn to cross the open meadow toward the big white house where it sat on a gentle southern slope. A woman's laugh floated out to him from behind the building, and Caddo couldn't help drawing up a little in his saddle. It always did that to him, even though he fought it.

A handler had brought a white mare and a fuzzy, long-legged, knock-kneed little colt up here for their inspection. The woman was fondling the colt as Caddo rounded the corner. She had a tall, statuesque figure and a finely chiseled profile, black hair worn in a long bob that caught the early morning sun in glistening ripples. The heavy leather skirt of her riding habit flapped against bare legs as she turned toward them. Her first sight of Irish Nyles drew a strange sort of surprise into her face, arching piquant black brows above her big, dark eyes.

"Finally got him to come," said Caddo, dismounting stiffly. "Irish, this is Mora Banner. She runs the Red Banner outfit. Maybe you've seen some of their cattle over Clear Creek way."

"Irish Nyles." She said it softly, something vaguely predatory in the husky tone, and then she chuckled, and said it again. "Irish Nyles."

"Yes, Mora," said Caddo.

She straightened perceptibly, turning toward him as if with some effort. "Caddo," she said, "I haven't seen you in so long. Where have you been keeping yourself?"

"I've been a week on this boy's trail," said Caddo. "I thought we might have some grub and a little shut-eye before he takes out after Comanche. We've been riding all night from Clear Creek."

Tommy Hart had been obscured by the horses until now. He came around from behind the mare, a tall youth, handsome in a florid way, with rich brown hair

14

worn in long sideburns. He had an arresting figure at first glance, with broad shoulders and long straight legs, the bottoms of his clean-pressed Levi's stuffed into black cavalry boots. It would have taken a second look to mark the thickness of his waist, or the softness of his hands.

"I didn't think you would be able to find him, somehow," he said, speaking to Caddo, but looking up at Irish in a strange, empty way. "Pegoes Oporto will be glad."

"The Brazilian around?" said Caddo.

"He's in Sheridan," said Mora. "Get down, Irish, we'll go in the kitchen for some food."

"Maybe he'd better eat with his hands," offered Hart.

"Don't be a fool, Tommy." Mora laughed, tossing her gleaming head. "Come on, Irish. What's the matter?"

The boy sat his buckskin without moving. His eyes were on Caddo. Mora looked from Irish to Caddo, and for a moment a nebulous, wondering expression crossed her face. When she spoke again, it was softer.

"Caddo will come, too, Irish."

They had pot roast and pan bread and black coffee left over from breakfast, and then went down to the bunkhouse. Caddo had a hard time getting Irish to enter the building and bed down in one of the bunks, but the boy was too weary for much argument. Caddo left him undressing and stepped outside to put his sweaty saddle in the sun to dry. Then, somehow, Mora was there.

"I thought you stayed at the house," he said.

"A strange, wild creature," she murmured, "isn't he?"

"Orphaned," said Caddo. "Lived with the Indians a while. There are horses like that. You can never tame them."

"I never saw one *you* couldn't tame," she said. "Even this one. He wouldn't move without you."

"Interest you?"

"Why not?" she said defiantly.

"You're sort of wild yourself," he told her. "I always thought it would take more of a man than Tommy Hart to tame you."

"You, Caddo?" she said in a soft, tantalizing tone.

He started to answer. Then he saw the mocking look in her eyes, and closed his lips over the words. He drew in a heavy breath. "I guess I got no right, have I? I guess you're a little rich for my blood."

Tommy Hart came around the corner of the bunkhouse and stopped when he saw them. "I'd like to talk with Caddo a minute, Mora."

She shrugged, turning to walk back toward the house. Hart came over to Caddo; jowls were already marking their faint formation on either side of his jaw, and the tautness of facial muscle beneath these was barely visible. He cleared his throat.

"I suppose you're taking right off after you get some sleep?"

"Might as well," said Caddo. "The farms were pretty near on our way into the Crow country. We needed a pack horse and some extra duffel anyway. Ever hear of Tripp Garretson?"

Hart drew in a short breath, clearing his throat again that way. "Name's familiar. Doesn't he ride in the shade?"

"Nobody ever pinned anything on him. He tried to stop me from finding Irish Nyles." Caddo was watching Hart's face when he said this, and he saw something pass through the man's eyes. "What's up, Hart?"

Hart seemed to hesitate. Then he put his hand on Caddo's arm. "I don't know, Caddo. But I . . ." — he hesitated, searching Caddo's face — "I don't think you'd better go out. There's something . . ."

Again it was that hesitation, and he dropped his hand from Caddo's arm, motioning with it as if trying to find words. Caddo pursed his lips. "I was wondering," he said, "to whose interest it would be *not* to have Comanche found."

The snow-capped peaks shone under a hot afternoon sun that drew perspiration from Caddo as he halted in the shallows of the Little Horn River behind Irish Nyles's buck-skin. He motioned toward the low hills on their right, covered with white-domed columns of rank beargrass.

"Yonder's Custer Hill, according to the Indians. When Hart sends us up here with mares, we turn them out at this spot and leave. If we stay within five, ten miles of the place, Comanche won't show up at all."

"That's why we traveled in water the last day," said Irish. "There won't be no scent of us."

"You plan to lure him in with that mare?" said Caddo. "Picket her anywhere and Comanche'll scent man on the rope before he comes within sight of it. I tell you he's uncanny."

"No picketing," the boy told him. "You can see how the Little Horn cañon narrows near the south end between the Wolf Mountains and the Big Horn foothills. There's only shore on one side of the water, and there ain't no tracks in that sand. That means he enters the cañon from the north if he waters here at all. The wind blows through the cañon from that direction, and, if we do our work down here, he won't be able to scent us. We'll stay in the water all the time so as not to leave any smell on the ground."

They chose a tall cottonwood with roots undermined and weakened by the constant flow of water, and, standing their animals in the shallows, it took both of them to pull it over once they had roped it. This blocked the narrow section of waterway. They chopped down several aspens farther south on the shore and dragged them up to lay across the shore with the foliage still on. Then they rode several miles back downstream to picket their saddle horses in a hidden gully. With nothing but their guns and dally ropes and a saddlebag full of grub, they mounted the mare bare-back and rode double back to the cañon. They turned her loose just north of the felled trees. Then they walked through the shallows another two miles to the northern end of the cañon, choosing a place where the water reached the very bottom of the cliff, and climbed this escarpment fifteen or twenty feet to a wide ledge. Irish gathered a handful of larger stones and piled them near at hand, and Caddo drew forth some jerked beef and stale pan bread for their evening meal. Then they settled down to wait.

"You don't think this is the way," said Irish, munching on the pan bread.

Caddo saw how narrowly the boy was watching him, and shrugged. "We tried doing it with pens before."

"Not this kind of pen, I bet. And you had your saddle horses along to cause a big commotion before you even saw Comanche."

"I'll admit we never tried it quite this way," said Caddo. "But how will we nab him on foot? He's as quick as greased . . ."

The sound across the river stopped him, and both of them raised up slightly, straining to see through the gloom. Then, with the remainder of the pan bread in one hand, Nyles scooped up one of the rocks and heaved it outward. It clattered against the cliff on the opposite side, and Caddo heard the snorting sound above the gush of the water, and could make out the mare now, rearing in a startled way and turning back downstream. He felt a growing admiration for this youngster's remarkable talents.

Several more times that night the mare tried to get out of the cañon, and each time they threw rocks across to spook her and turn her back. Caddo dozed in his blankets during the small hours of the morning. It was near dawn when a nudge in his ribs woke him. He did not move. Irish was lying utterly silent on his belly beside Caddo, peering in a tense, expectant way at the river. Then it came. A dim, feral snort. A stretch of

19

thick silence. Another snort. Finally, an answering whinny.

Caddo was lying on his back, unable to see across the water, and all he could do was watch Nyles's face. It told him as much as he needed. The boy had been running his tongue between his lips. Abruptly he stopped, and his mouth opened slightly and his head raised a little more. The expectancy in his face changed to satisfaction. Without looking at Caddo, he moved out and began to climb down the cliff. Caddo rolled from his blankets and followed, holding his coiled rope and gun above his head with one hand as he plunged into the icy water. It was a short swim, but the heavy current swept them far downstream before they reached footing on the other side. Trying to keep from breathing too audibly with the cold water and the violent effort, Caddo crawled out onto the sand. Irish Nyles was already moving down the shore. They had trotted about half a mile when they heard sounds from ahead. Nyles broke into a sprint, shaking out his rope, and Caddo followed suit, catching sight of the dim shapes moving there.

One of the horses whinnied, and made a tentative dash toward them. Caddo had a vague impression of a wild, tousled mane, and flashing eyes, and then the animal reared up and wheeled the other way, heading downstream at a dead run. The second animal followed without as much enthusiasm. Both horses disappeared around the turn, and the men ran after them. It was heavy going in the deep sand with high-heeled boots, and Caddo was already winded. The boy ran like a deer, his moccasins hardly touching the sand, a smooth wild grace to his movements. He was far ahead of Caddo, and disappeared around that turn after the animals. Caddo was almost to the curve himself when he heard Irish shouting.

"He's come up against those trees now and he's turning back! Get ready with your rope, Caddo. If I can't snare him, it's up to you. Here he comes. Get ready with your rope, Caddo . . ."

It was still too dark for Caddo to make anything out clearly as he rounded the turn. He had a sense of the wild beast charging straight down that narrow strip of white sand toward them, and of Irish's wild yell, and the twisting motion of the boy's gaunt body as he made his throw.

There was a momentary interval of flying sand and unreal movement, and then the horse's hollow, grunting sound as it hit the end of that rope. The sand shook beneath Caddo as the animal went down.

"Get in there with your tie-downs!" yelled Irish. "He's crazy and I can't hold him a minute! Get in there, Caddo!"

Caddo was already dashing for the downed animal, but before he could throw a loop on its flailing legs, the horse had managed to wrench enough slack in the rope to scramble erect before Irish could pull it taut again. The loop was around Comanche's neck, and, instead of pulling back or trying to jerk away as most horses would do, the animal wheeled toward Irish Nyles and broke into a run with its head down like a wild steer. Caddo was on the left side and made his throw in a desperate attempt to get the loop across Comanche's shoulder and catch his hoofs, but the animal was traveling too fast, and with a sinking feeling he felt the whole of his rope fall slackly in his hand.

Irish waited till the last moment, then leaped aside, still hanging grimly to the rope. If Comanche had gone on past, the rope would have drawn taut again and thrown him. But the wily animal stiffened both forehoofs and came to a halt that shuddered the earth, wheeling to charge back at the boy.

"Let go the clothesline!" bawled Caddo, running toward Irish. His own rope was stretched out uselessly on the ground. "You can't hold him like that. He'll trample you, boy!"

"I got him!" shouted Irish hoarsely, barely dodging the animal's next charge. "I ain't letting go. Get your rope again. I'll give you time. Hurry up, Caddo!"

Comanche wheeled once more, so that his rump was toward Caddo, and Caddo had watched maybe a thousand horses rear up before this, and knew exactly how the muscles tautened and rippled across their rump as they shifted their weight. Irish was down on one knee, still thrown off balance from that last violent dodge. Caddo saw he could never snake in his own rope in time for the throw. There was only one thing left.

Dropping the end of his dally, Caddo threw himself at Comanche. The horse was halfway in the air, with Irish crouched helplessly beneath its lethal forehoofs, when Caddo's body struck its left shoulder. It knocked Comanche to one side. His front hoofs struck the sand less than a foot from Irish. With a wild whinny, Comanche whirled his rump inward, trying to roll over on them both. Caddo could not get out from beneath in time, and all he could do was catch that matted, tousled mane and throw himself atop the animal, meaning to dive on over the other side as Comanche rolled. But the horse's weight shifted as he felt the man atop him, and, instead of going on into the roll, he caught himself, staggering a little, and then he was standing utterly still beneath Caddo.

Irish had thrown himself aside to escape the roll, and he stood there, staring at Caddo. For that moment, neither of them dared speak. Caddo sat Comanche tensely, hand twined in the mane, waiting for the first violent buck. But the horse did not move. It stood there in the sand, trembling from the violent action, hide wet and glistening, nostrils fluttering. Finally Caddo started speaking, in a low, soothing tone.

"That's a boy. Just take it easy, boy. I think we got him, Irish. That's it, that's it. He must still remember being ridden. Quiet now, Comanche, quiet now, boy. See if you can get close enough to throw a war bridle on him with that rope. Easy now, Comanche . . ."

It was the shot that cut him off. With the sound echoing back and forth between the cliffs, Comanche jerked beneath Caddo in a startled way, and then wheeled wildly, whinnying in fright, and broke past Irish in a gallop. Caddo would have been thrown off the rump but for his grip on the mane, and he threw his weight forward, knees pinched in against the heavily muscled shoulders. There was another shot, and sand made its pale spurt a few feet ahead of the horse. The old warhorse dodged as if it had been a cannon ball falling there, and slammed up against the cliffs. It tore Caddo's leg back and he roared with the pain, unable to keep his seat as he was swept off the horse. He lay there in the sand, stunned, dimly conscious of Comanche's charging on up the cañon toward the open end, and then of Irish Nyles running to him and dropping to one knee.

"You all right, Caddo, you all right?"

Caddo groaned, rolling onto his belly, then rising to hands and knees and shaking his head. "I guess so. Just knocked me off."

"We had him, too," said the boy, tears shining in his eyes. "We had him."

Caddo was looking at the cliffs across the river. "You got your gun?"

Irish's head turned toward him in a quick, comprehensive motion. "I dropped it back there fighting Comanche."

"Get it then," Caddo told him, still looking up there. "You might need it."

CHAPTER
THREE

An early morning haze dimmed the pattern of corrals about the Hart house, and Caddo Adair had come out of the bunkhouse with the last of his breakfast bacon in his hand, when he caught sight of Mora Banner coming in on the Sheridan road. Caddo had personally trained the colt Tommy Hart had given her three years ago, and he took as much pleasure in its high, collected action, coming toward him, as he did in the smooth way she handled the animal. *It would be nice . . .* , he started to think, and then wiped the back of his hand across his mouth in a bitter gesture.

"Heard you were back," said Mora, drawing the five-year-old to an easy halt before him. "Had some trouble up north?"

"We had Comanche," Caddo told her. "Somebody spoiled it for us."

She dismounted, turning toward him. "You actually had the horse?"

"I was on his back," said Caddo. "He was fighting like a Sioux up till then. Memory, or something. I don't know exactly. Anyway, he quit cold the minute I hit his hide. We could have brought him in like a lamb if somebody hadn't started pot-shooting. The gun sounds sent him wild again. I guess that's memory, too. Spilled me off. We tried to find who'd been shooting, but they'd already shucked their kack."

"When you going out again?"

He felt uncomfortable, somehow, under her gaze. "We tried to track Comanche. That wasn't no good. Lost him through the snow in those Big Horns. Ran out of grub and gaunted our own animals. I figure we skeered Comanche up so he won't show for a long time now. We just have to sit around till word comes down he's been sighted again. It's going to be a long process."

He sensed that Mora's attention had not been on him for the last part of his speech, and he turned in the direction her glance had taken. Irish was leading a bay from the barn. Although not yet mature, it already displayed the slightly dished-face and long level croup so typical of its breed.

"Take it easy on that horse, Irish," Caddo told him. "You're not handling a bronc' now."

The boy took a swift breath to say something, then held back the words, shrugging sullenly. Over one arm he had the bitting rig, composed of a padded back band and a crupper attached. Caddo laid the back band over the horse's back and ran the animal's tail through the crupper.

"You've got to be careful no loose hairs are in between the tail and crupper," he told Irish, buckling the surcingle in place. "Their tail's more sensitive than you know. Hurt him once in these early stages and you'll spend a week regaining his confidence. Now put the bridle on him and take him in the corral for fifteen minutes. I want to see you gentler than you were yesterday."

"I don't see why we have to drive him in that sulky," Irish complained, slipping the snaffle bit into the bay's mouth. "We aren't working him for trotting, are we?"

"I told you this ain't one of your bronc's," said Caddo. "It increases a horse's commercial value if it's trained for driving as well as riding. Makes it all 'round gentler and safer."

"It gives him a high, stylish, and fast trot that is desirable in all pleasure saddle horses, too," said Mora.

The mockery in her voice made them both glance at her. Watching her with a puzzled frown, Irish fastened the side straps to their rings on the back band and the bit. Then he climbed in the sulky and clucked his tongue. With the horse walking toward the corrals, Caddo spoke to Mora.

"What's your idea?"

"On the contrary," she said. "What's *your* idea? You sounded like a schoolteacher. I never heard you take the trouble to tell anybody that much about it."

Caddo shrugged, uncomfortable again. "He's just got a talent for horses, that's all. You should have seen the way he handled Comanche. He might as well be put to work while we're waiting around here."

"With you as teacher." She smiled. "You sort of like that boy, don't you?"

He turned partly away. "All right. Why not? Isn't often you find anybody with the feel for horses he's got. Time I passed on a few of my tricks, anyway. What's the word?"

27

"Protégé." She smiled again. "Do I make you nervous?"

He started to turn back, but Bob Ligget came down the corral fence. He was as tall as Caddo, but his great breadth made him appear shorter until they stood together. His legs were set far apart beneath wide hips, and it gave him a quick, square, catty stride that swung his whole body from side to side with each step, only lending, somehow, to his whole impression of potent force.

"Will you help Irish?" Caddo asked him.

"No," said Ligget.

The flat, emotionless tone of it drew Caddo up sharply. He stood there a moment, staring at Ligget. "What's the matter, Bob?" he asked finally.

Ligget wiped a grimy hand across his thick, flat lips, his small, bright, brown eyes meeting Caddo's defiantly. "You coddle your own dogies, Caddo. That kid don't know any more about working a good horse than an Indian. He still thinks he's breaking bronc's."

"You had to learn when you first came here," said Caddo. "You'd been working horses all your life, and you had to learn all over again."

"It isn't the same."

Caddo was aware of how Mora's eyes had narrowed, watching them, and he felt something tight enter his voice. "I guess it isn't," he said. "Why don't you want Irish to stay here, Bob?"

"It isn't that . . ."

"There was a man named Tripp Garretson who didn't want me to find Irish in the first place," said Caddo.

Ligget's heavy black brows lowered till his bright eyes were almost hidden. "Don't try to connect me with that."

"You're doing a pretty good job yourself, Bob."

"I . . ."

"You going to help the kid?"

Ligget had started to move the same moment he started to speak, and Caddo's voice cut it all off. Ligget was poised there, with all the weight forward on his toes, his breathing stirring his chest more perceptibly. The word came out on that breath, as toneless as before.

"No."

Caddo's chin lowered till there were two deep furrows in the leathery, unshaven flesh beneath his jaw. "Then I'll stop asking you, Bob. It's an order now." Ligget's breathing was audible. His eyes were locked with Caddo's and his weight had not settled back yet. "I guess you know I'm not one to take little differences like this to the boss," said Caddo firmly. "Don't make me put my hands on you, Bob Ligget."

He could see a faint slack appear in the waistband of Ligget's dirty jeans as the muscles tensed across the man's stomach, drawing it in. For a moment he thought Ligget was going on from there, and a dull excitement leaped through his own body. Then Ligget settled back on his heels, expelling his air through the nostrils with a harsh, rasping sound.

When he had turned and gone toward the corral, out of earshot, Mora allowed a faint, enigmatic smile to spread her lips. "I'm glad I saw that," she said, looking strangely at Caddo. "I'm really glad I saw that, Caddo."

There was a twenty-foot rope with a snap fastening it to the ring beneath the snaffle bit, and Ligget held the other end of this while Irish drove the horse in a circle about him. Mora had left to see Tommy Hart at the big house, and Caddo watched from the corral fence for a few minutes.

"Ease up on those reins, Irish!" he shouted. "Now turn him around and trot him the other way. That's it. Easy. Always easy. You got ten minutes left. Put him back in the barn after that. You'll find me in the loft."

They had gotten in a fresh load of grain from Sheridan for the winter, and Caddo went to the big hip-roofed barn to check the men storing it in the bins. It was a sweaty, grimy job, with dust from the feed filling the loft in choking clouds, and Caddo had lost the measure of time when the commotion started from below. Perhaps it was the small shudder in the wall of the barn that first drew his attention. Then someone's shout. A horse started whinnying wildly, and the barn shook again to a volley of kicks. The run-down heels of Caddo's boots made a dull *thud* across the thick carpet of grain spilled on the loft floor as he ran toward the ladder. He climbed about halfway down, and then dropped off, landing on bent knees in the aisle between the stalls. Down at the far end the violence was growing. A man ran toward him going that way, and, over the screams of frightened horses and the clatter of kicking hoofs, Caddo could hear him shout.

"The kid, the kid, he's in the stall with that punchy colt, he'll get his brains kicked out . . ."

Something caught at Caddo's vitals, like a big hand, twisting them in a knot, and, although he had to rise and break into his own run while the other man passed him, he was the first one to reach the other end of the barn. Just before he got to the last stall, the bay Irish had been working backed out of the stall, squealing and kicking, and wheeled suddenly out the door of the barn.

Other hands were coming from that direction, however, and one of them stopped the horse.

Through the door, Caddo could see Irish dodging about in the narrow box stall, trying to escape the convulsive viciousness of a big gray colt, his face streaming blood. The gray tried to crash through the door, but in its frenzy caught the opening broadside, and only succeeded in shaking the upright supports. His failure to escape that way only added to the animal's rage, and the colt whirled back, rump striking the edge of the loose, swinging door, and knocking it shut with a bang.

"Get out, Irish!" roared Caddo, pushing the door open again. "Climb over the wall. He'll kill you. He's punchy in that stall."

Caddo saw Irish leap for the wall, but the boy was weak from fighting, and, as he tried to claw his way over, the colt came up against him broadside in its frantic struggles. The boy screamed in a sick, broken way, slipping down. Face contorted, Caddo swept a lead rope off its hook on a post and jumped inside.

Irish was crumpled beneath the wild, flailing hoofs of the colt, and Caddo threw himself against the hot, sweaty hide of the animal. It knocked the colt off balance and he staggered across the narrow space, using his hoofs to keep from falling rather than for kicking. Caddo followed the animal on across, heaving his body up against its side to keep it going, slinging the lead rope beneath the animal.

"Get him out now!" he shouted hoarsely at the other men, fighting with the animal to pull that rope about its forelegs and throw it, "get the boy out now, damn you, get him out . . ."

With his shoulder and head shoved into the hot, fetid, shifting flank of the colt, he was dimly aware of Ligget and another man finally jumping in to drag Irish from the stall. With the boy out, Caddo tried to jump back. With the man's weight releasing him suddenly, the colt lashed out wildly. One of the hind hoofs caught Caddo in the belly, knocking him against the side wall. Wheezing in pain, he fought to his feet, still clutching the lead rope. He knew what Irish must have felt, now, as a shift of the colt's awkward body blocked him from the door. The animal was frothing at the mouth in wild excitement, the whites flashing as its eyes rolled in its head. The barn shuddered with his violent movement against the stall supports, and outside a hubbub of shouting, shifting men filled the aisle. Coughing in the sawdust, Caddo jumped at the horse, trying to anticipate the next kick.

He saw the shift of the colt's weight and twisted around to be carried in close. His body caught the hind leg before it could lash out, aborting the kick, and then, with his weight in against the horse, pinning it momentarily against the wall, he bent to sling that lead rope at its front hoofs once more. He missed the first time, and the colt whinnied shrilly, trying to back away. Keeping his shoulder against its rump, Caddo took another throw. This time the lead rope went around, and he caught the other end as it swung back. He stepped back to let the colt shift away from the wall and give him room to fall in. The animal tried to wheel his rump toward him and lash out with the hind hoofs. Caddo gave a yank with both hands on that lead rope. It pulled the colt's forelegs from beneath him.

The animal was not yet fully grown, but he was a big colt, weighing close to 700, and he shook the ground in falling. Caddo sprawled across the forelegs, throwing a couple of half-hitches in the rope.

"Get in here with your tie-downs!" he yelled, and in a moment a hand appeared in the doorway with another short length of rope. The man jumped past Caddo, going down to catch the heaving rump with one knee and forcing it into the ground so he could throw a loop on the flailing hind legs. Caddo rose, then, wiping sweat and dust off his face.

"Leave him lie like that," he panted, "till he quiets down," and, holding his stomach, he stumbled out the stall door. Irish was sitting up with his back against a support across the aisle, the cowhands milling about him. Caddo lowered himself before the boy. "You all right?"

"I guess so," muttered Irish.

"I told you to stay clear of that colt in the stalls," said Caddo, anger sweeping him now that he saw the boy was not hurt badly. "He's punchy in close quarters. He's already put one of our hands in the hospital. How in hell did you get in with him?"

"I didn't know he was there," said Irish. "Mora told me to put the filly away in that stall."

It took a moment for that to strike Caddo, and then his words came out in a hollow, unbelieving way. "Mora . . . told you?"

CHAPTER
FOUR

The Red Banner spread its corrals and outbuildings across a long meadow of lush grass as blue as Kentucky graze. Mora Banner's father had come from England with the influx of English capital into the Wyoming cattle market, and he had designed his house along the lines of his native rural architecture, with low roof lines and half timbering of dressed pine. The scrape of a fiddle emanated from the opened windows as Caddo halted his horse atop the last rise before the road dropped down into the compound.

"When Mora gives a party, every blade in the country comes," he said sourly. "You won't even get a chance to see her, boy. She'll be so dizzy from dancing she'll think you're a fence post. I don't see why you wanted to come at all."

"You wanted to come yourself," said Irish, grinning, "and don't try to deny it, Caddo. I seen the way you watch her."

Caddo turned soberly to him, studying the wild refinement of the boy's face a moment. They had prevailed upon him to wash his hair and it formed a shining golden mane now, paler streaks of ash blond burned through the top by the sun. A week of good steady meals had filled him out a bit, and he looked more mature in the clean Levi's and white shirt they had given him.

"You know she's out of our class, don't you?"

"Why?" said the boy, gazing at him.

"I . . ." Caddo hesitated, unable to put into words what years of environment had instilled in him.

"You take too much for granted, Caddo," said Irish, that vagrant grin making its flash in his sun-darkened face. "Just because you're a foreman and Tommy Hart's your boss? What's wrong with being a foreman? You're the best in the territory, they tell me. That's something to be proud of. Is Hart as good at his job? If I wanted a woman like that, I'd take her."

"You're a kid . . ."

"I'm old enough. And so are you. Age doesn't matter as much as that. You letting it stand in your way? Ten years' difference in your ages, maybe. You're still twice the man any of those fancies are she goes around with."

Caddo settled a little deeper in his saddle, nudging his sorrel on down the road, the thoughts stirring in him somberly. He might have reacted to that a few days ago. He might have begun to wonder if the kid were right, if there were a chance. But now, somehow, it failed to arouse him. He kept remembering who had told Irish to put the filly in that stall. He couldn't figure it out. Or maybe he didn't want to.

They hitched their horses among the others at the racks before the house and crossed the stone porch, halting a moment in the open door. The Banner living room ran almost the whole length of the house, furnished in Sheraton that James Banner had imported from England. At one end, by the fireplace of smooth round boulders from Clear Creek, was the fiddler and a pianist Mora had hired from town. The rest of the room was overflowing with men and women from the surrounding spreads. Caddo could see how many of Hart's type there were — gay, laughing young men in impeccable fustians or steel pens. Hart himself was standing by a large sideboard that held cut-glass decanters of liquor, and his fleshy face was already flushed deeply. He turned part way around to see who was in the doorway, and a surprised look passed through his glazed eyes, and then something else.

"It's all right, Tommy, I invited them."

Mora's voice reached Caddo over the hubbub of talk and the waltz being played, and then she was sweeping through the crowd, three or four of the younger men following her. She had on a green silk overdress, caught up at the sides by rosettes, and her hair was arranged in braids and pinned close to her head with one long ringlet coming from the braids on the left side and hanging down over her left shoulder. It changed her face, somehow, for Caddo, who was used to seeing her hair hanging long and free, and he didn't know that he liked it this way. She took each of them by the hand, speaking to Caddo, but smiling at Irish.

"I didn't think you could really get him to come, Caddo."

"I couldn't hold him back," said Caddo, a faint frown drawing its furrow in his brow as he felt their eyes on him. Or were they on him? He saw the vague

37

smile on Hart's face. The man was looking at Irish. They were all looking at Irish.

"Shall we dance?" There was something behind Mora's smile. "Do you dance, Irish?"

"I used to swing the squaws up on the Rosebud." The boy grinned.

"Did you," said Mora, and threw her head back to laugh, and the rest of them joined in. "Let's dance, then, Irish."

"Wait a minute." Caddo's voice came from him more loudly than he had anticipated, and Mora turned toward him sharply, something inquiring raising her brows.

"Jealous already, Caddo? You'll get your chance."

"It isn't that," said Caddo. "I don't dance. I think maybe we better . . ."

"Come over and have a drink, Caddo." It was Tommy Hart's hand on his arm, pulling him insistently toward the sideboard. He tried to jerk away, but Mora had already swung Irish off through the crowd, and the fiddler broke into a faster waltz. Caddo felt the heat of a sullen anger rising in him, and he moved stiffly to the sideboard with Hart's hand on his arm, watching the crowd narrowly. A few of them were dancing, but they had left an open space around Irish and Mora, and Caddo could see how they were watching the two. Caddo felt his breath coming out more heavily, and he tried to pull away from Hart again.

"Whatsamatter, Caddo . . . ?"

But he had already stopped. It was the boy's wild grace again. It was astonishing, how swiftly he comprehended the form of the dance. He was swinging Mora around smoothly, that vagrant grin coming and going in his sunburned face. Caddo felt Hart's hand slide off, and turned to see a faintly puzzled disappointment in the man's face, and almost laughed out loud. It was the same in Mora's face. That veiled, waiting speculation had been in her eyes and her smile, looking up at the tall youth, but now it was something else. A perceptible flush tinted her cheek as Irish swung her around and her eyes were sparkling.

Hart must have interpreted it the same way Caddo did. He made an abrupt, clumsy movement beside Caddo, and shoved his way through the crowd, knocking into the dancers. He tried to cut in, but Mora only threw her head back, and her laughter pealed out above the music as Irish swung her away from Hart. Diffused blood swept into Hart's face, darkening it, and his sensuous lips moved in words Caddo could not hear. He seemed about to go after them again when the music stopped abruptly. It was not the end of the song, and Caddo did not understand for a moment, and then he saw how the couples had stopped, one by one, and had turned toward the doorway. Caddo turned to see who was there. It was Tripp Garretson.

A horse by the hitch rack shifted nervously. A light afternoon breeze ruffled the aspens brooding at one end of the long stone porch. Caddo dropped the butt of his cigarette, grinding it morosely beneath his heel, and rose with a grunt from the chair he had been sitting in the last half hour. Hart came heavily out the front door, obviously carrying a heavy load, and Caddo's movement caught his eye.

"Wondered where you went," he said. "Why'd you leave?"

Caddo shrugged. "Wanted some air, I guess."

"You looked sort of uncomfortable," said Hart. "Can't blame you, with all those fops."

"Why did she let Garretson stay, anyway?" asked Caddo. "She knows who he is."

"Excitement," said Hart, dropping heavily into the chair beside Caddo. "You know Mora. Anything for a little excitement. She's as wild as that kid. It'll take something of a man to hold her, Caddo. I thought I could. I'm beginning to wonder."

Caddo shuffled his feet uncomfortably, staring at the worn toes of his boots. "I don't like it. Garretson has some reason for coming here."

Hart looked up stupidly. "You still worrying about that kid? Irish can take care of himself, Caddo. Didn't he prove it to you? I told you Mora'd do anything for excitement. Thought they were going to have a laugh? Thought maybe he would jump up in the air and whoop like an Indian or something?"

"I saw it," said Caddo savagely. "I didn't think Mora would do a thing like that."

"You got a lot to learn about Mora," said Hart. "I guess it's the kid who got the laugh today, though, isn't it? He's in there making the rest of those men she runs around with look like clumsy cows. He and Garretson have taken over the whole show . . ." He trailed off, staring at the porch floor a while. "How's it going, Caddo?" he said finally.

"I understand there's a Crow buck in Sheridan wants to see me," said Caddo absently. "Might be that Comanche's been spotted up there again."

"You're not going," said Hart, rising clumsily and lurching forward to catch at Caddo's shirt front, blinking at him with bleary eyes. "Not after they tried to kill you that time, Caddo."

"I should think you'd be the first to want me to go," said Caddo. "I went over the books again yesterday with that accountant. You're bankrupt, Hart. If you don't sell out within the next few weeks, you won't even get from beneath this with a clean shirt. And you won't sell, unless Comanche is found for Oporto."

"I know, I know," said Hart, sinking into a drunken melancholy. "I'm no good, Caddo. I've drunk and gambled and played around till I haven't got anything left. I could have been rich, with what I had there. I could have been a big man in the territory. Help me, Caddo. You've stuck by me. You're my best friend, Caddo. If Oporto buys me out, it'll leave me with fifty, sixty thousand clear, anyway. You're my friend, Caddo, help me . . ." He leaned heavily against Caddo, patting his shoulder with one hand, breathing the thick sweet smell of peach brandy into Caddo's face. Suddenly he pulled back, eyes widening in a strange fear. "You aren't going, Caddo, not this time . . ."

"Hart," snapped Caddo, grabbing him by the lapels. "What do you know?"

Mora stopped Hart's words, coming from the door between Garretson and Irish, holding each by the arm. "Come on, Tommy. We're going to see some fancy riding. Tripp brought a horse he bet Irish can't ride."

There was a slack-lipped grin on the kid's face, and it struck Caddo what was happening. He started after them, opening his mouth to call Irish, then clamped his lips shut over the words. He waited until Mora had released Tripp's arm so the man could go in among the horses at the rack and unhitch a mean-looking roan with scarred flanks. Then Caddo came up beside Irish, speaking in a low, intense voice. "You've been drinking."

Irish turned toward him. "Sure. Why not? That corn *tiswin* the Crows brewed doesn't compare with this. Whyn't you try, Caddo? Loosen you up a bit."

Caddo caught his arm. "Don't be a fool, kid. Don't try any fancy riding like this. I don't want you hurt."

The boy's grin faded. "I won't get hurt."

"Oh, leave him alone, Caddo," pouted Mora. "He's all right. He only had a couple of drinks. You can't run his whole life."

"Sure," said Irish. "You can't run my whole life."

"I'm not trying to," said Caddo desperately. "You're just not in shape for anything like this. Please, Irish, don't be a fool . . ."

That old, sullen withdrawal flashed through Irish. "Don't call me a fool."

"What's the matter, Caddo," said Tripp from the other side. "You aren't afraid, are you? I thought your boy could ride anything."

"I'm not *his boy!*" said Irish hotly.

Caddo turned toward the man. Tripp Garretson stood with his legs spread a little in that arrogant, sway-backed stance of his, both thumbs tucked into his gun belt, a mockery lying turgidly in his strange, catty eyes. Dana Border had come with Garretson, and he took a step that moved him in beside Caddo, hunching his shoulders more deeply into the buffalo coat. A vagrant movement on the other side impinged itself into Caddo's consciousness. Although it was rigid custom that the handlers did not mix with their employers at affairs like this, Bob Ligget had accompanied Tommy Hart to take care of the horses. The movement had come from him, on that side. A nameless suffocation caught at Caddo, and he drew in a heavy breath.

"Tripp," he said. "The boy isn't riding that horse."

"Isn't that his business?" said Garretson. "Take the roan out to the corrals and saddle him up, Dana."

"Don't touch that horse, Dana," said Caddo.

They had a brutal war bridle on the horse instead of bit and reins, and Dana turned to take the loose end of the hemp from Garretson's hand. Caddo took a swift step forward to reach out and tear the rope from Garretson's grip just before Border did. It put him in between the two men, and he no more than had the rope in his fist when from the corner of his eye he caught the change in Border's intent. The man had been holding his hand out to grab the rope. He left that hand out, but shifted his weight to the other side. The significance of that flashed through Caddo all in an

43

instant, and the dull, sullen frustration that had been building in him the whole afternoon suddenly exploded.

He dropped the rope and whirled toward Dana, blocking the man's right hand blow with an upflung left arm and shifting on in to sink his right fist into Border's stomach. The man was softer than he had expected, beneath that buffalo coat, and his gasp came hot against Caddo's face. Caddo knew what was behind him, and he threw himself against Border, knocking the man back. The movement carried both of them two or three staggering steps, and Caddo heard Garretson's explosive breath behind him, as the man missed whatever he had been going to do. Caddo shifted his weight to sink his other fist into Border's belly, taking a savage satisfaction in the man's gasp of agony.

"Stop him!" he heard Mora cry. "Oh, stop him, somebody."

He knew Garretson would not miss this second time, and he whirled to meet it. He heard Border fall to the ground, behind him, and then the other man entered his vision, lunging at him. Caddo bent in low and tried to catch Garretson the same way he had Border. But Garretson was harder in the middle. He took the blow with a gasp, and then had his own blow, and, bent in low like that, Caddo couldn't block it. Garretson's fist came in from above in a chopping, hammer-like way to catch Caddo on the cheek, and it knocked his head down, putting his face into Garretson's hard, sweaty belly. He got his arms around the man's lean hips to keep from falling, and felt the writhe of steely muscle through those flanks as the man shifted his weight to follow the first blow with a second.

Caddo squatted and grabbed Garretson's calves and heaved upward. The fist struck the back of his neck, but its force was aborted as Garretson went over backward, both his feet sliding down between Caddo's spread legs. Before Caddo could raise up, someone came in from the side. He sensed the swing of an arm more than saw it. A brilliant light flashed before his eyes, containing all the stunning agony in the world. Then it blinked out.

CHAPTER
FIVE

The year's first snow had dropped a light mantle over the ground, and its chill struck Caddo as he awoke in his bunk. He lay there a moment, the squawking of a flight of ducks dimly in his ears as they passed above, flying south. The throbbing pain in his head sharpened as he rose up, throwing the blankets off and swinging his legs to the floor. He felt Ligget's gaze on him from the other bunk, and raised his eyes. He saw the look in Ligget's eyes, and dropped his own, unable to meet that.

"You sure made a fool of yourself yesterday."

Caddo slipped into his Levi's, not answering, because he knew the man was right. He turned his back on Ligget, reaching for his shirt. The movement sent a new flash of pain through his head, and he rubbed it tenderly.

"Dana hit me with a gun?" he said.

"Dana?" said Ligget. The tone of his voice caused Caddo to turn and glance at him. Then Caddo became aware Irish Nyles's bunk was empty. Ligget saw his eyes on it, and shrugged. "What else do you expect? You never was exactly a little tin god to the kid, no matter how bad you wanted to be. Tripp's more the type to appeal to a boy like that. Wild and reckless and dangerous. They went into Sheridan about an hour after you left the Banner spread yesterday. I'll bet they put the reddest coat of paint on that town it's ever seen."

"Irish . . . with Tripp?" It came from Caddo incredulously. Then the full significance of it struck him, and he whirled around with his shirt tails flapping, to grab his gun belt. Buckling it on, he ran out the door. He was halfway across the compound when he saw the horsebacker coming down the Sheridan road. Caddo turned that way, still running. They met by the corral, and Caddo caught at the boy's stirrup leather, staring up at his puffy face and bloodshot eyes.

"What happened?" he said. "What happened?"

Irish stared at him stupidly. "Nothing."

"But you went with Tripp!"

"Sure," said the boy. "What of it? I can go with whoever I please."

"I don't mean that," said Caddo. "Didn't anything happen?"

"We had a good time in town." The grin caught momentarily at the boy's mouth. "To put it mildly."

Caddo still could not believe it. "You mean . . . you just went into Sheridan . . . ?"

"And had a helluva good time," said Irish. "Yes. Now let go. I'm going in and get some shut-eye."

"Wait a minute." Irish had started to gig horse forward, but the tone of Caddo's voice stopped him. It had changed inside Caddo, now. It was only a dull, insistent anger. "You're still working for me. Whether we're out tailing Comanche or here at the outfit, you're working for me. Whether the hands want to go into town and get drunk every night or not is their own business, but, either way, they're expected in the corrals at seven o'clock every morning. You're already half an hour late. I'll give you fifteen minutes for breakfast."

Irish stared down at him a moment, a sullen resentment flushing his face. Then he put his moccasined heels into the horse, moving it away, his seat in the saddle stiff and angry. Caddo held his hand, starting to say something, his face twisting. Then he dropped the hand, and stood there, staring after the boy, a hollow, blank look to his eyes . . .

Fifteen minutes later, Irish was leading the bay from the barn. Caddo met him at the number one corral, speaking in a cold, impersonal way.

"You won't need the sulky today. He's through driving. Get one of those Pelham curb bits out of the tack room and a light Cheyenne rig off the rack."

After Irish got the outfit, he dropped the Cheyenne saddle on the ground in order to put the bridle on. Caddo stood by, directing him in that same dispassionate way. "Take it easy, now. This isn't one of your rawhide hackamores. The snaffle should rest on the lips. Keep that curb just above the tusk so the chain rests flat against the groove under his chin . . ."

"Tripp said you were pretty good with a gun," Irish said casually, heaving the saddle on.

"Not so rough, kid," Caddo told him.

48

"I used an old Ward-Burton mostly," said Irish, slipping the latigo through the cinch ring, jerking it up tightly. "Never got around to handguns. Long as you're so all-fired enthusiastic about teaching me how to handle these Arabians, how about throwing a few lessons on the six-iron in?"

"What do you want them for?"

Irish was still turned toward the horse. "It might come in handy sometimes."

"In Tripp Garretson's string?"

Irish wheeled toward him defiantly. "Why not? What's wrong with Tripp? He knows how to have a good time."

Caddo gazed at him soberly, taking in a long breath, then letting the words out on that. "I thought we had something, kid. It isn't often a man comes along I like real well. I thought . . . maybe . . ." Caddo trailed off as Irish turned back to the horse, tucking the free end of the latigo strap away and dropping the stirrup leather. He stared at the stiff, unyielding line of the boy's back a moment. "I guess I did make a fool of myself yesterday, didn't I?" he said finally. Irish did not answer. Caddo drew in another breath, stepping toward the horse, and, when he spoke again, it was in that casual, impersonal way. "Put the reins over his head so I can get them and hold him by the bridle while I mount. If he starts bucking or jumping around, take it easy on him."

He put one hand on the bay's withers, the other far back on its rump, and gave several small hops off the ground. The horse shied nervously but not too

49

violently. Then, still hanging with his hands, he let his weight pull the animal over to one side to give him the sensation he would receive when he put his foot in the stirrup. This time he shied aside with more force, and tried to rear up.

"Come back here, you coon-footed cribber!" yelled Irish, yanking him back down.

"Take it easy on his mouth, I told you," said Caddo, almost thrown off as the horse responded to the brutal pull with a jerk.

"Might as well teach him who rods this outfit now as later."

"Not that way, you don't teach him," Caddo told him, letting go of the horse. The release of his weight caused the animal to try and shift sideward, away from the boy's pressure on the bit. Irish jerked the bridle angrily toward him. It hurt the horse and he reared back again, whinnying shrilly and jerking his head from side to side in a growing frenzy.

This time the boy's jerk was even more cruel. "I'll pull your tusks right out . . ."

"Let go that animal!" yelled Caddo, leaping at him. "I told you this isn't any bronc'."

"I don't care what it is," Irish panted hoarsely, refusing to release the bit as Caddo tried to tear his hand away. "A little cold blood don't give him no right to act this way on me. Settle down, you snake-eyed stump-sucker . . ."

"Damn you!" roared Caddo. "I told you." His backhand blow caught the boy fully across the face, knocking him backward across the corral to come up hard against the bars. Irish would have fallen if he had not caught at one of the rails. The released horse wheeled and ran across the corral, snorting and squealing. Irish straightened against the fence, wiping the back of one hand across his face. He stood there, staring at Caddo a moment, and the terrible, blank opacity that crossed his eyes struck Caddo, more than anything else, with the full significance of what he had done. He held out his hand, that twisted look in his face.

"Irish . . ."

"Never mind," said the boy in a flat, dead voice. "I guess that's about all you can teach me. I guess I'll have to learn about the gun from somebody else. Garretson, maybe. And when I do, Caddo, you'd better not let me see you. I won't forget this. I won't forget it for a long time."

CHAPTER
SIX

The gaunt, thorny stems of wild rose bushes formed a dark pattern against the snow, here and there, and the fir trees huddled together in the hollows as if to escape the morning chill. Caddo had made camp by a frozen stream in a grove of barren aspen, and he sought to warm himself by taking the last cup of his breakfast coffee in one long, scalding gulp. Nearly three weeks of travel and bitter unending labor lay behind him, and he rose from his hunkers wearily, washing his tin cup out with snow, and rolling it along with the pot into his sougan. Then he stripped off his Mackinaw and lifted the double-bitted axe from before the fire and moved downstream past the hobbled horses to seek more timber for the corral he had begun here the day before.

He found some good young spruce and went to work with the axe. Soon the sweat was soaking his shirt and streaming down the furrows on either side of his mouth into the scrubby beard he had grown. When he had felled half a dozen of the young trees, he lashed a dally about them and went back for a horse to drag them to the corral. He had built the pen in a sheltered cove of the creek, backed into a steep bank on the north end that broke the cruel wind from that side, protected in the other direction by thick growths of mountain oak. Three sides of the corral were already up, and with the freshly cut timber he began lashing the bars of the fourth side to the stout cedar-post uprights. He was lifting the last bar, when a horse raised its head and whinnied.

Caddo whirled, dropping the axe. He had his gun out by the time the rider appeared, silhouetted a moment at the top of the steep bank above the corral, a slim figure turned bulky by a heavy sheepskin coat.

"Mora," he said blankly.

She turned the gaunted horse down the bank past the corral, and her pack animal came into view, following on a lead rope. She slid her saddle mount down the snowy bank and stepped off. They looked at each other a moment, and Caddo could find nothing to say, and knew she must feel the same way.

"You've had a ride," he muttered finally.

"Comanche?" she said.

"Not yet," he told her. "I'm working something out. That Crow in Sheridan three weeks back said the horse had been sighted up in the Big Horns west of Lodegrass."

"And you're trying it all alone," she said, and then reached out a gloved hand impulsively. "Caddo . . . I've been wrong."

"Come all this way just to tell me that?"

"I thought it was excitement I wanted," she said. "I was young and wild and restless and I thought Tommy and the rest of those stupid, shallow fops he runs with were the kind of men who knew how to live and I . . ."

She trailed off helplessly, holding that hand out to him as if for aid.

"What brought all this on?" he said warily.

"I don't know exactly." She shrugged. "Maybe it started that day you faced Ligget down when he wouldn't help Irish with the colt. I don't think he would have taken that from any other man. Or maybe the day of the party. Ligget told me you thought you made a fool of yourself then, Caddo. You didn't. Standing up against the bunch of them that way, for a kid? None of the others would have done it. If only Irish had realized why you were really doing it. He thought you were just trying to exercise more authority over him, trying to show him up as a kid in front of them all." She moved in closer. "I got to thinking of those things these last three weeks, Caddo. More and more. It frightened me, somehow. It shook me. And finally I couldn't stand it any longer, knowing you were up here, all alone, facing this."

He shifted away from her deliberately, stifling an emotion within himself by a great effort, his words coming out stiffly. "Something been in my mind a long time. I got to ask you. You were the one who told Irish to put that horse in the stall where we kept the punchy colt?"

"Ligget told me to tell Irish," she said. Then her jaw dropped faintly. "And you thought . . . I . . . ?"

She stopped again, unable to finish it, and he shrugged his shoulders, studying her face somberly. "What else was I to think, Mora? And when you let Garretson in to your party that way."

"And you still think it," she accused him, stiffening. When he did not answer, she caught his arms, speaking swiftly, intensely. "Caddo, you've got to believe me. I don't know anything about this. Bob Ligget told me to have Irish put the horse in that stall. Is that what they were trying to do?"

"I don't know how Ligget fits in," said Caddo. "Garretson was the first to reach me. He warned me not to find Irish Nyles."

"That's partly why I came up here," she said. "If Garretson's mixed up in it, then so is Irish, now. The boy's riding with Garretson."

Caddo's face paled, and he turned back toward the pole. He took up a strip of rawhide, staring at it without seeing it. He felt Mora move in closer behind him.

"What was it about Irish, Caddo?" she said.

"I don't know," he muttered. "I'm almost old enough to be his father. Maybe that was it. A man needs something like that. He had a lot of good qualities. A lot of talents. It was nice to watch them come out, under the right treatment. A man needs something like that . . ." He trailed off, still staring at the rawhide.

After a while, she spoke uncomfortably: "What have you got there?"

"I've been building a string of pens like this all the way from the river into the Big Horns," he told her. "Each one has a roofed lean-to for shelter in case of bad weather. A horse could keep in good condition a week or so in a corral like this. I brought along about a dozen ponies from Hart's string of work animals. I'm going to plant one in each of those corrals. Comanche was last seen somewhere up in those hogbacks behind me. Soon's I'm finished here, I'm going to track him down. Then I'll drive him back in the direction of this corral. The horse here will be fresh when I reach it. I'll keep pushing Comanche as hard as I can right down this line of corrals. They're about twenty-five miles apart. You drive a horse a hundred and fifty miles without a chance to even stop and drink and he's going to be so played out a baby could snare him."

"Sounds a little risky to me," she said. "Do you think one man could drive him in a given direction that long?"

"I've been working horses a long time, Mora," he said. "I figured the angles down pretty close. They work horses this way on water holes farther south with good results. The spookier a horse is of a man, the easier he is to drive. Just show up a mile away on one flank of him and he'll turn the other way. It will be easier to find him, too, with this snow. It's too deep on the top lands for him to stay there, and there's only a few good sheltered pastures left in the valleys."

"I'm going with you."

He smiled, in a faint, patient way. "No, Mora. It isn't for fun from here on in. Might a week go by without any sleep. Once I find him, there won't be any stopping till the end. A hundred-fifty miles on those terms is an awful lot of *pasear*."

"Two could drive him better than one," she said hopefully.

"I can't let you," he said.

She drew herself up. "You can't stop me."

★   ★   ★

Indian Notch cut through the Big Horns on top of a rugged hogback, swept by a ceaseless wind that blew the horses' tails between their legs and ruffled their manes with bitter, whining fingers. Caddo's eyes were squinted painfully in a raw, reddened face as he searched the lowlands below for any movement, and the girl was bent dispiritedly over in the saddle, eyes shut with weariness. They had ridden the ridges for three days now, hunting some sign of Comanche, without success. Caddo's saddle had not been thoroughly dry in a long time, and it creaked soggily with his shift, as he turned toward her.

"I'm taking you back," he said.

She straightened up, eyes flashing wide open. "Caddo, I told you, I'm not spoiling it for you now. You've got to finish it this time and you won't be able to if you do anything like that. I'm still good for . . ."

She paused, her glance directed beyond him. After a moment, he turned to look down the snowfield into a bare patch of the valley where a row of conifers had protected a stretch of meadow from the snow. It was a moment before his aching eyes caught the movement.

"Deer?"

It came from the girl in a soft, breathless way, and he waited a long time before answering. "Likely be more'n one if it was that. Let's drop down easy-like."

It was that way in him, too, now, as he eased his horse through the snow toward the trees, breathless and excited as a horse-runner with his first outlaw, all the exhaustion of the past days dissipated by the possibility of this. They reached the trees and moved carefully through the limber pine. It seemed an endless stretch of time before Caddo spotted the movement again. This time they were close enough to recognize it, through the somber, white-floored lanes of timber. The protection afforded by this thick stand of trees on the upper slope had left a strip of meadowland uncovered here, and the horse was nibbling at the sparse brown grass still left in patches. Suddenly he raised his head, wheeling toward them, and they were close enough for Caddo to see his nostrils flutter. Then he wheeled and plunged on down the valley and into the leafless scrub oak covering its lowest section.

Caddo cast one glance at Mora, and then gigged his horse into a run that carried the animal across the meadow and into the oak. It was rough going here, with patches of freshly fallen snow lying deeply in the coulées, and he had to slow a bit. Mora caught up with him in there, coming in beside him, and there was a strange expression in her face.

"That Comanche?"

He nodded. "What is it?"

"I don't know." She looked ahead, frowning vaguely. "Something's wrong. Didn't you see it?"

"What?"

"I don't know. I told you. Something. I didn't get a good enough look. His face. His tail."

There was no time for that now, and he turned his horse to one side. "We can't hope to stick on his tail with these nags. Only way to drive him is to get on opposite slopes. That way he'll head straight down the valley. That'll open onto Badger String and my first pen. Think your horse'll last it?"

"Think yours will?"

He couldn't hold back the grin at that, and then she was gone, cutting off through the oaks. He rose out of the trees and gained enough height to see Comanche against the snow ahead, going up the opposite slope toward the ridge. Then Mora appeared on that slope, slightly higher than Comanche. The horse saw her and turned back down. Caddo kept out of sight in timber till Comanche had reached the bottom again and took a straight line out the valley.

It was close to midnight when they reached that first pen at Badger String, where Mora had first found him. Knowing she would be with him, he had left her pack horse here along with the one he had intended, and that gave them each a fresh mount. He tore the saddle off his jaded mount and heaved it on the new horse and turned the used-up animal into the pen and swung aboard again as soon as he had given Mora's latigo a last tug, and the two were off once more, seeking the slopes so they could sight Comanche against the white snow under the dying moon.

The excitement had worn off now and it was a steady, bitter pull, working on their nerve. The first wild run, almost killing their saddle mounts, had tired Comanche enough so that he was willing to settle into a steady trot now. With each of them riding an opposite slope this way, it was not hard to keep him running a pretty direct course down the valleys, not allowing him

59

to stop long enough for a drink when they came to streams.

They pushed him through Big Horn Cañon a little after dawn, reaching the second pen. Here was only one horse, and Caddo took it himself, as Mora's lighter weight had not tired her horse as much as he had his mount. It was a nightmare of snow fields and browning valleys and barren aspens along unnamed streams now, and that running, trotting, walking, shifting shape of Comanche, dark against the white carpets ahead.

At the third pen it was Mora who got the change. The ride was beginning to tell on her, and he tried to get her to stop here, but she would not. Without time to argue, he turned the used-up animal into the pen and lifted up the drop bar, lashing it tightly, all without having dismounted. They reached the fourth pen near evening, and Comanche was beginning to show definite signs of tiring. His tracks were closer together in soft earth and his efforts to seek escape on either side of the route they were driving him had become more infrequent with each passing hour.

By the time they reached the fifth corral, Caddo had gotten his second wind, and was sitting in a sort of lurid daze, feeling nothing but a numb determination to finish this now. They were in lower country, with stretches of open terrain that would have let a fresher horse turn aside often seeking escape, but Comanche was going in a dogged, desperate trot. He had even ceased trying to stop at the watering places. Caddo knew it had settled down to the last stage.

The sixth and seventh corrals passed by and Caddo was waiting for Mora to fall from her saddle any moment. They passed through the night, and by dawn that terrible, ceaseless trot had turned into a walk. They reached the Little Horn River, and Caddo understood where Comanche was headed. He had reckoned on this to start with, and had predicated the line of his pens on that reckoning. Comanche was going to make his last stand where his master had, so many years ago.

Up the river they followed the stumbling, adamant Comanche to where the eighth corral formed its dim pattern, rising out of a thick morning haze that fogged the low swales here. Both were too exhausted to waste effort in speech now, and Caddo unsaddled Mora's animal for her and gathered himself to heave the sweaty corus on the back of the fresh horse, leaning against the animal as he hitched up the latigo. Then he helped her aboard, and climbed back on his own mount, spurring the weary beast ahead. They had lost sight of Comanche in the fog, but Caddo urged his horse ahead, drawing blood with his gut hooks before he could get the jaded animal to gallop. It was the broken country Custer must have seen on his way into the Sioux camp, matted hummocks of cattail that dropped abruptly into coulées chocked with bitterroot and serviceberries, a stand of leafless haunted alders looming out of the dim haze, the thorny fingers of a bullberry bush rattling against the animal's legs.

Then, ahead, still in that dull, dogged walk, Comanche appeared out of the ground fog like one of the spirits of the 7th returned to his defeat. Comanche's stride broke noticeably as he crossed a high bluff. He seemed about to halt. Then he moved on. Caddo and Mora passed the bluffs, crossed the open flats. Finally, ahead in the streamer of mist now being dissipated by a belated sun, Caddo sighted Custer Hill. He watched dazedly as Comanche leaned forward against the rising ground, climbing to the peak of the low crest, turning slowly around to face them. They drew to the bottom of the hill, near enough now to see how Comanche was trembling with exhaustion, barely able to keep his feet. He gave a feeble snort of defiance as they climbed the hill toward him. They both stopped their animals about the same time, staring at the horse. Caddo realized, dimly, what Mora must have meant back there.

"Funny," he said dully, still unwilling to believe it, "all the time I've been chousing the horse. Even when Irish and I had him there in the cañon. It was too dark to see. This is my first real close look at him. I had no idea."

"I told you," she said. "His head. The eyes are too small or something. All those colts you have at the Hart Farms show a dished face."

"You're right," he said. "No full Arabian has a face like that. His back's all right, though. They have one less vertebræ that makes them shorter than the other breeds. You can see that in him."

"His croup isn't level enough," she said. "And the tail's too long. I thought they had one or two less vertebræ there, too. Caddo, this can't be Comanche."

"On the contrary," said a soft, purring voice from behind them, "it can very well be Comanche."

Caddo's saddle creaked as he turned. Tripp Garretson stood in the damp buffalo grass at the foot of the hill. Behind him stood Tommy Hart. It took a long moment for the full significance to seep through Caddo's exhausted mind. At last he turned his horse around to face them, looking at Hart.

"It was you, behind this, then?" he said emptily.

Hart made a vague, reluctant gesture with his hand. "I . . . I couldn't help it, Caddo. The thing grew by itself, somehow. You're right about Comanche. He's not pure Arabian. He's got a little Suqwali blood in him somewhere. You can see it in his back, his action. Enough to start the rumor that he was an Arabian. The farms weren't going at all. It was Ligget's idea to take advantage of the Comanche legend. We thought about letting you in on it, but your principles were too obvious. We saw to it that Ligget always got the job of trailing those mares up here to be serviced by Comanche, instead of you."

"But the colts," said Caddo, a bitterness entering his voice. "They were unmistakably pure."

"They were sired by pure studs," said Hart. "All that hokum about mating the mares with Comanche was just a show we put on to cinch things up. The colts wouldn't have been worth a tenth of the price we got without Comanche's name as their sire. You know what a gold mine the story has made for the Hart Farms. Arabians are too new to the West, despite their real value, to be worth much without something like that to sell them. When Oporto wouldn't buy the farms without capturing Comanche, I had to make it seem I was willing, on the surface. I hired Tripp to keep the horse from really being caught. If it came out that Comanche was just a cull, the whole thing would blow up in my face."

"That was you potting at us in Little Horn Cañon, then?" Caddo asked Garretson.

"That's right," said the man. "We're really sorry you finally caught up with Comanche this way. We didn't think you could do it without Irish. I had some idea of getting Irish out of it that day at Mora's party. I even had something in mind to get rid of him when we rode into town. But he's a pretty tough kid. I saw it would be safer to let him break with you and step on our side of the fence. He's riding our wagon now, Caddo."

"Look," said Hart feebly. "Can't we make some sort of deal, Caddo? Surely you can see how this would ruin me if it got out. What's the difference? They're all good Arabians. Who cares if the sire wasn't Comanche? Everybody seems well satisfied."

Garretson waited a moment, watching Caddo's face narrowly. "I told you that wouldn't be the way, Tommy, with a man like Caddo. I told you how it would have to be, if he ever found out."

"But . . . Mora," said Hart emptily.

"It all depends on how much this means to you, Tommy," said Garretson. "You'll be finished if it gets out."

"But not . . . a woman . . . Tripp . . . not this way . . ."

Caddo comprehended now and couldn't help the shift he made in his saddle.

"Don't," said Tripp sharply. "You'll get your back filled."

Caddo turned far enough to see what he meant. Dana Border had come over the crest of the hill, a few yards to one side of Comanche. There was someone else with him.

"Irish," said Caddo, his voice filled with a profound defeat.

"Yeah?" The boy's tone was flat, unrelenting.

"Mora." Hart was trying again, his face pale. "Surely you . . ."

"What about me?" she said edgily.

"You can't get around it, Hart," said Garretson. "She's in it for good."

"No . . . no," said Hart. "Can't you see it, Mora? Come down. We'll let you. You're one of us. You've been one of us. Surely you can see your way clear. What's it to you? Oporto will buy the farms and we'll be out from under it in a few weeks. They'll never find out. Nobody else could ever get Comanche."

"And if I came down," she said, "what of Caddo?"

"It's got to be that way," said Hart. "Don't you see? It's got to. Tripp told you why. With Caddo it's got to be. But not you."

She let her eyes move over to Caddo, and he met them. "It's your chance, Mora. Don't be a fool."

"Yes," said Hart. "Come down, Mora, give us your answer."

"I'll give you my answer," she said, and it was in such a calm, dispassionate tone that the violent movement which followed it took them all by surprise. She raked her horse with her spurs before she was finished speaking, and jerked the reins against its neck at the same time. The horse screamed in surprised agony and leaped to one side, slamming into Caddo's horse. He felt her body come up against him, carrying him off the saddle. He struck the ground with Mora on top, rolling through the wet buffalo grass with the sound of screaming horses and the flat explosion of that first shot in his ears. They rolled into a shallow gully, Mora still on top, Caddo sprawled beneath her on his belly. He got a shoulder between them and rolled from under her body onto his back, and his arm was free enough to grab his gun when he saw where Garretson was.

The shot above had evidently come from Border, who was now running downhill. Garretson had thrown himself aside to escape the bolting horses, and only now was coming up off his knees and throwing himself toward the gully.

"All right, Caddo!" he shouted, and clawed out his Colt. Savage satisfaction twisted his face.

"All right, Tripp," Caddo said, and shot the man through the middle of his chest, and watched him take two more steps on through the soggy grass, that satisfaction changing to surprise as he tried to pull his half drawn gun on out, and failed, and then fell over on his face. Border's gun began again, and Caddo convulsively tried to shift over on one side, pulling his gun across his hip. But Border had been firing as he threw himself to the ground, and was down now, invisible above the lip of the coulée. Irish was not in sight up there, or Hart. Caddo grabbed Mora about the waist, half carrying her down the cut toward a stand of scrub oak choking the coulée between her and the river. Within the trees, they stopped, crouching to be completely hidden by the low growth, breathing heavily. Her face turned toward him, and he read it in her wide, dark eyes.

"I'll do it if I have to," he said between his teeth.

"You can't," she sobbed. "You loved him like a son, Caddo. You can't and you know it."

"I'll do it if I have to," he said again, in that hollow, bitter way. But inside him, like an insidious voice, were her words: *You can't and you know it.*

They both wheeled toward the sound outside the fringe of trees within which they crouched. There was still some ground fog left, swirling through the soggy, furrowed trunks, but the sun was growing stronger, and it drew a sweat from Caddo, as he leaned toward the noise. Irish? Something clogged in his throat, and he tucked his chin in to swallow.

"Caddo . . ."

It was Mora's voice behind him, a small, hopeless, pleading sound. He blinked his eyes, wondering if he could, if it were possible for a man . . . ?

Then it was the other noise, behind them, from the river end of the coulée. He started to turn that way, and then stopped, because he caught the dim movement in the foggy trees before him. The sun caught brightly on yellow hair. Caddo's arm jerked upward involuntarily, but the sight was gone as swiftly as it had come, blocked by the gnarled trees. He held the gun stiffly in his fingers, calling in a soft, hoarse voice: "Kid? Don't be a fool. You didn't come for this. You didn't know what you were riding for, did you? Tell me you didn't. Don't come in, kid. I can't have you gunning like this with Mora in it. She's right beside me, Irish. Tell me you're quits. Tell me you won't . . . ?"

"I told you what I'd do back in the corrals that last time." It was the boy's voice.

"We were friends once, Irish."

"Tripp and I were friends, too," said Irish.

"You got your dally hitched on the wrong leg. He came at me . . ."

"He's dead back there. He taught me how to use a gun, Caddo. I'm going to use it now."

"Mora . . ."

"Tell her to get out of it. I don't care about her. Just you and me, Caddo."

"She can't, Irish. Someone's coming in from the other side. Don't do it, kid, don't make *me* do it . . ."

"I'm coming, Caddo."

There was the *crunch* of undergrowth beneath those moccasins, soft, insistent. Then Mora was shifting against him with a small, choked, indrawn breath. Then it was that flash of sun on yellow hair again, and Caddo's arm came up.

"Irish!" he cried, but it wasn't in him.

The instant they stood there, staring at each other, seemed the longest measure of time Caddo had ever spent, and then Irish Nyles's gun boomed. There was a muffled echo, aborted by the trees, and Caddo wondered why he felt no pain. Then he saw the boy's gun was not quite lined up on him. He heard the sound

68

Mora made from behind, and turned part way around. Dana Border was crouched on his knees, hugging himself with a grimace of awful pain, and the gun he would have used on Caddo lay at his feet. Caddo turned back to Irish. The boy put his gun away.

"Tripp didn't teach me very good, anyway," he said uncomfortably. "You could've had me if you'd wanted."

"Irish!" shouted Caddo, and caught him by the shoulders as he came forward, pounding him on the back and grinning, and Irish was grinning, too, and neither of them knew what to say.

"Tommy?"

It was Mora's voice, from behind Caddo, and Irish answered her. "Hart won't cause us any trouble. He's sitting out by the river, afraid to make a move for fear he'll run into Caddo. He's through and he knows it."

"Yeah." Caddo sobered. "I guess he is. Along with the Hart Farms. When this gets out, a horse from there won't be worth a Crow buck's short bit."

"The farms wouldn't have to be through," Mora said. "As much money as Tommy's made there, he's drunk and gambled it away to the point of bankruptcy. It will go into receivership. A man could get it from the hands of the receivers pretty cheap. If people knew it was being run honestly again, it wouldn't take long to build up a market on a different, more solid basis. You've been putting it away in the sock ever since I knew you, Caddo, for a time like this. It's your chance. If you haven't enough, there are a dozen men around Sheridan who would loan you the balance, including me."

69

He looked at them both, the thought of it warming him, somehow, till he felt a faint, excited flush in his face. "I'll need two things," he said.

"What's that?"

"I won't be satisfied with any moon-eyed wrangler to handle those horses," he said, looking directly at Irish. "I'll want a man I can make the best ramrod in the Territories."

Irish dropped his eyes to the ground in a pleased discomfort. "I'll come, Caddo."

"And I won't be satisfied living in the big house by myself," said Caddo, turning toward Mora. "I'll want a woman there to make things complete."

Mora did not drop her eyes from his. "I'll come . . . Caddo," she said.

THE LEGEND OF
YALLOW HOLE

"The Legend of Yallow Hole" was Les Savage, Jr.'s original title for this short novel. It was submitted to Fiction House and accepted on May 31, 1945. The author was paid $480. The title was changed to "The Brand Twisters" prior to publication in *Lariat Story Magazine* (3/46).

CHAPTER
ONE

I guess it was dumb, but I was tired as a horse after roundup, and I'd left Bibo at the shack that morning. I come through that downslope meadow so thick in blue root the smell almost gags you and got down off my blowing dun in the pines out front and slung my sweaty kack off, all without even looking at the cabin. I unbridled him and gave him enough slack on the picket rope to graze a little and had to kick open the door because I was carrying the saddle inside. Then I realized no light was showing inside the place.

"Bibo?"

"Come on in." It wasn't Bibo's voice. "I have a gun on you. Shut the door afterward."

Maybe I was too played out to feel much. The loose board near the threshold squawked with my weight when I crossed it. That was about all the farther I went. I let the saddle down and shut the door behind me.

"Now you can turn up the light. It's on the stool to the right of the door."

We'd found an old hurricane lamp when we came here, and I got me a match out of my Levi's and lifted the cracked glass shield to get at the wick. My hands weren't shaking, but they was sort of tense by now. I wasn't surprised when the light revealed her.

"Running Iron Smith?" she said, and looked me up and down, and a smile began to grow on her face, and it was different when she said it again, and I didn't like it. "Running Iron Smith."

I'd been around a little, and I'd seen a few women, but never anything to sit a fancier saddle than this. There were two bunks at the back end of the room, and she sat on the lower one. No hat on her head and hair like midnight parted in the middle and hanging, long and glossy, down around her shoulders. If you never saw that gleam in an outlaw horse's eyes, you don't know what I'm talking about.

There was a cayuse down in Cheyenne I tried to tame once and never could. Nobody else could, either. They said the devil made him and then had to kick him out of hell. His eyes looked just like this woman's. She had on tight Levi's that showed off bigger hips than a girl would have, and I figure maybe thirty. Her Justin boots looked custom, and her leather jacket must have come expensive, too. The gun was one of those old Spencer falling-block carbines across her knees.

"Where's Bibo?" I said.

"Safe," she told me, still studying me that way. It was almost like a hand feeling my face to have her eyes there. She had full red lips that should have looked nice when they smiled, but I knew what they were smiling at, and they didn't look nice to me. *All right, lady,* I thought, *I never claimed to be a Handsome Harry.* Then her glance dropped down my dirty white shirt to

74

where the hardware hung. Not many people would have taken in those nail scratches across the top of my holster, but they're usually a good sign, and she took them in. Suddenly she laughed. It was low in her throat and husky like a man's. "How do you get your pants off?" she said.

"I'm sensitive about my bowlegs, lady," I told her. "If you don't tell me where Bibo is, I'm coming over there and get that gun."

She jerked the rifle up at that, and it was the way I'd figured; she was a little spookier about this than she wanted to let on. She saw it in my face, then, and tried to settle down a little.

"That's one for you, Running Iron," she said. "I told you Bibo was safe. He'll remain that way if you tell us where you've cached those Cut-and-Slash cattle you appropriated last Tuesday." She saw me looking at the smashed table then, and the broken chair, and she shrugged. "He's just got a bloody nose."

"You didn't have to do that," I said. "He's an old man."

"A stubborn old man," she said, standing up, and I saw her eyes beginning to smolder like banked coals, and it was the same way as in that horse. "He wouldn't tell us where the cattle were. Now you're going to. He's an old man, and we know how much he means to you, and we won't even have to bloody your nose. Where are the cattle?"

"You from the Cut-and-Slash?"

She saw what I meant. "It doesn't matter. Let's just say there won't be any trouble with the law in this if

75

you tell. As soon as we have the cows, you get Bibo back and twenty-four hours to shake the dust of Sweetwater County from your hocks."

My fists ached, and I realized they had been clenched like that since I saw the busted table. I still had those scars across my cheeks from the time some ranny worked me over down Austin way, and they never found out what they wanted. But Bibo . . .

"You let me see him first?"

"He's too far away by now," she said. "We weren't taking any chances. I'm getting impatient. Let's have it."

"There's a pocket near the upper end of Horse Creek," I told her. "We got 'em there."

"You'll have to show me. I've lived around here some time and never heard of any pocket there."

"That's why we put them there," I said. Then I turned around, to get my saddle. While I was bent over, I felt the tug at my belt. I started to straighten up, then stopped. I hadn't heard her come up behind me, but I knew what it was. The mad was beginning to build up in me now. I felt like kicking myself for walking in this way. But what else? I picked up the kack and opened the door, and, when I walked through, my empty holster flopped against my leg with every step. The dun didn't want the saddle again, and he puffed up, and that only riled me worse. Then I saw why I hadn't spotted her horse. She gave a swing to those nice hips and was on my dun and made me walk in front of her through the upper meadow. A mockingbird was singing from the Douglas firs along the ridge top, and I was puffing by the time we reached her horse, a classy-looking black with four white socks, tethered in a coulée on the other side of the ridge. I got a good look at the silver-mounted Cheyenne rig she climbed into, and figured I would remember it next time I saw it. We dropped down through a little talus, that scared her black some, to a string of cottonwoods beside the stream in the next valley, and then I turned northward toward Horse Creek, and now it was beginning to reach me. If she was from the Cut-and-Slash, it didn't set right about no trouble with the law if I told. A rancher running a straight rope would more likely have a posse right on the spot. And if she wasn't with the Cut-and-Slash . . .

"Don't strain your brain about it, Running Iron. You're hardly in a position to be looking in the other fellow's poke."

That almost made me jump out of my kack. She had come up beside me, smiling that way, a little twisted on one side, the way you'd smile at a greenhorn, maybe, and it aggravated me.

"You a mind-reader?" I said.

"No," she said, "but you aren't a poker player, either. At least you wouldn't make a very good one. You just show me the cattle and leave the figuring to men with a few more marbles."

Up to now I'd been so mad about walking in on this and about Bibo and about the way she riled me with this smile that I hadn't rightly appreciated her. Maybe it was the way the moonlight glistened on her lips, or the way her thigh curved against the horse. Bibo and

77

me don't travel a trail that takes in many women. The last one was that Mex gal down in Austin. I found myself suddenly wondering if this woman's kisses wouldn't taste even better than the Mex gal's, and then I give a jerk on my reins that made the dun jump, because how could I be thinking of that, when they had Bibo?

Horse Creek itself was nigh onto dried up, and the timbered slope above its bed was where the railroad got a lot of its ties. We kept passing piles of pole ties with only two sides surfaced and slab ties with three sides and quarter ties with four, and finally I pulled up onto the higher slope for fear we'd hit some of the tie cutters. The only way into the pocket was along the bottom of a dry stream that used to run into the bigger creek; the willows and cottonwoods were so thick here a man wouldn't see the dry bed unless he fell right into it. We'd busted out a lot of the serviceberry bushes and ripped through most of the vines driving those critters in, but even then it would have been hard to find. The bed cut the ridge and dropped down the other side between some high shoulders into a little cup of a valley with another stream watering its bottom. The whitefaces were lying around on the sandy banks or standing knee deep out in the gurgling water, and looked happy enough.

The woman got off her black to look at the brand on the hip of a heifer. "You haven't changed it yet," she said.

"That's right," I told her.

"Then you might as well start doing a little decorating," said the man sitting his horse where he had come out of the timber behind us.

He had a load of hay on his head thicker'n bunchgrass, and it was mostly gray, but that didn't tell anything. He was an ageless ranny; his face must have been carved out of granite with a dull Bowie, and it probably looked the same when he was weaned as it did now. There was a faint pattern of scars across one cheek that struck a familiar chord in me, but I couldn't place it right then. He was big enough to hunt bears with a switch, and his mare must have been seventeen hands tall, if it was one, and by the heavy way he sat the kack I figured the poor horse was nigger-branded from withers to hocks. He must have weighed 220 on the hoof, and his chest like to bust out his plaid shirt every breath he took, and his hips so negligible I wondered how he kept his .45 from sliding down his legs.

"You weren't going to follow us," said the woman.

"We changed our minds, Ardis."

"Damn you," she flared, "I told you not to . . ."

"Oh, hell" — he swung off his horse, heavy dark brows almost hiding his eyes when he frowned — "what does it matter?"

"All right," she said, those black eyes snapping, "all right. If you're going to let him know our names, it might as well be formal. Running Iron, this is Wolffe Farrare. He's too tough to kill, and too mean to die, and, if he carved a notch in his gun for every man he dusted off, there wouldn't be any handle left . . ."

79

"Never mind, never mind," he said. "Someday somebody's going to get tired of that hot head on you and slap it off."

She got so stiff she looked like a Sharp's ramrod. "It won't be you!"

"No?" he said, and took a step toward her.

"No," she said, and he stopped, looking at that falling-block gun she had pulled up till it leveled on him. He let his breath out his nose like a bull does when it's disgusted, but he didn't go any farther toward her. "I told you I'd come back and tell where the cattle were, didn't I?" she said. "How did you know he wasn't just bluffing?"

"What's the difference?" Wolffe asked her. "I didn't show till you found the cattle, did I? If he'd been leading you a blind trail, I wouldn't have come out. Now we've got the critters, there's no use hiding the old man from him longer. Cadaver!"

That last was louder, and it called a man from the trees, so narrow he could take a bath in a shotgun barrel. He looked about as happy as a duck in Arizona. His black, flat-topped hat sat squarely on his thin head, and his black tailcoat hung down over the back of a horse as gaunt as a gutted snowbird. Then I saw who was riding the cayuse behind him.

"Bibo," I said.

"Couldn't help it, Running Iron," Bibo said, taking a swipe at his nose with his bandanna, and I could see it was still bleeding. "They come up on me so quiet I didn't know they was there till they was inside the cabin. I wish you hadn't brought them here."

"What's a few cows?" I said.

"It ain't the cows." He stopped his horse in front of me, slouching over in his saddle, and I saw what else they'd done beside his nose. "It's our reputation. Those coots down in Austin never made you talk."

"But this is different . . ."

"Ah" — he waved the bandanna disgustedly — "you getting soft or something? You know I wouldn't've talked if they'd had you."

I knew different, but before I could say anything, Farrare jerked his arm at me.

"Get that iron off your saddle and start to work. Cadaver'll build you a fire. We want that Cut-and-Slash changed to an A Bench."

Cadaver kicked away some growth till he had clear sand and began hunting for dry wood. It was springtime, and most of the cottonwood was green nearby, but finally he found an old dead one and built his fire. I got my running iron from under my saddle skirt and put it in the blaze to heat. Not much else to do, considering that hogleg the dark damsel kept swinging my way.

The mournful gent took off his black coat and uncoiled a dally off his horn. I couldn't see how he got that bag of bones he rode into a trot, but in a minute he was hazing in a big steer, and his throw was good enough to drop it six or seven feet from the fire. I had my rope, and hog-tied the critter, and got my iron. It squalled and flopped around some, getting sand in my eyes. Before I let it up, Farrare came over to see the brand. Ardis followed him, and I found myself

81

wondering how hard it would be to jerk that falling-block gun out of her hand.

"Hell," said the big man, jerking a hairy hand at my work, "that's too good. Time it cools, not even a brand inspector could tell it had been worked over. Nary a one. Never."

"What do you think I am, an amateur?" I said.

"You are this time, whether you like it or not," said Farrare. "Next one, you botch it a little so an ordinary hand could spot it."

"You can't talk to my boy that way," Bibo told him. They had made him get off his horse, and he had been lying down on his back trying to stop the nose bleed, but now he had jumped to his feet. "Why do you think they call him Running Iron Smith? He's an artist. He never botched a job in his whole career. If you took all the hides he's decorated and laid 'em tail to snout, you'd have a rawhide road from here to the border and back again, and not one of 'em that ain't so perfect they could pass every brand inspector west of the Mississippi. I taught him that. I taught him all he knows, and I ain't letting you ruin his rep any more than you already . . ."

It was a backhand blow. Farrare didn't even turn toward him to do it. He just swung with his arm coming out, and the back of his hand hit Bibo in the face, and Bibo must have dragged his heels through the sand ten feet before he went down for good. I already had both hands out for Farrare, and my knees bent for the jump when I heard that sharp *click* at my side. The woman stood there with her hand still holding the lever down on her Spencer, and she knew I'd heard it, and she didn't say anything. I looked at my hands, and they were shaking like fillies spooked by a rattler. That's how much I wanted to get them on Farrare. Finally I put them down.

"I'll kill you for that someday," I said slowly.

"Never mind the dramatics," said Farrare. "Finish blotting these brands. And do it the way I tell you."

There were two dozen head, maybe. Cadaver certainly hadn't looked like any top hand, but his work on the rope opened my eyes, and I've seen the best there are. The morning star was out, by the time we finished. Farrare had got a coffee pot off his saddle and boiled some java for him and the gal, not offering us any. She sat there with the firelight catching those outlaw eyes, and I felt her watching me more than I liked. After the last steer was decorated and Cadaver was circle-riding them into a little bunch to quit them, Farrare got up and dumped the coffee, sloshing the pot in the river. He went over and talked with the mournful man, and pretty soon Cadaver started working the cattle toward the dry bed that led out of the pocket. Ardis stood up.

"I guess that's all," she told me. "Texas is a mighty pretty country in the spring, they tell me. Nice and far from Wyoming."

"Nobody's going to Texas," said Farrare.

The woman turned on him. "Wolffe, don't be a fool. They wouldn't be loco enough to stay around here after we found them with Cut-and-Slash cattle!"

I began to understand what Farrare was driving at, and I looked over toward Bibo, because we'd come up against this sort of tight once or twice before. Bibo's eyes were on the last embers of the fire where the long running iron still lay, and he was closest to it, and that's what decided that.

"Nobody's going to know our connection with these cattle," said Farrare, looking straight at Ardis.

"Then why did you make him blot the brands?" she said. "We could have let them go before."

"Blotting the brands don't matter," said Farrare. "Just knowing we were interested is enough." He moved his right hand toward his gun. "If you don't like it, you can go on with Cadaver . . . Ardis!"

She had swung that rifle on him. "No. I won't let you, Wolffe!" He tried to jump back and knock her rifle aside and go on drawing his big Smith & Wesson Shofield all at once. Bibo'd already taken the dive and rolled through the fire, catching at the running iron and throwing it while he was still rolling. It struck Farrare across the face, and I've heard the big cats scream the same way in Texas swamps.

As Farrare staggered back, dropping his Shofield and pawing at his face, Ardis tried to whirl around toward me. But I hadn't been wearing hobbles, and I went into her even before she started around. She tried to keep her feet, and it carried us back through the brambles. She tripped in some thick chokecherry, and, still fighting to keep her from getting that falling-block gun in line, I went down with her, and we rolled over and over into the trees.

84

I've stepped on enough broncos to know how to be on top when it's over, and that's where I was when it ended up against a juniper, both of us hitting the trunk so hard the alligator bark showered down on us with a crackling sound. I had the rifle by then, twisting it from her hand.

"Damn you!" she panted, and I don't like that in most women, but it seemed to fit her like a custom-made kack. Before I could do anything with the rifle, she started clawing at my face, and I heaved the gun aside in order to grab her hands and stop that. I finally got her wrists crossed above her head, holding them there in one fist while I used my other to snake my own gun out of her belt. Behind me I could hear someone crashing through the trees, and I had that last minute with her body, warm and writhing, against mine. I couldn't feel mad at her, really, and I had wanted to kiss her for sometime now.

She stiffened, suddenly, beneath me, and stopped breathing, for that moment. Maybe I stopped breathing, too. I hadn't meant the kiss to be quite like that. My ears began to roar so loudly I couldn't hear that noise behind us, and I forgot all about Farrare and everything else, and, when it was over, I couldn't have told how long it lasted — a minute, or a year, or a thousand. I let her hands go and raised up a little, looking at her face.

Then someone was shaking me by the shoulders and shouting in my ear. When I got up off Ardis, she didn't even try to grab me, just lay there looking up with that startled look on her face. Bibo pulled me through the trees upslope, jerking on my arm like he wanted to pull it off.

"What the hell's wrong with you?" he said. "The horses spooked and ran up thisaway."

I could hear Farrare coming through the trees. My Bisley felt good in my hand. We were breathing hard, by the time we spotted the animals near timberline. I was running behind Bibo because he didn't have a gun, and I kept looking behind me, but I didn't know how close Farrare really was till he came into plain view from behind some junipers all of a sudden and opened up. It must have been his second shot that got me. My leg gave way, and I fell flat on my face. I rolled over on my back and sat up and threw down on one with my .38–40 that made him jump back into the trees. Bibo tried to get me up, but I waved the smoking Bisley at him.

"Get out. I can't walk. I'll hold him here till you're skeedaddled. Go on, damn' old fool. Getting soft or something?"

I eared back the hammer, hearing him stumbling off through the last of the timber back of me. Beginning to feel the pain of my leg now, I rolled up my Levi's and wondered if the slug had smashed the bones in my calf. Those Shofields always did throw a wicked hunk of lead.

"Come on out, Farrare. I'll give you one for Bibo. What's the matter, Wolffe? Come on out."

He tried it from behind a juniper, and my Bisley bucked in my hand, and I saw alligator bark fly from the tree about the height of his head. The snort behind me made me jump like a roweled bronco.

"I could only get one," said Bibo. "Now give me that gun and climb into the kack. I'll hook on behind."

It was some job getting in that saddle. Bibo kept Farrare back, and he was the one who taught me to sling that Bisley iron, and Farrare didn't have much chance to do any shooting. Then I felt the horse grunt with Bibo jumping on behind, and he gave it a kick in the kidneys that made the critter start off like a jack rabbit. Farrare's last shot sang over our heads, and then we were in talus above timberline and across the ridge top. I don't know when Bibo started shaking me.

"Come out of it, boy, come out of it. You get hit that bad?"

"Pretty bad," I said, and didn't mean the bullet. "You know, I was right about that Mexican gal."

"What Mexican gal?"

"The one down in Austin. She was a piker."

CHAPTER
TWO

Down where Horse Creek runs into the Green, the balsam poplars were dropping their red blossoms and perfuming the air. We'd got shuck of Farrare, although he and the woman tried to follow us when they corralled their nags, and washed my leg out at a crick that night. It took a good hunk out of my calf muscle, but no bones, and I'd tied up worse wounds than that with Bibo's bandanna. The horse he'd snagged was the gal's black, and carrying both of us two days hard running had played him out some. Bibo sang:

> Swing yo' partner, form a ring,
> Figure eight an' double L swing.

"Quit jiggling around," I told Bibo. "You'll have this pore horse so low he has to climb a ladder to kick a grasshopper."

"Can't help it, can't help it," he cackled. "Smell that wheat grass, boy. Spring in the air. I feel like singing. I feel like dancing. I wisht we was at one of them old square dances they had down Austin way."

> Ducks in the river, goin' to the ford,

Coffee in a little rag, sugar in a gourd.
Swing 'em once and let 'em go,
All hands left and do-ce-do . . .

He went on that way, and I couldn't help laughing, hanging onto his skinny old waist with his stringy gray hair in my face and all his smells of dirty leather and sour tobacco and sweat fanning my face. I'd been with this old ranny most of my life, and the old home I remembered was a saddle beside him or a sougan next to his. But other thoughts were still with me.

"You know," I said, "those Cut-and-Slash cattle. There was something going on there."

"When the beef smells bad, it's the smart man who leaves it to the coyotes," said Bibo. "Though it did rile me to have them horn in on our deal there. We could've got ten dollars a head at least out of those Cut-and-Slash critters. We'll find that Farrare gazebo someday and take it out of his hide."

"He wasn't going to sell those cattle?"

"Not the way he had you blot those brands," snorted Bibo. "A greenhorn could've spotted the botch. That don't add up." He had stopped the horse and was looking around.

"What's in your poke?" I said.

The brim of his battered old John B. was always flopping down in front of his watery eyes, and I guess I've seen him shove it up that way a thousand times, or a million. "This place looks familiar."

"We never hit the Green country before," I told him.

"Something about those hills I recall," he said.

"Or the cattle," I told him.

"Ah?"

"Look at the earmarks on those whitefaces."

He was looking toward the animals grazing on a slope to our right, then gigged the jaded black, crossed a rutted road, and stopped just beyond. That's what the earmark's for, to spot a longer distance away than you could see the brand. It was a steeple fork and that had been the earmark Farrare had made me put on those Cut-and-Slash cattle.

Bibo was squinting at the brand. "These ain't your decorations."

"These ain't the kind of cattle I work on," I said. "They've only been branded oncet. That A Bench is a stamping-iron job."

"Like the looks of our cattle, gentlemen?"

We had been too interested in the critters, and the road was still soft enough from the last spring rain to muffle most of the noise that rig had made coming down the hill. It was a nice new spring wagon with a pair of neat little bays, and the girl sitting in the seat had hair the color of ripe corn above her sunburned face, and blue eyes so big I could see them from where I was. Always equal to anything, Bibo turned our black around as calm as you please and walked him over toward them. The man beside the girl was tall and gaunt except for his shoulders, which were broad and heavy and stooped, more like a farmer's than a rancher's. His shirt sleeves were rolled to the elbow, revealing long-sleeved red flannels beneath, and his mop of gray hair might have been the same color as the girl's once, because his eyes were as blue as hers, except they weren't as big, or as soft. It was the man who had spoken, and Bibo answered him, scooping that battered Stetson for the girl. "We are interested in your cattle at that, sir. Adams is my name, Adams, and my friend here is Mister Smith."

I could feel the girl's glance drop across me from the top of my matted hair down through my brown stubble beard and dirty shirt to my Levi's that would probably stand up themselves by now. She didn't stop at the gun, the way Ardis had, or take in those scratches across the top of the holster, and that might have been one way of knowing how she was different from Ardis.

"Smith?" she said.

"Yes . . . uh . . . R.I. Smith," Bibo told her. "We're up this way looking for cattle . . ."

"Or horses?" said the gray-haired man, and lifted a scatter-gun from beneath the seat and laid it across his lap before I realized what had happened. "I think you better come with us, Bibo."

This is one time Bibo lost the reins. "Would you mind chewing that hay a little finer?" is about all he could say.

"What I mean is," said the other man, "around here they usually hang horse thieves."

The A Bench wasn't a very big spread, and the house was set down between two spur ridges, the narrow valley in front of it widening to a slope that ran down toward the Green River. The road wound over the north ridge and cut down its side through a snake fence, flattening out when it passed the pack-pole corrals and shabby-looking barns. There were a couple of horses hitched to the ring post in front of the long porch the house sported. It was one of those steep-roofed Wyoming buildings with no windows on the north side on account of those winter blizzards.

I slid off the black as easy as I could, but I almost fell as it was. The gray-haired man stiffened up, suspicious as a dog smelling a stranger on the street.

"What did you do to your leg?" he said.

"I . . ."

"Got it hurt when his horse rolled on him," Bibo finished for me. "Yeah, when his horse rolled on him. It was a big fat nag, and you should have seen . . ."

"Shut up!" said the man, and then it was the woman, opening the front door of the house and coming out on the porch, and he turned toward her. "Ardis," he said, "we found the men who took your horse. Sheriff Hale is riding out this way this afternoon. I won't even have to send Marval for him."

She stood there with those outlaw eyes staring at Bibo and me, and she must have been as surprised as we were. I had to admire her then, because her laugh was easy, and she came down the steps swinging her hips that way. "Took my horse? I guess you gave them a scare, Leo."

"Damn' right," he said. "I'll give 'em a bigger scare when they see that rope." He was looking at Bibo in a strange, tight way, and I've never seen so much bitterness in one man's eyes. "And that's too good for 'em to begin with."

92

"Don't be a fool, Leo," said Ardis, swinging her head so's that long bob spun black and glossy around the white line of her neck. "Nobody took Satan. I was up at Daniel last night and he pitched me coming home."

He looked like he hated to believe it. "That why were you so late?"

"Why else?" she said, and I could have answered that. "You were all asleep when I got in, and I didn't want to wake you to hunt the animal. Everybody around here knows him, and I figured somebody would pick him up sooner or later. All you've done is scare a couple of saddle bums out of a year's growth." She turned to us, and the smile was mocking. "Where did you find the horse?"

"Up near Horse Creek," said Bibo, and he was smiling, too, because he could appreciate something like this. "Yes, up near Horse Creek."

"You mean he ran that far and you brought him clear back here all in one night?" asked the blonde girl.

"You know what kind of a horse he is, Marval," said Ardis angrily. "Look at the sweat caked on him."

"But Horse Creek . . ."

"Never mind," snapped the older woman. "Will you take Satan to the barn for me when you put up the buggy? I think you might as well put that shotgun away now, Leo, and let these men go."

The one named Marval had hitched the black to the buggy. "I think we ought to at least give them a meal for the trouble we caused them," she said. "Looks like they could use it."

"A meal?" The man hadn't put his shotgun away; he stood there with both barrels pointed at Bibo's belly. "I should give them a meal?" He laughed suddenly, and it was harsh and short, like a gun going off, with just about as much humor. "I should give them both loads of this Greener. I should kill you right where you stand, Bibo Adams. I don't know what holds me back. I'll give you just about a minute to clear off my A Bench."

Bibo bent forward a little to peer at him. "I never told you my first name."

"Don't try and tell me you don't remember," the man said, and the muscles around his mouth began to twitch, lines deepening there till two grooves pulled his lips down toward his thin jaw. Bibo was still bent forward, and he pushed his hat brim up, staring at the man.

"Leo? That what she called you?"

"Manners," said the man flatly. "Leo Manners."

"Oh," said Bibo, pursing his lips. "Oh." He straightened, and his voice was sort of soft. "It's been a long time, Leo. You've changed a lot."

"You haven't, Bibo," said Leo Manners. "You're the same filthy conniving lying two-faced son-of-a . . ."

"Dad," cried Marval, catching Manners' arm. "What's the matter? What is it?"

Manners jerked his arm away so hard I almost jumped for fear that scatter-gun would go off. "You better go, Bibo," he said. "You better go before I empty this Greener in your gizzard."

94

"You better turn that shotgun around, Leo," said Ardis. "It looks like it might be of more use pointing that way."

I guess we all saw them, then. They were coming hell-for-leather down the ridge road, a big pot-bellied man forking a buckskin in the lead.

"It looks like our old crimes is catching up with us fast, R.I.," said Bibo. "That's a Cut-and-Slash brand on the buckskin."

The horsemen rode up and pulled their horses to a halt. The man on the buckskin leaned back in the saddle to compensate for his bay window, and his face was red and beefy.

"What are you up to, Newcastle?" Manners called to him. "I told you . . ."

"You ain't telling me anything, Leo!" shouted the fat man, and waved his arm toward the men behind him, and I saw how many of them had their saddle guns out. "Get his Greener, Farley."

They were all around us now with their Winchesters laying across their pommels and pointing at Manners or me or Bibo, and the one Newcastle had called Farley swung off his horse and wrenched the scatter-gun from Manners. He didn't make any fuss about what he did, turning back to his horse and lashing the shotgun behind his cantle with swift, skillful jerks, and then untying his forty-foot dally rope from a thong on his skirt. Right then I got the idea.

A couple of riders had swung in behind Manners, and their horses kept knocking him in toward me. I couldn't move any farther forward because the pot-bellied jasper had his lathered buckskin up there, and I was already bumping up against it and slopping myself all over with that lather.

"We found twenty-three of my cattle down in Sioux Coulée with my Cut-and-Slash changed to your A Bench, Manners. What kind of fools do you take those brand inspectors for? A tenderfoot could tell the brand had been worked over."

"Don't be a fool!" shouted Manners, fighting at the horses that kept bumping into him from behind. "I never even saw your cattle. Why should I be crazy enough to rustle them and then leave them with their brands changed right on my own land? Newcastle, I swear . . ."

"You better pray instead!" the fat man yelled at him, and those little veins were beating in his jowls. "We've been bled dry by you these last months, Manners. Every cattleman on the Green. I'm glad I was the one to find out who'd been doing it. You know what I said, Manners. I vowed I'd hang the rustlers when I found them."

"Dad!" called someone from outside the horses, and I realized it was the girl, "Dad, where are you? Newcastle, you leave him alone. What are you doing?"

The man behind Manners had his rope out, too, and snaked the loop down over Manners' head and jerked it tightly around his arms before he could struggle out. Then it was me. I tried to throw up my arms and double forward and slip the loop off, but he'd let it out community, and it caught me anyway, jerking me back up when he pulled. Bibo was the only smart one, but that didn't last long. He ducked under that tall buckskin, trying to get free of the horses, but a rider came in broadside from farther out, pinning Bibo against the buckskin as the old ranny came out on the other side. I saw Newcastle jerk his six-gun free, and it flashed in the sun going up, and down, and I heard Bibo grunt, hard.

"Pick him up," said Newcastle. "That poplar will do."

With the stink and sweat of those horses gagging me, they dragged and jerked me along with Manners toward a big poplar growing near the barn. I guess I fought a lot, choking in the dust, swearing at them most of the time. Somewhere outside the bunch of horses I could hear Marval yelling at Newcastle.

"You can't do this to him! It's murder! You can't do this to him, Newcastle, you can't, you can't . . ."

A lot of help she was, I thought. She sounded half loco, taking a big sobbing breath every now and then that sounded fair to rip her apart, voice breaking and choking on her words.

Reaching that poplar, three of the men got off their horses. They tied my hands around behind me and set me up a skittish little pinto. Farley French had thrown three ropes over the limb and the loops were black against the sky, and suddenly, sitting on that pinto, I quit fighting. The animal rage had passed, leaving only a full realization that this was it. I wanted to vomit.

Bibo was conscious now, sitting on the horse next to me, and he met my eyes. "I'll introduce you to the devil when we git there, boy." He grinned. "I hear he plays a right good game of stud."

I tried to laugh. It had a cracked sound. Farley French adjusted the noose around my neck, drawing it snugly, looking up at me with that impersonal ice in his eyes. Manners was sitting stiffly on the horse beyond Bibo, staring straight ahead of him. Out farther the other riders had bunched their horses in front of Marval to keep her from this, but I could hear her crazy little cries and see her corn-yellow head moving behind them. French had the ropes all adjusted now and all they had to do was whip the horses out from under us, and we would dangle. Newcastle jerked his arm that way, shouting at French.

"All right, Farley, all right!"

Marval stopped screaming suddenly, and the riders quit shifting over there. I could feel the pinto gather itself beneath me as if sensing what was coming. Even the breeze stopped through the foliage above us. Farley French raised his arm to slap my horse's rump. And right then and there it came.

"You hit that horse and it'll be the last thing you do on this earth, Farley French!"

CHAPTER
THREE

French stood there with his arm held up, his whole body stiff as a poker. Then he turned toward the voice. We were all looking that way now, and I saw what had happened. In order to do his work here, French had hitched his own horse to a scrubby cottonwood between this poplar and the house, with that shotgun of Manners's lashed on behind the saddle. With all the attention on us, Ardis had been able to reach the horse and jerk the Greener loose, and now she stood there with her legs spread apart and the double-barreled iron across her belly and that outlaw look arching her black brows up over her burning eyes. There isn't anything to hold a crowd of men like a shotgun, and, when she jerked it at me, Farley French moved fast enough. I guess he knew her.

"Get him down," she said. "Get him down."

French let the rope slacken so it wouldn't stretch my neck when he got me off the pinto, and untied my hands. I got his gun out and tossed it over by the tree, and then pulled my own Bisley and watched the rest of them while French let down Bibo and Manners. They let Marval in, and she threw herself in her father's arms, crying and shaking like a dogie with the colic. It

99

was when I turned away from this that I saw another rider coming down the road from the ridge. He brought his gray to a stop near us and sat there a minute, taking time to check his chewing tobacco and spit.

"Having a little party?" he said.

Nobody answered him for a minute. Maybe he hadn't expected an answer. He wasn't big, but he wasn't small, and his gray hat was flat-topped and sat squarely on his head, so the brim threw a shadow that didn't quite hide his eyes. They were the same color as his hat and held about as much humor as the business ends of two 45s. There was a tarnished star on his blue serge vest, and he packed his Remington .45 stuck right in the middle of his Levi's waistband. Down in Austin, they had told me to stay clear of Sheriff Monte Hale of Sweetwater. I saw now what they meant.

He turned to Newcastle. "I told you what I'd do with you if you tried lynching anybody, Owen. I'm not having that in my county."

"And I told you what I'd do if I found the rustlers!" shouted Newcastle, gouging his buckskin with grappling irons big as the wheels on a Murphy wagon. "You stay out of this if you know what's good for you, Hale."

"If Manners has been rustling your cattle," said Hale, "I'll take him into Sweetwater, along with the evidence. I don't know but what I'll take you along, too, for this little lynching bee you tried."

"Hale, I'll break you . . ."

"Where's the evidence?" said the sheriff. "I swear, if you don't . . ." Hale turned to spit, and Newcastle jumped like he thought the sheriff was going to go for that belly gun. "Where's the evidence, Owen?"

Newcastle was trembling with rage now. "In Sioux Coulée. One of my hands is holding them there. The job was so sloppy a child could tell those brands have been worked . . ."

"We'll go get it. Who are these others?"

Ardis answered that. "Just a couple of saddle tramps who found a horse I'd lost. Leo brought them in."

Sheriff Hale turned toward Newcastle, and I wouldn't want his mouth to get thin that way at me. "And you were going to hang them along with Manners," he told the fat man. "Do you know what that would mean?"

"How do you know who they are?" yelled Newcastle.

"That's just it," said Hale. "And you were going to string them up." He turned to Manners. "Come on, Leo, let's go and see those cattle in Sioux Coulée."

I didn't particularly hanker after seeing any more of this lawman than I needed, and I didn't make any move to go with them, just stood there, leaning against the poplar while someone got a horse for Manners from his corral. Marval got herself a little pied nag, too. Sheriff Hale necked his dun over to me, and leaned forward out of the saddle.

"When we leave," he said soberly, "you and your friend better shake this county's dust off your hocks as quick as you kin. I guess you can see it ain't exactly a healthy place for strangers."

Then they all filed off up the ridge road, Newcastle sulling like a Texas steer tied to a mesquite bush, Hale turning once to spit. When they were out of earshot, Ardis came over to us, still holding the Greener.

"Now you get out," she said. "If Wolffe ever sees you again, he'll kill you. I'm giving you this chance. Get out."

I took a step away from the tree, and my leg gave out from under me, and I went down. Bibo came over to help me up.

"You give us a horse," he said. "Running Iron ain't in any fix to hoof it."

"You think we give horses away to any saddle bums that come along," she scoffed. "I don't care how you get out. I don't care if you have to crawl. But get out!"

I guess that made Bibo mad. "What are you doing here?" he said.

"I'm Leo Manners's sister-in-law."

"Bibo didn't exactly mean that," I told her. "Your little frame-up almost got out of hand, didn't it? Why didn't you just let them hang Manners? That would have gotten him out of the way for good."

I saw her hands tighten around the shotgun. "You're running across slick rock."

I looked at the dilapidated house, the shabby barn. "Sort of a scrubby spread to go to all this trouble for. You still got to get rid of Marval."

"If you think I'm doing this for the . . ." She stopped herself, then bent forward. Her teeth were small and white, biting her plump underlip. "Are you going, or do I call the sheriff back here and tell him who really altered the Cut-and-Slash brand on those twenty-three cows?"

Bibo cackled. "You won't do that, honey. We'd just as soon let him know how you're in on the deal as not. You give us a horse and we'll go."

She took a breath through thin lips. It looked like something was going on inside her. "I can't give you a horse," she said finally, shaking her head from side to side in a frustrated way. "Somebody rustled Leo's string of cow animals, and Leo and Marval are out on the last of the saddle stock."

"Rope that," said Bibo, grinning slyly at me. "Somebody rustled their saddle stock!"

She caught the mocking tone of his voice, and her eyes narrowed at him. "How long have you been working Sweetwater?"

"Why, you know we wouldn't touch another man's horse," said Bibo. "It must be some other fellers doing all this rustling. We're just pore honest saddle tramps that got mixed up in all this, innocent as a pair of newborn dogies. How about your horse?"

She looked at Bibo a moment longer, then shook her head savagely. "I couldn't let you have Satan even if I would. He's known all over the county, and somebody'd just pick you up again for horse stealing and bring you right back here." She shook her head again. "Oh, damn you, damn you . . ."

Bibo cackled. "It looks like you're saddled up with us till this boy's leg's healed enough to hoof it away from here. Funniest part of it is you pulled the cinch tight on this rig yourself." He turned toward the house, rubbing his belly. "Can't say as I mind that, either. Been a long time since I et reg'lar. A week here on three squares a day would leave me right fat and sassy. What say we git Running Iron inside and look to that bullet hole?"

It had been a good house once. The kitchen had a wainscot of oak halfway up the wall, and a big iron kitchen range that must have come from back East somewhere, and an oak table as big as most kitchens I've seen. They sat me down on one of the heavy chairs, and the woman stood there a minute, looking at me like she didn't know quite whether to go on and squeeze the trigger on that scatter-gun she still held or put it down and look at my leg. Finally she put it down. She looked at my pants leg and went over to a drawer and got out a big carving knife. Then she hunkered down like a man would and slipped the tip of the knife in the bullet hole some below my knee and slit the pants leg clear to the bottom from there. She didn't need to do that to get the pants leg up, and I had to grin.

"You're the smart gal, ain't you?"

"And you're the dumb boy," she said, taking a couple more slices at the bullet hole till it was no longer plainly recognizable.

"How do you expect anybody to believe that story about a horse rolling on you with the bullet hole plain as daylight in your Levi's?" She had unwound Bibo's bandanna, and the disgust was plain on her face when she saw the wound. She jerked one hand at Bibo without looking at him. "We'll need some hot water first. Well out back."

"You know," I said, after Bibo was gone, "I'd like you even better if you were all bad."

104

Something wild about the way that black hair always tossed when she turned her head to look at you. "What do you mean?"

"That soft streak in you," I said. "You couldn't let Wolffe kill us the other night. And today, with your little frame fitting so nice around Leo Manners, you couldn't let them hang him."

"You're not so pure yourself." The look in her face made me think maybe she was ashamed of that softness in her, somehow, the way a boy doesn't want to be thought a sissy. She was looking at the wound again. "What on earth did you do here?"

"Tried to dig it out with a sharpened stick," I told her. "Without much success. You had our horses and Bibo's Bowie was in his blanket roll. Not even a Barlow knife between us." Then I was watching the top of her head where that part ran white down the middle of her black hair and was talking about the other thing. "I guess that's what's wrong with me and Bibo, too. We're not bad enough. I guess that's why we'll always be a couple of saddle tramps. That Wolffe Farrare, now. He'll go places. He's all bad. When he starts anything, you know just how he's going to ride his horse all the way down the trail, and, when he gets to the end, it'll be loaded down. What's he carrying here?"

"Never mind," she said, going to get a smaller knife and a whetstone out of the drawer.

"No use taking that attitude," I said. "If we stick around here, we're bound to find out sooner or later what you and Wolffe are after on the A Bench. *He* would have let them hang Leo, I wager."

"Don't try to play dumb." She had been honing the blade easily, but she took a vicious stroke against the stone. "You know what's going on here just as well as I do."

"You'll have to cut the deck a little deeper," I said.

"You know what I mean." She jerked her head up to look at me. "You came back with Bibo Adams, didn't you? You've been traveling with him. You know what's going on here."

"Is that why Leo Manners knew Bibo?" I said.

"Will you quit it . . . ?"

"I guess Wolffe Farrare was mixed up with them, too?" I said. "He's closer Bibo's and Leo's age than ours, isn't he? Sort of an old man for you to ride with."

"Listen . . ." — she took a step toward me, holding the knife hard on the stone — "when Wolffe was cutting his baby teeth on a six-gun, he was ten times the man you are, and, if he grows to be a hundred . . ."

"I sort of thought it was that way," I told her. "Did you tell Wolffe what happened?"

She waved the knife jerkily. "It isn't *that* way. I can kiss any man I please."

"I sort of thought the saddle was on the other horse," I said.

"All right. So it was *you* that kissed *me*," she said. Then the anger had slipped from her, and she was breathing heavier now so that her silk shirt sort of rippled in the light every time her breast rose against it. She took another step toward me, bending forward slightly. "You've had a lot of practice, Running Iron."

I looked at the way her lower lip dropped a little from the white line of her teeth and the way her pants fitted the line of her hip. "I had a stallion once," I said, "that liked the mares all right, but whenever he went after them, it was like he could take them or leave them, never tossing his head much, or pawing around like you'd expect. Then one spring a black outlaw mare comes down out of the monte, and my stallion snorts so loud they heard him in the next county and paws up so much ground the dirt farmers for ten miles around didn't have to do any plowing that year and tosses his head so high I thought he'd break his neck."

She bent forward a little farther, and the contour of her face seemed softer, more feminine. "I thought maybe it was that way." She breathed it more than spoke it. "I felt the same way, Running Iron. There have been other men. But never like that."

I licked my lips. "It's all right for a man to heat himself by a fire, but he's a fool to stick his hand in and let it burn him."

"Can you help it . . . now?" she said.

She was so close her breath warmed my face. "I guess not, Ardis. I guess Wolffe will have to kill me, after all, or I'll have to kill him. It won't be any different than that, will it, or any less?"

She took a breath. "I told you it wasn't *that* way."

"Maybe not with you," I said. "But it is with him. I've seen how he watched you. He doesn't mean to see anybody else's dally on you." Her hand on my arm burned the sleeve.

"Running Iron," she said, "maybe you're right about the fire. You're not burned yet."

"You asked me to leave before."

"It isn't for that, this time," she said, and, looking into her eyes, I could believe it.

"Bibo taught me a few things with an iron," I said.

"There have been other men, that way."

"Did you ask them to go?" I said.

"No," she muttered. "I told you it had never been this way before." Her fingers tightened on my arm, and the strength in them surprised me. "You don't know Wolffe, Running Iron."

"Then I'd better stay around and get better acquainted," I said. "Does he eat old six-guns with his breakfast?"

She looked into my face another moment, then straightened, taking her hand off, and that softness was gone from her. "You've picked the horse you want. You'd better cinch it up tighter than you ever did before."

I watched her face and thought: *Yes, I've picked the horse I want, Ardis, and I can't help if it's bad or good, and I guess I don't care much, because a man can't care much when it strikes him like this, and my boots are about as muddy as yours, anyway.*

Bibo came in with the water then, and Ardis told him to get the whiskey out of the cupboard and finished putting the sharpest point on that knife I've seen outside a stiletto a Mexican had once down in Durango. I took a couple of shots of the coffin varnish and licked my lips and got hold of the table with both hands. Ardis was hunkered down in front of me. She took one look at my face, then ducked her head and went to work. Bibo stood over against the kitchen sink, finishing the bottle.

"I recall once down in Van Horn a Mexican I was traveling with got his seat full of twelve-gauge buckshot whilst trying to entice some Elbow X cows across the Río with the help of his dally and sundry other aids they was using to influence cattle in them days. The man with the shotgun didn't have a very good horse, though, and me and this Mexican got acrost the Río before he could load up again and get close enough to put the second pair of barrels in a more effective place. I don't know how many chunks of lead that Mexican took, but he had about resigned himself to sleeping on his belly the rest of his days, when I tuk a ride into Van Horn, and there on a bulletin board the Rangers always keep in front of their office was a printed circular saying anybody finding a Mexican who didn't seem to enjoy his seat in the saddle would be perfectly justified in killing him on sight for a dirty, thieving, low down . . . ah, ah, you want another swig of this, Running Iron? No? I think you better have it. Get a better grip on that table."

He put the bottle to my mouth, and I spilled half of it over my shirt front because I couldn't get my teeth apart to let the whiskey through, somehow. Ardis was biting her lip so much the blood trickled down her chin. She looked up at me that way again.

"It's caught in between the bones somehow," she said.

I nodded, and she ducked her head again, and Bibo went back to the sink, taking a drink himself. "That was the attitude they had toward operators like us in them days, you see. A man even suspicioned of nefarious cow practice was perfectly legal bait for any rancher's gun, and I seen more loaded tree limbs down there than a man with a weak stomach should be allowed to. Anyways, I went back and told my Mexican friend about how he was marked for life. Everywhere he went with that tender seat of his, he'd be a direct invitation to a lynching party, and damned if he didn't pull out his Bowie knife and go to work right there. You can understand how awkward it was, but he wouldn't let me do it for fear I'd miss one. Dug that point in till he felt the piece of shot and then pop it out like a peon spitting piñon seeds. Must have tuk him nigh onto a week, working night and day, to finish the job, hunkered there like a turkey gobbler picking the thorns out after it's been getting elm mast in a cactus patch, and I'll be . . . ah, ah, Running Iron, get a holt there. Another little swig? You better."

I didn't even try to take it this time. The sweat in my eyes blinded me, and I could hear someone breathing like a winded horse, and didn't know whether that was me or Ardis. I guess it wasn't as bad as the time those rannies worked me over in Austin, but right now it seemed worse.

"Better take it before I finish it," Bibo said. Then he saw how it was and went back to the sink, tilting the bottle up. "Yeah. And would you believe it, that Mexican's saddle sitter healed up till he could sit down like any other man, and all he had to show for it was a bunch of little holes, like a bunch of smallpox scars, and he could ride right into Van Horn with the best of them and stand there, reading the circular they'd put up about him, and nobody ever knew the difference. Well, what do you know, all finished! How about painting your tonsils with what's left of this red ink?"

Ardis got the kettle and washed the wound.

"You must've treated more'n one gunshot wound without a doctor," Bibo told her.

"I guess I have," she said. She smeared the poultice on my leg and then on some clean cloth she'd got, and tied up the wound. Then she pulled the Levi's down over it. "Now, if anyone asks, your leg was so swollen from that horse falling on it we had to split the pants to get them off your calf and cut the flesh up a lot to remove the pus."

Bibo had a cackle like an old hen. "That about fills the poke, all right."

"There's a more comfortable chair in the living room," Ardis said. "Help me get him there."

They had me lifted up between them when the horse pounded up outside. We heard it slide to a halt and saddle leather squeak and then boots clattering up the back steps. Marval came in on the run, and Ardis let go one side of me to stop her, grabbing the girl by her shoulders.

"What is it? What hap . . . ?"

"They've got him." It came from Marval in a broken way. "Let me go. They took Dad to town. You know how long that will last. Newcastle's got the other

111

ranchers so whipped up now over those rustlers they'll be storming the jail by nightfall. I tried to stop them but I couldn't do anything. Let me go, Ardis. They'll lynch him. Let me go. Let me go!"

She tore free of Ardis but, in trying to get around her, bumped into me. Then I realized what it had taken for her to get even this far into the room, and why she had wanted Ardis to let her go. Like a Solado horse that can't run any farther, she sagged against me, almost knocking me over, and burst into tears, her whole body shaking like an aspen in a Texas norther.

"Let go the boy," snapped Bibo. "He can't hold you up like that."

He let go of me to try and get her off, but she clung to me desperately, the whole front of my shirt wet with her tears, and she was holding me up now as much as I was holding her. "They'll hang him . . . they'll hang him . . . you know they will . . . he never rustled a steer in his life, and they'll hang him, and I'll be here all alone . . ."

"Shut up," I said, riled by that, somehow, and began shaking her. "Haven't you got any guts. You're a grown woman now. They haven't put the rope around his neck yet. I've seen a newborn dogie with more starch in it than you. Bust out crying every time the wind changes, I swear. Shut up, damn you, shut up!"

She threw her head up, her eyes wide with surprise, and for that moment she had stopped crying, staring at me. Then she pulled free, taking a step backward. Finally she began moving toward the door leading to the front part of the house, her head turning toward me with that dazed expression in her face, but she hadn't started crying again when she disappeared. Ardis was watching me, too.

"Well," she said, "you really like them tough, don't you?"

CHAPTER
FOUR

A couple of days in that house and I was getting as restless as a thirsty cow smelling water over the next hump. Ardis left the second day. I saw her riding that black horse up over the ridge, swaying a little in the saddle with her easy, supple seat, and, after she was gone, it wasn't as crystal inside me as when I'd talked with Bibo. I heard someone outside and was turned from the window by the time Marval opened the door. She had on a pair of blue jeans with hay and dirt all over them, and there was a smudge across her face.

"Don't you have any hands?" I said.

"Never did," she told me, coming in, and with the plaid shirt on her shrunk really too tight from a lot of washings, I could see she wasn't as much of a girl as she looked, sometimes. "It isn't such a big spread. Dad was always able to handle things himself."

"Where did he know Bibo?"

"Your friend?" She was studying me. "I have no idea. You've been with Bibo a long time."

It was a statement. "Yes," I answered. "My dad sacked his saddle when I was about three, and Bibo's brought me up ever since."

"He's down in the kitchen getting drunk," she said. "Does he do that often?"

Only when there's a girl, I started to say, and then I stopped myself. He had done the same thing when I started going with that Mexican gal at Austin and, after he couldn't stand it any longer, conked me on the head and tied me behind his saddle and lit out for Wyoming. "I won't let him get messy," I said finally. "He doesn't anyway. Just goes to sleep."

She laughed, and it didn't have that husky sound Ardis always made. More like the bell in the Alamo, or a creek running over pebbles. "Same way Dad acts when he gets drunk," she said, and came on in. "I'm sorry the way I acted day before yesterday. It just hit me hard I guess, and Dad's the only one I have. Nothing's happened so far. I suppose I was wrong about the lynching. They have too much respect for Sheriff Hale's gun to try it. The trial's set for June Tenth, and I know Dad will be proven innocent then."

How, I wanted to ask her, how? I had turned to the window, wondering why I didn't want to look at her. Because of what Ardis was doing? Then I realized it wasn't that at all. I didn't feel guilt. It was more a distaste. That didn't seem right, either. She seemed nice enough now. And she really had gotten a jolt the day before. But I kept remembering how helpless she had been through it all, and I found myself wondering if she could have dug that bullet out of my leg, or even looked at the wound. Oh, hell . . . "You want something special?" I said.

"You seem to be getting around better."

"I could ride a horse, if that's what you mean," I said.

"I wasn't asking you to leave," she told me. "I wondered if you wouldn't like a job." I turned around at that, and there was a pleading look in her face, like a dogie begging for milk after three days of a dry mammy. She held out her hand. "I know it isn't very hospitable. If Dad were here, I wouldn't even mention it. You'd be welcome to stay till your leg got well. But I'm in a bad spot. If I leave spring roundup go any longer, Newcastle's riders will begin picking up all our unbranded stock and putting their Cut-and-Slash brand on. Dad's bucked Newcastle ever since the Cut-and-Slash was a shoestring outfit down on the Green, and Newcastle's always done everything he could to try and force us out. If I don't get our A Bench on this new stuff, there won't be any spread for Dad to come back to. Somebody has to stay here at the house, either Ardis or me. It isn't a very big herd, but one person couldn't handle it alone."

"I thought your string had been rustled."

"It was," she said, "but I can borrow a few cutting horses and ropers from our neighbors. Newcastle won't loan us anything, of course, but there are a few smaller ranchers still sticking by Dad."

I was about to refuse, but then I remembered Bibo, and that would be one of the few ways to snap him out of this bender he was heading for. "I won't be much good roping with this leg," I said, "but Bibo can make up for it. Now don't start crying again."

116

"I won't," she told me, swiping the back of a dirty little hand at her eyes. "I just don't know how to thank you."

"Don't," I said, turning back to look out the window. "When do we start?"

Next morning. And it was the rattiest string of cow horses I've yet laid my eyes on. The roper Marval had got for Bibo was just an oily little bronco ready to jump every time his own shadow did, and I couldn't see him working cattle from the hind end of a clothes line, somehow. I got a shad-bellied bone yard that passed for a cutting horse, its bed-slat ribs sticking out through a winter coat that hadn't finished shedding yet. No chuck wagon, either. Just a coffee pot and some bacon slung in a tarp on an extra cayuse. I tried to see Ardis alone before we left, but Marval stuck around too close, and the best I got was a good look at the black-haired woman when she came out on the porch to say good bye. Even then I couldn't look too long for fear Marval would see.

Manners had his line camp in Yallow Valley, and we dumped our truck there and started right out that afternoon to gather all the unmarked stuff we could find and be back at the holding spot before night. With only three of us, Marval decided it would be better to separate. I got a hogback called Medicine String that cut east and west along the south side of Yallow Valley, and lifted my shaggy bag of bones right up to the ridge top so I could see both slopes. I spotted my first bunch in a coulée down the north side and dropped in to cut out three cows with new calves and a couple of long heifers that had missed being branded last fall. By the time the sun was dropping behind Medicine String, I had about a dozen head, driving them through a saddle in the String that would lead back to Yallow. Bibo came up from behind with his own bunch, a-singing.

> Chase that 'possum, chase that 'coon,
> Chase that pretty gal 'round the room.

"You feel pretty good, getting me away from that Ardis, don't you?" I said. "Or is it something else?"

> How'll you swap and how'll you trade,
> This pretty gal for that old maid?

"I saw the way you looked at Medicine String, Bibo," I told him. "Same way you kept looking around when Manners first picked us up south of here. Is this part even more familiar?"

> Wave the ocean, wave the sea,
> Wave that pretty gal back to me.

"Maybe that's why you're glad to leave Ardis," I said, leaning toward him. "She knew what had been between you and Leo Manners?"

He didn't look at me, but he wasn't smiling. "It's a smart Injun that don't hunt for live coals in the ashes of a dead fire, and I always thought you was a smart Injun."

"I never asked you things you didn't want to tell me before, Bibo," I said. "But this is different. Don't you think it would be better if I knew, just this once? What's going on here? When did Manners know you before? What's Ardis and Wolffe trying to get off the A Bench?"

His saddle squeaked as he turned toward me. "I'll tell you what's going on. A boy I know is being a damn' fool. It ain't enough that the ranchers around here is liable to find out by some off chance just who it really was that's been relieving them of their stock. You're in with Ardis now, and, if that crooked dally she's throwing on the A Bench happened to snag on a bad steer, you'd be pulled off your feet right along with her, and Sheriff Hale'd be right there ready to hog-tie you afore you could get up again, and, if there's one brand of John Law I wouldn't want to have throwing a peal around my legs, it's Hale. And if it ain't the ranchers or the law, it'll be Wolffe Farrare wanting to know just what you're doing with his heifer in his pasture, and I don't think you're in any condition to do much answering, seeing as you can't stand only on one foot."

"All right," I said. "Forget it."

We rode along ringy as a couple of sulling steers, not looking at each other, till finally Bibo spotted movement on the slope to our right and waved his arm up there. "Couple of heifers in that high coulée. Holler if you need any help."

My nag jumped a little when I jerked it around. It was getting dark, and the old man's beard hanging on the firs on this north slope looked foul, somehow, and a dusky grouse was sitting on a branch with his tail spread and wings hanging, filling his neck pouches with air till they looked ready to burst before he started pumping his head up and down to deflate them and send his hollow hoot through the timber. It's the most mournful sound in the world when the timber's filling up with dusk, and I reached around for my Mackinaw, suddenly feeling cold. I had just unlashed one whang from the saddle roll behind my cantle when I spotted him.

"Never mind your gun, sonny boy," he said. "I had mine out first."

I sat there a minute with the grouse hooting through the trees, because I never had Bibo's recovery, but finally I got something past my teeth. "Smith," I said. "R.I. Smith."

"Glad to make your acquaintance," he said. "My name's Sean. You wouldn't happen to know the whereabouts of a man named Bibo Adams?"

"Adams?" I took my hand careful-like off the saddle roll. "Never heard of him. You want him for something?"

"Yes," said the man mildly. "I've been hunting him for some years. I'm going to kill him."

I don't know why that grouse should stop hooting just then. Maybe this Sean saw how I stiffened in the saddle. I couldn't help it. He stood there, shifting around as touchy as a teased snake, and for the first time I saw he was bare-footed. His jeans were patched in the seat and knees, and his buffalo coat was old enough to have been worn by General Custer.

"Git off the horse," he said finally. "We'll wait for Bibo."

"You've got your boots in the wrong poke," I told him, but I saw how tightly he held that gun and swung off anyway. "I don't know any Bibo. Smith is my name. I trade in horses."

"Looks like you ain't such a sharp trader," he said, taking a gander at my bag of bones. And that was when I saw his eyes. He had a beard shaggier than the buffalo coat, and it grew up high enough to make his eyebrows part of it. His face was pale and gaunt as a cow skull on the Cimarrón. I'd seen a Mexican hopped up on peyote once, and his eyes had the same look, like a fire was blazing inside him. "R.I." he said. "Could that be for Running Iron? Down in Austin they told me a man named Running Iron Smith had taken up with Bibo Adams."

"No," I said, "no." This had to be so fast it wasn't very good. "Real Injun. They called me that cause my pappy was Cherokee."

He bent closer, and he wasn't grinning when his teeth showed, and they were rotten and yellow. "Don't try to fool with me, sonny boy. I been waiting for Bibo Adams a long time. I thought maybe he'd come back to our old diggings someday. We'll just sit down and wait for him."

"But, pard . . ."

"Sit down."

I sat down. Then he did, too, lowering himself, cross-legged, onto the wheat grass without a sound. We couldn't see the valley from there, because we were

121

down in the bottom of the coulée, but Sean was facing toward the way Bibo would come from when he got tired waiting for me to ride back with those cattle I'd gone to fetch. Bibo and I'd been in some pretty narrow tights before, but I'd never sat down with a crazy man waiting for the old ranny to come so the loco could shoot him. *Oh, God, Bibo,* I began thinking, *don't come after me this time. I'm old enough to look out for myself, you old fool. Don't come after me, just keep riding down into Yallow and wait for me at the line shack.*

Sean began giggling, bobbing his head up and down. "Real Injun," he said. "That's pretty good. Be a long time afore anybody tops that. Real Injun. He-he. He-he."

"He-he yourself. Don't I look part Cherokee?"

"You don't."

"Look here, this Bibo ... Bibo ... what's his name ..."

"Don't try to pretend you don't know him, Real Injun. Adams. And I'm going to kill him."

He'll come right up over that hump like an old fool looking for me and get it smack in his pickled old gizzard. I was beginning to sweat; with that cold wind beating down off the ridge, I was beginning to sweat. *Bibo, for God's sake don't do it, not this time. I don't want to see you killed like this. You're the dirtiest old bull I ever threw a dally on, and you don't know enough to drive nails in a snowbank, but I've been with you too long for it to happen like this.*

122

"Bibo Adams," I said. "Yeah. Why you want to kill him?"

He jerked that rifle at me. "Quit moving around. You see that sump over there?"

It was the first time I saw what was left of the old mine workings on the lip of the coulée above us, a bunch of smashed supports reaching out from the granite and some rotten old hemp dripping off them. Seepage was turning the stone dark and working down the shale to form a foul pool in the bottom of the coulée behind Sean. It didn't make too much impression on me then. That grouse was still calling up in the timber, and I felt like I couldn't breathe. *Don't, Bibo, please, Bibo, don't.*

"That's why I'm going to kill Bibo Adams," said Sean, and his eyes blazed like lanterns in the gathering dusk. He leaned forward, and his voice sounded like a fiddler on a tight string. "I'm going to kill him and dump him down the old Yallow Hole because that's where he belongs. You see how it's seeping. It's full now. It's just a sump. Once the richest mine north of Laramie. Two hundred dollars to the ton once, and now just a sump. Bibo's sump. He did it, and he's going to rot in it."

"Did what?" The grouse was still hooting, and that wind was whining now so I couldn't hear what I was listening for behind us. *Did what, you crazy old coot? Bibo, for God's sake . . .*

"Piney Creek," said Sean. "That's what backed up into it, and nobody could pump it out, and the richest vein north of Laramie was lost. I been waiting a long time for this."

No, Bibo, no. Was it something else beside the wind, now? My gun felt like a ton of buffalo bones against my hip, and I was watching him like a painter ready to jump a sheep, and he knew what I was doing, and he was waiting. *Bibo, please don't . . .*

"Well, it's about time, Bibo," said Sean, and jerked his rifle away so it pointed past me.

But I threw myself at him the same instant he spoke, because I'd been waiting for that. I never saw anything move so fast. Or maybe I didn't see him move. He had to jerk the gun back to keep my body from knocking it aside, and then he was gone from in front of me, and I was rolling into the stagnant pool and knowing it was all over now and waiting for that shot and thinking: *Why did you have to do it, you damn old coot, why?*

Then I could sit up in the water, and I realized Sean hadn't shot. He stood there, tall and skinny and knobby-kneed in the dusk, holding his rifle across his belly toward the lip of the coulée. The figure skylighted there was as tall as the crazy man, but his shoulders were heavier. His whole body was heavier. He was just about big enough to hunt bears with a switch.

"Running Iron Smith," he said, and dropped down the shale in a walk that swung those great shoulders like on old Texas Cimarrón on the prod. "I've been wanting to see you. About Ardis."

"Wolffe," said Sean, "you promised me . . ."

"Shut up," said Wolffe Farrare. "You'll get what you want when I've tended to Mister Smith here. Hold your gun on him. And now, Running Iron, I want you to unbuckle your Bisley there right easy."

"Couldn't you do it just as easy without that?" I said.

"No," he told me. "Drop your hardware."

There wasn't anything else I could do. I stood up in the pool, and my iron made a splash when it slid down my legs. Then he unbuckled his own gun. Even in the dark, he must have seen the surprise in me.

"It appears you don't know Ardis very well," he said.

"What's Ardis got to do with it?"

"Do you think I don't know what's going on between you and her?" he said. "She was up here the day after they tried to lynch Manners. She'd changed toward me. I know the signs, Running Iron. There have been other men. It happened the same way. It isn't as simple as just killing you."

"You were willing enough to do it in that pocket above Horse Creek," I said.

"That was for the cattle," he said. "I didn't want anybody wandering loose knowing how we were connected with those Cut-and-Slash cattle they found in Sioux Coulée. But this isn't for the cattle. I wish it was. I wish it was that simple. But it isn't. Not with Ardis. Just killing you wouldn't be enough. I'm going to give you a beating. I'm going to give you a beating you can take back and show her, and every time she looks at you, she'll know who gave it to you."

"I thought you said you knew what was between me and Ardis," I told him.

"I'm not blind."

125

"I think you are," I said, and all the time he was coming on. "You're treating it like we were a bunch of cows in a pasture. Ardis isn't a heifer that'd take a bull just because he beats all the others. She's a woman. You won't stop what's between me and her by just beating me up."

"She's closer to a heifer than you think." He grinned. "She's a very elemental woman, Running Iron. She's the kind of a woman wants a man, if nothing else. When I get through with you, there won't be enough man left in you to attract a female heel fly."

Calling her a heifer was what made me mad. "Come on, then, Wolffe. There ain't nobody sitting on your shirt tail."

I stood there in the water till I heard him grunt. That was when he jumped and his body came at me so big and black it was all I could see. I doubled up and stepped aside, but he wasn't as dumb as he was big.

Another man would have gone hell-for-leather on forward and tripped over that foot I left behind, but Wolffe was ready for something like that, and even though he couldn't stop himself, he was twisted around far enough to grab my arm and pull me down with him. We rolled into the pool, and, when he came on top, he let me go and jumped up, and right there I knew why that pattern of scars on his face had struck a familiar chord when I'd first seen it. They call it logger's smallpox, and it comes from being stamped on with a caulked shoe, and the lumbermen from Calgary to Santa Fé are marked that way, because it's the way they fight, and it's the way he was fighting now.

126

But Bibo Adams had taught me a few things besides what to do with the two irons, running, and shooting, and, as soon as I saw Wolffe shift his weight onto one leg so's his other would be free for kicking, I rolled over on my side without making the mistake of trying to rise, and was already grabbing for his foot when it lashed out. I caught the boot and kept on rolling and pulled him right off his other foot. He came down with a crash loud enough to make the bucks in Montana shed their velvet three months early, and this time I was the one to get up first.

"I can fight with my feet, too!" I yelled, and I was already running for him when he rose.

He whirled around with his arms out like a grizzly, not meaning to get out of the way of anything, wanting to come to grips again, no matter how. Maybe he wasn't expecting me to take off that way. I hit him feet first and they went into his belly so deeply I thought I'd get them caught there. It carried him back against the rock wall with all the air going out of him in a hoarse bellow. Then I was down on my back in front of him with my feet still in the air, and before I could roll away, he dove. His face was shut hard enough to bust his nutcrackers, and his eyes were closed tighter than a sleeping 'coon's, and his hands pawed out in front of him like a jumping painter's. I let his chest hit my feet and rolled him over me, using his own momentum. The ground shook when he hit, and I was already coming out of that backward somersault onto my feet. He came to his hands and knees, shaking his head, shouting: "Sean, Sean!"

127

I saw the crazy man standing there with his rifle pointed at me. He waked up, still looking like he'd give his last boot to let me have it. "Real Injun?" he said, and laughed like a coyote on a moonlit night. "Real Injun."

I was blowing like a boogered bronco, and I tried to reach Wolffe before he got off his hands and knees. I let my whole body strike him, and we rolled over and over, and every time I came up with my right arm free, I hit him in the face with everything I had. I don't know how many times I let my knuckles go into the front of his skull before we came to a stop. All I know is my whole fist looked like a chunk of hamburger, and my arm was filled with lead, and he was still fighting as hard when we stopped as he had been when we started. I came up straddling him and caught him by the hair and beat his head against the rocks.

He grabbed my arms, trying to jerk loose, roaring savagely — "That's it! I guess you see how it is now. That's it, that's it!" — like he enjoyed it, and then he had my elbows pinned so I didn't have any leverage, and I had to let go of his hair. His head smashed into my belly, and I went backward with the whole world exploding.

I tried to get up, but he hit me before I had my feet under me, and I couldn't keep myself from staggering back until I hit that granite slope. Then with his sweating bloody body holding me against it, he grabbed my ripped shirt by the collar in one hand and began hitting me with the other. I must have fought like hell, because I could hear him grunting and shouting, and feel him writhing back and forth to avoid whatever I was doing, but that free fist kept blowing up in my face, and pretty soon I couldn't see anything or feel anything but the way my flesh ripped under his knuckles and the way my bones cracked, and then I couldn't feel anything.

It was the snapping sound at first. The snapping sound, and then someone's low voice. I had trouble opening my left eye; my face felt all wet. Then whatever sensations came was pushed away by waves of pain lapping at me like the water coming up the ford at Horse Thief Crossing when the Pecos is bank full. I guess I didn't even hurt so much that time the wild bronco tromped me.

"Who was it, who was it?" somebody kept saying. Marval? I tried to focus. At first I thought it was the moon. Then I saw it was her yellow hair shining from the light of a fire. I felt the heat of that fire on my left side now. She was washing my face with a rag dipped in warm water. "Adams wondered what took you so long and found you like this in that coulée on Medicine String. Who was it, Mister Smith?"

I caught Bibo's face behind her, puckered up in a sly way. "Some loco ranny," I told her.

Bibo's cackle was pleased. "I guess he's still a little foggy."

"Some Cut-and-Slash men?" she said.

"Some Cut-and-Slash men!" I echoed.

"Oh, those fools . . ."

"That mine." I waved my hand and that hurt, too. "Those diggings . . ."

"The old Yellow Hole," she said. "Dad and Uncle bought it when I was a little girl. They had pay dirt all right, assayed so much they incorporated. Dad had a lot of influence around here, and everybody bought shares up to the hilt. It was about that time Uncle married Ardis and brought her here. But Piney Creek backed up into the shafts they sunk and no amount of dredging would empty the water out. It ruined Dad completely. He did what he could about paying off the shares with his private fortune, returned about twenty-five cents on the dollar. All we had left was this land the mine was on. After that nobody would trust Dad for anything. You can understand how it's turned him bitter."

"And your uncle?"

She shrugged. "He lost everything, too. He went out of his mind for a while. It was a pretty hard time for Ardis. Then Uncle disappeared. They found him dead in Laramie a couple of years back."

It was something in the back of my mind that made me ask. "What was his name?"

She looked surprised a little. "Sean," she said. "Sean Manners."

CHAPTER
FIVE

Nights like this north of Kemmerer the stars were so thick and so close it looked like heaven was having a Christmas party and you could reach up and pull one of the candles off the tree for yourself. I lay there awake a long time after Marval had rolled into her sougan, staring up at the sky and trying to piece it all together through my pain. I could hear Bibo singing out where he was circle-riding the herd. He doesn't croon a Texas lullaby like most night herders, but one of those damned square-dance tunes, and I never will stop being surprised that it doesn't stampede the critters.

Rope the cow and kill the calf,
Swing your partner 'round and a half . . .

Then it was the other sound. Marval's sobbing. The old line shack's sod roof had caved in and we were all bedding outside by the fire. I gritted my teeth with the ache it brought to raise up on an elbow. I might have known it. I had a lot of trouble getting out of the sougan and slipped on my Levi's over my long flannels. I didn't know what I was going to do. I just couldn't sleep, listening to that, and it made me mad, somehow. I grabbed her by the shoulder.

"Listen, you've got to stop that. Nothing to do that for now . . ."

Marvel had turned over so suddenly I didn't know what it was till she was in my arms, her whole body shaking against my chest. "I can't help it, I can't help it. Those Cut-and-Slash men are out to stop our branding. Next they'll be stampeding what few cows we've collected. Newcastle isn't satisfied with having Dad. He has to ruin us completely."

"But it wasn't Cut-and . . ."

I stopped myself, and she turned her wet face up to me. "What?"

Holding her like this was different than Ardis. "Nothing," I said, and I didn't know whether I was mad at myself now, for feeling this way, or at her. "Nothing." And then she had sunk that yellow mane against me and was bawling again. I couldn't help it. Her head rocked back when I shook her so hard I heard her teeth click. "Will you stop bawling like a puking dogie? I swear you ain't got clabber for guts. What's the matter with you?"

"Go ahead," she said, her head thrown back, "go ahead!"

That stopped me. "Go ahead and what?"

She was rigid in my grasp. "You looked like you were going to hit me. Why don't you? I'm just a girl. I couldn't fight back like those Cut-and-Slash men. Go ahead and hit me."

"Oh, hell" — I let her go, shoving her away from me — "you ain't worth hitting. If I thought a few knocks could bring a horse's guts out in the open, I'd quirt him right enough. But when they got a streak of yellow down their spine so broad it laps over their brisket bones, I wouldn't even bother putting a hackamore in their teeth. Go ahead and cry. I'll go out with Bibo."

"Mister Smith." I'd turned away, but her voice turned me back She sat there leaning on one arm, firelight lining down one curve of her wet cheek like a piece of ripe fruit. Her underlip was quivering. She bit it. "You've had a hard life, haven't you?"

"It doesn't matter what kind of life a person's had. It's what the top screw put in them to start with."

"I guess you're right," she said, dropping her eyes from mine. Then she noticed something and pulled out of her blankets.

"Your bandage is coming off."

"No . . ."

That's about all I got out. She was close enough to reach my pants leg without moving and pull it back off my calf, and there it was, the bandage all pulled down off the wound and trailing around my spurs. She didn't even have to bend closer. Finally she looked up, a strange, new expression in her eyes.

"Ardis knew it was a bullet hole?"

I licked my lips. "I reckon."

She took a heavy breath, getting to her knees and unwinding the bandage. "R.I. Smith?" she said. "Running Iron? I guess I should have known it."

"Word spreads," I said.

"Trail hands passing through here have spoken now and then. The way they talked, I didn't exactly know whether you were real or not. The way you were supposed to handle a running iron, I mean." There was something tender about the way she rewound the bandage. She looked up quick-like then, reaching out one hand and not quite touching my arm. "Running Iron, if you're in trouble . . ."

"No more than you're in," I said.

"I mean . . ." — she hesitated, and then the fingers touched me — "I mean I want to help you."

"Why?"

"Because you helped me. You took that beating for me."

"You know what I am."

"More than you think," she said. "Maybe that's why. I guess I wasn't wrong about the way you've lived. Bibo brought you up?"

"And taught me all I know."

"The running iron, the gun, the owlhoot" — she jerked her head impatiently, then looked at me again, as if hunting for something in my face — "I guess you're a lot like me. Maybe I have it in me to be brave, but nobody ever taught me how before. Maybe you have it in you to ride a different trail, but nobody ever showed it to you."

"What's wrong with my trail?"

"Don't you know?" she said. "Are you so stupid as to try and convince yourself cutting out other people's cattle and changing the brands is honest and good?"

"I never worried much about bad or good," I said. "They're just words. Most people seem to have them mixed up pretty well anyway. They wouldn't let a man like me in your Kemmerer church, but Newcastle goes there every Sunday and everybody tips their hats and licks his boots like he never heard about sin. How do you justify that? He's appropriated ten times as many cattle as me. He's broken men like your father from here to Texas. Every time a bunch of homesteaders gets pesky or gets too strong, Newcastle whispers a word in his assemblyman's ear, and the grangers find a new law that puts them off their land and out of Newcastle's way."

"Running Iron . . ."

The surprise in her face maddened me. "Don't pretend you don't know. Maybe you don't know everything about him, but you know enough. And he ain't the only one. The cottonwoods talk a lot plainer along the owlhoot than your minister does in his pulpit. We got a grapevine that'd make Sam Morse blush for shame, and I know enough about half the big, honest, good ranchers in this county to send them to hell on a hot shutter. I've probably made a few men curse with the cattle I've borrowed, and Newcastle's made a few die with the deals he's pulled, and they'll make him governor someday, and hang me. So now ask me what I know about bad and good."

"Oh, Running Iron, Running Iron." She had me by both arms now. "Is that what Bibo's taught you? Haven't you ever tried to figure it out for yourself? You were brought up by him and never knew any other teachers, and he was already so far down the wrong trail you couldn't see where you'd turned off even if you looked back, and I can't blame you for the way you've lived. But haven't you ever tried to think it out for yourself? Would you take my cattle from me?"

Her eyes were big and bright and blue, and I couldn't meet them. "I . . . I . . ."

"That's what I mean," she said. "You wouldn't, because you know how it would hurt me. It's all we have left, and you know how it would finish us, and you wouldn't touch them. That's what bad and good is, Running Iron. Not what people think of you. Not what they say of Newcastle because he's rich and powerful and goes to church and hides what he does, or what they say of you because you're a known rustler. Bad and good is inside yourself. You'd know it if you ever tried to think it out for yourself. The good in going to church isn't the mere fact that you're there. The bad in rustling isn't in the rustling itself but the harm you do to others by it. You've got just as much good in you as anybody, and just as much bad. The only trouble is all anybody ever showed you before was the bad."

Talking to me like I was a kid or something that way. But somehow it touched me, like a hand would touch you. I shook off her arm and turned away from her face, and then got up and limped off a bit toward the herd. I realized she was right. I'd never thought about it before. I'd had plenty of time to, a thousand nights, or a million, lying beneath the stars with my head on my arms, and all I'd thought about was the way that Mexican gal in Austin kissed or how nice the beef we'd roasted for dinner tasted or how good that ride down through the timber had been beside Bibo with a posse yapping at our heels. I'd never asked myself if it was bad or good to kiss the gal, or bad or good to eat beef that wasn't yours really, or bad or good to have a posse chasing you all over Texas. I just liked things, or didn't like them, and that was enough, the way Bibo took it, the way he had taught me to take it. I felt like an animal suddenly. A hog that had been rooting around with his snout in the dirt after onions because he knew they tasted good, and then had looked up to see the sky and realized it had been there all along, if he'd just got his nose out of the dirt long enough to take a gander.

My head jerked up, and I didn't know what the sound had been at first. Then I realized Bibo wasn't singing any more. I had my Bisley out and was already running toward the herd. "Bibo? Bibo?"

I must have fallen a dozen times on that bum leg before I reached the cattle. They were milling around, spooked by the gunshot, and I knocked a couple of wobbly calves over before I could get through the bunch to where the horse stood. It had been a good roper once, and, as soon as Bibo left the saddle, the animal must have stopped. The reins were still on the horn, and he lay on his back in the deep wheat grass. I started to go one way, then the other, and finally almost jumped on the horse.

"Nev' mind, boy," said Bibo. "They did it from the timber over there, and you might as well try to find hair on a frog as trail them. Help me up. Got something to tell you before I sack my saddle." By the time I lifted his head he'd got his shirt all wet bleeding at the mouth, and there was a funny, glazed look coming into his eyes. He waved his hand toward Medicine String. "Funny. I pulled so many deals I forgot some of them, I guess. I'd forgotten this one, till we met Leo Manners. I knew the country smacked familiar, somehow, but I couldn't recollect anything. Didn't even recognize Leo, remember? It was the Medicine String, boy, I should have recalled. Twenty-odd years ago. Before I put you in my poke. Twenty-odd years ago and now it's starting all over again. Funniest part they never did know the real truth. Piney Creek backed up into it, and they never did know the real truth. They still think it's rich. Doing all this because they think it's rich. Even Leo. Leo and all of them. And it's salted. Not like you'd take a shotgun and blow some dust into a rock. A ton of good rock, see. Packed in on mules and dumped down the hole. That's really salting it up right . . ."

"Running Iron, what's he talking about?" Marval had crouched beside us now, her face white in the dark.

Bibo saw her and cackled. "Like corn, ain't it, boy, yellow as a Kansas cornfield. This is the one for you, boy. You got your heifers mixed. Ardis'll give you a crooked ride and a knife in your back at the end. All the time you thought it was that hellcat, and it should have been Marval here. You need her, boy. You're all hard, and that ain't good. I guess I made you that way, didn't I? I couldn't help it, boy. We had a good ride anyway you look at it, didn't we?"

"We had a good ride," I said.

"You can be soft with her, boy," he babbled. "You can be soft with a woman and that ain't weakness. It's something you got to learn I couldn't teach you. Neither could any of the women you ever knew. Marval can. Let her teach you, boy. A man sees the last ridge ahead, and a few things are clearer. She can give you softness and you can give her guts . . ." He shuddered in my arms and for the first time I realized how really little and dried-up he was. He waved his arm again toward the Medicine String, so hard it almost knocked me over. "Don't let them do this to her, boy. Tell 'em old Bibo salted it. Tell 'em they're doing all this for a bunch of salt. A ton of it. That's all, boy. A ton of it, and then they're through. Salt, boy, salt . . ."

CHAPTER
SIX

A high wind was coming down out of the Salt Rivers
when we got back, and a loose shutter was flapping
somewhere on the second story of the A Bench house.
There was a gaunt sorrel standing hipshot at the hitch
post in front of the porch, and I pulled up just below
the top of the ridge.

Marval turned in her saddle, pulling her animal to a
halt. "It's not Sheriff Hale's sorrel, if that's what's
worrying you."

"Looks familiar," I said. It was three days since Bibo
had died in my arms, never even answering my
question. I'd finished branding for the girl because I'd
promised, and I wanted to see if I could find something
on who murdered Bibo. But I didn't find anything.
Even the trail into timber had petered out in shale, and
an Injun would have been hard put to trail, and I'm no
Injun. It had been too big a shock at first for me to feel
much, or even realize Bibo was gone. But now it was
beginning to come when I was alone in my sougan at
night, and I felt mean as hell right now. I took out the
bullet. It had gone clean through him and been stopped
by the cartridges in his belt at the back, and, when I
buried him, it had dropped out his shirt.

"I still can't figure any of the Cut-and-Slash men in on that," she said. "None of them would use a steel-jacketed slug in their saddle guns."

I could have told her I never figured the Cut-and-Slash from the beginning. "This doesn't come from an ordinary carbine. It looks a little bigger than Thirty-Thirty."

She was watching me closely now, and strangely. "And when you find the gun it came from?"

I put the bullet away without answering, turning my horse on down the road. I could hear her animal trotting up behind me.

"Running Iron, you can't do it that way, you can't just go out and take vengeance like a wild animal. I thought you understood that night, before Bibo was killed, I thought I'd showed you it was in your face, your eyes. Killing someone else won't help now. Two rights don't . . ."

"Keep that in your own poke," I told her. "Nobody bothered about right or wrong when they dry-gulched Bibo. And when I find the man with the gun this shell came from, I'm not going to bother about bad and good. I don't know whether it's bad or good. All I know is Bibo's dead and they killed him."

"You didn't understand that night." She spat it like a treed cat. "I thought there was something good in you, something decent. I thought you'd just been given the wrong horse. But you would have picked that horse even if Bibo wasn't there to rope it for you. You're no better than a wild animal. You're worse than an animal. At least they don't know any better . . ."

We were at the porch then, and she was almost crying again. I dropped off my horse and threw the rawhide reins over its head, my face clamped shut. *All right, so I'm an animal . . . I feel like one. I'd like to get something in my hands and tear it apart.* Thinking that, I limped onto the cool stone porch. It was then the door opened, and I knew why that gaunt sorrel had looked familiar. Ardis came out behind the man and introduced him to Marval.

"This is Mister Carnes, Marval," she said.

"Cadaver Carnes?" I said.

"What?" said Marval.

"How did the branding go?" asked Ardis quickly, and seemed to cover it up because Marval's mouth pouted out and she took a heavy breath.

"Not good, Ardis. Not enough to make a day's work for Running Iron, and him not able to get around very well as it was. I don't think the cattle alone will see us through this fall, even if we sell the whole herd."

"Running Iron?" said Ardis, turning toward me.

"Yes," I said, watching Cadaver Carnes. "Bibo didn't get a chance to do any branding. Somebody killed him."

The rich color left Ardis's face, and her mouth opened without any sound coming out. She put up her hand to indicate something, then dropped it again. The mournful man's features never changed. He held his dusty black flat top against one side of his dusty black tailcoat, and three cartridges in his gun belt glittered between the front edges of his coat, and he stood without moving, my gaze making no visible impression on him. Finally Ardis could speak, and her reaction was genuine enough. She said something about how inconceivable it was or how terrible, or something, I didn't hear rightly, and then we were moving into the big living room. Ardis nodded at a mahogany Morris chair with reversible cushions and four reclining positions the way it's advertised in the Sears, Roebuck catalogue, and Cadaver took it. She kept looking at me, and I decided she wanted me out of it.

"I'll go wash up," I said, rattling my spurs across the hooked rugs to the kitchen door. They expected me to go on outside to the wash rack the hands must have used, and I knew that, and it was why I closed the kitchen door and went to the tub they had inside. It had enough water in it, and I could hear well enough through the door what they were saying.

"Mister Carnes is here for Headway Lumber," Ardis told Marval. "They're still willing to buy that strip along Medicine String."

"Yes." Cadaver's voice was hollow and dusty. "We're hard-pressed to fill our tie contracts with the U.P., and we're willing to up the price we quoted last fall."

"I know" — I could hardly hear Marval; she was across the room — "but Dad didn't want to then, and I can't . . ."

"Your father was just being stubborn, Marval," said Ardis. "Unwilling to sell the String because of his fool sentimental attachment for the Yallow Hole. Newcastle's out to get you now, and, if you don't have hard cash when this next payment comes due on that trust deed he holds, he'll foreclose and get the whole A Bench, including Medicine String. Sell the String to Headway now, and it will give you enough to see you through this year regardless of how your beef turns out."

Marval hesitated a moment. "But Dad . . ."

"Yes," said Ardis, "what about your father? Do you think you're doing him any good stewing around like this? With money you could fight Newcastle. It's the only thing that can fight him. If you don't care about the A Bench, at least think of Leo. It's for his own good now. You're lost, if you don't see that Marval. You'll just have to sit here and let them railroad your father to the pen or a lynch rope and then come and take the A Bench right out from under you."

Marval's hesitation was longer this time. Finally she sighed. "I guess you're right, Ardis . . ."

"I have the contracts right here," said Cadaver.

"What good will that do?" Marval asked.

"Your father being imprisoned loses all his civil rights," said Cadaver, "consequently the title to his property falls under the jurisdiction of the legal heir. You being of age, your signature on the deed ratifies it completely. I have pen and ink in my case here, and, if you'll just sit down at the table . . ."

"Don't do that, Marval."

The three of them turned like I'd jerked a string, all at once, to stare at me where I had opened the kitchen door. The blonde girl was sitting at the sideboard with a bunch of papers spread out across its cracked glass top. Ardis flushed dark, and her lips twisted around the words.

"You were eavesdropping!"

"I sure was," I said. "My ethics don't prevent peeking through the fence when a couple of old mossyhorns are trying to hornswaggle a pore little dogie. You leave those papers alone, Marval. As long as your dad hasn't been convicted, he remains in full legal possession of his property. Whatever you're trying to do here, Cadaver, you jumped the gun a little."

Cadaver's voice was expressionless. "I don't think I've jumped any gun, Mister Smith. I didn't want to be the one who broke the sad news to Miss Manners here. The circuit judge arrived a week early from Kemmerer this year. Owen Newcastle brought pressure to bear and had Manners's case shoved to the head of the list. A jury was sworn in last night, and all the necessary witnesses subpoenaed. The trial was already over when I left town this morning."

"You mean Newcastle bulled it through like that without even giving them time to notify me . . . ?" Marval had almost knocked the chair over, getting up, and then it struck her fully, how he had finished. She stared at him. "Dad . . . Dad . . . ?"

"Was convicted," said Cadaver.

Marval collapsed into the chair, still staring up at him, then she buried her head in her hands, body shaking like a dogie with colic as she sobbed.

"You better go, Cadaver," I said.

"Miss Manners hasn't signed the papers yet," he said, and somehow his coat had got shoved back far enough for me to see all the cartridges in his gun belt and the big black-handled Colt in its slick holster.

"Any other time I might try to reason with you," I told him, "but right now I feel mean enough to eat off the same plate with a snake. Either you get out right now or you pull your gun, and I don't care which."

The only sign Cadaver made was the way his big sad eyes suddenly grew opaque, like water when a cow stirs the mud up, but Ardis must have seen it the same as me, or known it, because she was speaking. "Don't be too quick with your reins, Mister Carnes," she said softly, "you're on the toughest bronc' in the String this time."

Cadaver stood there another minute. Then he turned toward the door, his tailcoat making a soft dry whisper in the hush, and left without speaking or looking at any of us, and we heard his saddle leather creak outside, and then the sorrel passed the open door going up the road. Marval was still crying, and I didn't know whether I was going over and slap her face or leave the room, that's how mean I felt. Then I turned and went out through the kitchen. The air smelled fresher outside, and I stood there sucking it in a while, and then went around front to unsaddle the horses and turn them out just for something to do. I'd slung all the kacks on the opera seat and was just closing the corral gate after the horses when Ardis came down from the house. I took a hitch in the rawhide latching and stood there, waiting for her, knowing what was coming.

"So you had to butt in," she said.

"Why didn't you let Cadaver go on?" I asked.

"I didn't want him to get killed," she said. Then she was standing up to me, bosom heaving, face flushed.

"Listen, Running Iron, I told you how I felt about you and that won't ever change, no matter what, but it has nothing to do with what I'm doing here."

"Just what are you doing here?"

"Don't bother acting dumb," she said. "You know what's going on. You know more about it than I do. You and Bibo thought you could come back and cash in a second time? That's all right. I can forget that. I told you what we're doing here has nothing to do with the way I feel about you. But if you try to stop it, Running Iron, no matter how I feel about you, I'll kill you. Do you understand that? If you try to mess things up now, I swear, I'll kill you!"

That bronco in Dallas held his mouth the same way when he kicked me, all twisted up, the outlaw in his eyes turning them hot and blazing. "I understand," I said, and I did. "That's the kind you are, isn't it?"

"Yes, that's the kind I am," she said, and then leaned back a little, something like a smile catching at her mouth. "And it would take a man like you to understand it."

I shrugged. "Wolffe said it right, maybe. Elemental. I never knew what the word meant before, exactly."

She reached up to touch my face, and, where Marval's fingers had felt soft and cool, this woman's were like hot pokers touching me. "Looks like Wolffe did more than explain my character to you."

"What do you mean?" I said.

"No other man would mess you up like that, Running Iron, no other man could. It was Wolffe, wasn't it? He did it deliberately, didn't he?" She

147

laughed suddenly, pulling her hand back. "So you thought he was a little old for me?"

That riled me so I grabbed her by the shoulders, and her flesh was hot against my dirty hands through the thin silk shirt. "Maybe Wolffe was right. Killing me wouldn't have been enough. Any man can pull a gun and kill another one. That wouldn't have been enough. He had to beat me up so you could see. Is that it? Like a couple of bulls in a pasture goring each other to see who gets the heifer."

"Don't call me a heifer!"

"I guess that's it, then. He was right. Elemental. Just beat me up so you can see who's the best man . . ."

"You fool, do you think that matters? Do you think he could change anything that way? Do you think it's that simple, now?" She almost shouted it, to stop me, and then her body was up against me, heaving with the breath passing through her, and it was like that first time back in the pocket by Horse Creek, only more so, and all the meanness that had been in me at Bibo's death left in a flood, and all my anger at Ardis, and all of everything, except the terrible burning consciousness of her there against me. She had her eyes closed when she finally took her mouth away. "Now tell me Wolffe was right," she breathed.

"I guess he didn't know his woman as well as he thought," I said.

She pulled away. "I've got to do something now, Running Iron. This will end it. When I come back, we can go away or do whatever you want."

148

★　★　★

She carried with her a saddle gun and a leather case, and I realized what the case was. "You mean you got Marval to sign that deed, after all!"

Ardis nodded. "Carnes left it on the table. It's for her own good, Running Iron. The A Bench is through without that money."

I grabbed her wrist so hard she let out a cry of pain. "Don't try and tell me you're doing it for the girl's own good, Ardis. You're doing it for her dad."

"Do you think I care about Leo?" she said, trying to tear loose. "Blind, bigoted, miserly old fool. Do you think I give one damn what happens to him. I saved his life. That's about all I would do. Whatever else happens to him is his own fault. He could have sold the Medicine String a year ago and saved himself all this, but he wouldn't listen to reason."

"Forget Manners," I said. "I saw what he was. What about the girl? I'm not going to stand by and see her hurt."

She drew up. "Oh, aren't you? Why the sudden solicitude for Marval? Maybe you kiss her like that, too, when you're out branding her cows . . ." The way I squeezed her wrist made her cry out again. Panting, she tried to tear loose once more.

"You know it isn't that," I said. "She's just a kid, that's all, caught in this, and I can't see you or anybody else hurt her any more than she's hurt now."

"Hurt?" She almost laughed. "She was never hurt in her life. She doesn't know what it is to be hurt. She'd bawl like a sick dogie if you so much as gave her a hard

149

look. She's a spineless, sniveling little brat. A spineless sniveling little brat and a bigoted miserly stupid old man, Running Iron, and you don't know what it's been like having to live with them, and I don't care what happens to either of them now."

"Why have you *had* to live with them?" I said. That stopped her, and she stood there, licking her lips, staring wide-eyed at me. "Because of Sean?" I said.

I hadn't expected such a violent reaction. Her face turned the color of dead ashes and with my fingers on her wrist I could feel the stiffening of her body start from there. She took a breath through her teeth.

"What do you know . . . of Sean?"

"I met him up on Medicine String," I told her. "He said he was hunting for Bibo Adams to kill him."

It came out of her brokenly. "Sean . . . ?"

"Yes," I said. "Your husband. As crazy as locoweed. Now, Ardis, don't you want to tell me what's going on here?"

"No . . ." She tore loose this time and turned and started running toward the front of the house where her horse was hitched. "No, Running Iron, you know what's going on as well as I do, and, if you try to stop me now, I told you what would happen."

My leg hurt badly, trying to run after her, and she was already at her horse by the time I reached the corner of the house. She jammed the saddle gun in the scabbard beneath the left stirrup leather and lashed it in with a tie thong. Then she ran in the house again, and I could hear her boots clattering around in the front room. When she came out, she was stuffing a handful of shells into the pocket of her Levi's, spilling a couple of them as she half ran across the porch. She threw a look at me, but I didn't move from in front of the porch, because that outlaw light was flashing in her eyes, and I could see there would be no stopping her. She knocked the reins off the hitching post and threw them over the black's head and jumped up like an Indian, hooking under the horn with her left hand and kicking her right leg up so it carried her into leather without touching the stirrups. She jerked the black around, jamming her boots into the ox-bows.

"Don't try to follow me, damn you, don't try," she spit at me, and then she wheeled the animal and raked it with her can openers and jumped it into a gallop up the ridge road. I stood there till she had topped the rise, trying to decide whether I wanted to follow her or whether the feeling for her was so strong inside me I didn't care about anything except waiting for her to come back and then going away with her the way she had said. I turned around and went up the steps, and something bright caught my eye. Marval came to the door about the time I stooped to pick it up.

"Where did Ardis go in such a hurry?"

I didn't answer. I fished in my shirt pocket for the bullet that had killed Bibo. I held it up with the cartridge I had picked off the porch.

"Running Iron," said Marval, "what is it?"

I turned around and walked back out to the corral and got a kack off the fence. Marval had followed me, and it must have been about then she understood. I put the saddle on one of the horses I had turned into the

151

corral, and led it back out, and closed the gate, and stepped into the stirrup. I turned the horse up toward the ridge road.

"Running Iron!" screamed Marval. "You can't! Not Ardis, Running Iron, for God's sake, not Ardis!"

CHAPTER
SEVEN

Up where the blue spruce sheds its needles so thickly your horse sinks into the carpet like a bog, and the black bear roots through the chokecherry for wild onions, and a marmot startles the quaking aspens with his shrill whistle from some higher talus. Up where the air is so pure it hurts to breathe, and the piney smell is so strong it almost chokes you when the wind is right and the silence is so big a pine cone dropping from a tree sounds like a cannon going off. Up where Bibo belonged. Sitting there on the first ridge of Medicine String, that's what I thought. How many times had he and I sat our horses on a top land like this, drinking in the sweetness of spring in the wind and sounds of a country where a man knew how free a bird felt in flight? How many times had we . . . ? *The hell with you, Running Iron,* I thought, clamping my teeth shut, because to think of anything now was only pain. My nag was no equal to that black stallion Ardis forked, but I had managed to follow her this far, trailing her most of the time, guessing her direction some, sighting her once or twice when I got to a ridge behind her. Now remembering what was in my mind all that ride, looking back, it seemed a black emptiness of purpose.

But there must have been thoughts. Hate and anger and love and passion and bitter reluctance and driving vengeance all spinning around, each trying to top the saddle and ride roughshod over the others, none clear enough or strong enough to do it.

From this ridge I could see Yellow Hole above the cut I had been driving the cattle through that day, and, when I saw movement about the rotting workings of the old mine, I turned my weary horse that way, dropping down through thick strands of spruce that were crowded out finally by juniper on the lower slopes, riding in the darkest shadowed lanes and avoiding every open patch until I reached the spot where I could no longer approach mounted without showing myself. I stepped off and hitched my horse and stood there watching for a while.

Down in Yellow Valley the cedars clung, warped and stunted, to the bases of the foot slopes, but up here they were like tall queens, and they were the last patch of timber I moved through before the Hole. A black stallion was tethered to one of the shattered supports of the shaft. It nickered as I stopped at the edge of the cedars.

"Wolffe, is that you?"

It was the voice of Ardis, from the mouth of the mine, and I walked out without answering. That first terrible craving for vengeance had subsided in me now, and I felt dead inside, somehow, knowing only that this had to be done, that I couldn't live with myself past this day if I didn't do it, that I couldn't die without doing it.

"Wolffe . . . ?"

She started to call again, but I had appeared at the mouth of the cave. I could see her dimly inside, staring at me, the pale blot of her face, the mature line of her hip in those Levi's. I walked on in, boots sinking into the boggy ground here, taking the two bullets from my pocket.

"I want you to know why I'm doing this, Ardis. Bibo would want you to know." I held up the lead slug and the fresh cartridge. "This steel-jacketed Forty-Five-Forty is the bullet that murdered Bibo. And this steel-jacketed Forty-Five-Forty is one of the shells you dropped when you left the A Bench."

"You fool" — it was almost a gasp — "you shouldn't have followed me. Running Iron, you shouldn't." It wasn't what I'd expected. There wasn't even any fear in her face as she clutched at me. "Please, get out, get out before it's too late!"

I tried to tear her loose. "You don't seem to understand."

"I understand," she said. "It's you who doesn't understand."

"I've come to kill you."

"Running Iron! Please, get out of here. I told you not to follow me . . ."

"Didn't you hear me?"

"I heard you . . ." She stopped, clinging to me, and her face was turned past me. Then I felt her arms tighten around me. "Wolffe!" she screamed, "Wolffe!" — and slammed me up against the wall of the tunnel as the shots thundered from behind. I got my Bisley out while I was rolling across the floor. I struck one of those

155

rotten timbers, and it crashed down somewhere to one side of me. Choking and gagging in the wood dust it raised, I got to my feet. I heard someone running down the tunnel and couldn't see Ardis any more between me and the lighted end and thought she had gone on in. I thought of Wolffe in that moment, but I didn't want to lose Ardis — I wanted to reach her while this was still strong and black enough inside me, and I turned on into the mine.

The floor was rotten mud that sucked me down sometimes to my boot tops, and after a few feet I couldn't run. Then I struck a strata of rock and some old timbers fallen across the bottom and made my way a little faster, jumping across deep pools of water in the bottom. She couldn't go far, if this mine was filled with water like they said. I could hear somebody coming in behind me now. Wolffe?

It was too dark to see finally, and I began feeling my way along one wall, and it was then I came to the first branch tunnel. I stood there, realizing what that meant. No telling how many of these branches were ahead. Without a light, I'd have about as much chance of finding Ardis as I would finding hair on a frog.

Rope the cow and kill the calf,
Swing your partner 'round and a half . . .

I don't know how long I stood there after it came. It chilled me so I was actually shuddering when I recovered from the first shock. Then I tried to tell myself it had been in my head. I clamped my face shut

156

and started moving on down the main tunnel. The water sucked at my legs with a sloppy, mournful sound. The dampness of the earth around me seemed to press against my body like a cold hand. The darkness was suffocating.

> Ducks in the river, going to the ford,
> Coffee in a little rag, sugar in a gourd.

Bibo? It welled up in me and slapped against the roof of my mouth, and I didn't know whether I had said it aloud or not. *Bibo? Don't, Bibo, please. Ain't it hard enough without that? Ain't it dark enough? I'm after her, Bibo, she's right ahead somewhere.* I began stumbling faster through the muck, bumping my head against rotting timbers, knocking a support down with a crash, lurching into a rusting ore car on a siding that turned into the next branch tunnel.

> You swing me and I'll swing you,
> We'll go to heaven in the same old shoe . . .

"No, Bibo, please. For God's sake, Bibo, don't plague me like that. I'm doing the best I can, Bibo . . ." I stopped myself, crouching there, realizing how far I had gone gibbering in the dark like that. I never was afraid of anything I could fight. But this was different. I clutched the Bisley out in front of me, trying to make my call quiet. "Bibo, if that's you, come out. I'm here. Running Iron. If you're not dead, come on out."

And if you are dead . . . ?

157

Swing 'em once and let 'em go,
All hands left an' do-ce-do . . .

"Bibo, damn you, quit it, quit it. Bibo, damn you, quit it, quit!" I stopped myself again, my breath coming in hoarse sobs. It was Bibo's voice, all right, no denying that. And his laugh. I could hear it ringing down the mine, that crazy old hen cackle. Not in my head now. I knew it. Nobody else. Nobody else could sing the old square like that, or laugh like that. *Oh, please, Bibo, for God's sake, Bibo, don't. Please . . . come on out of that hole . . .*

How'll you swap and how'll you trade
This pretty gal for that old maid?

Bibo. I started running wildly down the mine through the water then. *Bibo.* The tunnel had a deep slant, and I went headlong more than once, keeping my gun out of the water by instinct more than intent. *Bibo!* I don't know what I meant to do, all I knew was I couldn't stand there in the dark and hear him singing like that. *Bibo!*

I followed the sound of his laughter through a maze of tunnels, turning off the main one into a branch, turning off that into another. First I thought it was the woman mocking me, but she couldn't have made her voice sound like that, or laughed like that. Then I thought of Wolffe. But he couldn't have done it, either. Finally I stopped the loco running, crouching there with my own breath deafening me. The rotten timbers were dripping ooze constantly around me. The water was up to my knees, freezing cold now. Then I heard movement. Ahead? I took a step that way before I heard it again. Behind? I whirled around. *Oh, damn you, Bibo, damn you . . .*

The shot stopped that. It sounded muffled. I moved toward the sound, then saw the light filtering into this end of the tunnel, revealing the framework of supports and buttresses. The opening it came from was in the ceiling, and I had to holster my gun to climb up the timbers and claw through the hole. Sunlight hit me like a blow, and I couldn't see for a minute. I rolled over, and what I did with my right hand was automatic. Then I could see. I was on a slope, and below me about ten feet were two men, one of them lying stretched out on his back. The other man stood above him, twisted toward me with the tail of his long black coat shoved away from the black butt of his six-gun. We had both reached that point about the same time and now both stopped there, the way two men will when they're equally surprised, both waiting now for the other one to make the break.

"Go ahead," I said.

He did. There was no sensation in me. It's always that way. Feeling nothing from the time I saw his move till when my Bisley crashed in my hand. Cadaver's long body jerked to the .38–40, and stiffened, and hung there with his right hand gripping the gun he had gotten halfway out of its slick holster. Then all the muddiness went out of his eyes, and they turned glassy,

159

and he fell over on his face. Bibo had been a good teacher.

I got to my knees, staring at the man lying on the ground. Sean Manners. He gurgled on the song, and I could see the blood all over his chest. Cadaver must have plugged him and been putting his gun away when I arrived. I stepped over Cadaver's body, kneeling beside the loco man.

"It was you in the cave," I told him. "Singing Bibo's song."

"This pretty gal for that old maid," he choked, and one of his hands was lying across that Spencer falling-block. "Bibo's song? I'll kill him. Where is he? I'll kill him."

"Never mind," I said, and I understood now why Ardis's reaction hadn't been what I expected. "You've already killed him."

They made two tiny figures down on the river. Sean Manners was dead behind me, and I had turned down the slope, seeing them below me. I was close enough to recognize them now. In late spring like this the lumbermen float their ties down the streams like Horse Creek and Piney Creek and stretch cables across the streams at a wide spot to boom the ties, holding them there till the spring freshets have filled Green River to the proper depth for driving the ties on down to the town of Green River. The ties had jammed up here till they were solid from one bank to the other, and Ardis was already out on the boom, crossing the water that way, with Wolffe behind her. The slope here was mucky, like the water from Piney Creek might have backed up here in flood season, and I could slide down most of the way like a kit beaver, reaching the sandy shore before Wolffe was very far out onto the boom. It was only then I realized he had been chasing Ardis. She had Cadaver's briefcase with the deed in her hands and was too far ahead to have been with Wolffe.

"You'll have to take care of me before you get that deed, Wolffe!" I hollered, and it turned him around, like I wanted. "Is that why you wanted Medicine String? How long has the water been out of Yallow Hole?"

He swayed back and forth on the bobbing ties, having to shift his feet constantly to keep from slipping down between them. "Come on then, Mister Smith. You know as well as I do how long Yallow Hole's been dry. When Bibo Adams sold Yallow Hole to Leo and Sean Manners twenty years ago, he knew it would be full of water within six months. Leo and Sean could never empty the Hole by dredging because they were working at the wrong stream. They thought the water came from Piney Creek here, because of those seep holes it had made in the bottom of Number Two shaft during flood season. But that only put two or three inches on the floor of Number Two. The real water was coming from the underground source of Horse Creek. Bibo must have tapped it sinking his first shaft. When Bibo heard Horse Creek was drying up, he thought he'd come back and cash in a second time, is that it? Only we happened to be here first. Manners hadn't been to Yallow Hole in several years. It was me discovered the Hole was drying when I was cutting ties in the timber on that slope."

All the time he had been shifting around, trying to get a solid footing in order to shoot when I drew near enough. I was on the boom now and could hardly keep my feet on the treachery of bobbing, jerking, twisting ties. And all the pieces were together for me now, and I knew what Bibo had been babbling about just before he died.

"Leo wouldn't sell you Medicine String?" I said, the constant clatter of the ties almost drowning my voice.

He spread his legs a little, and I knew I couldn't get much closer before he started it. "Leo was a stubborn old fool. We represented ourselves as Headway Lumber, tried to buy the String off Leo. He thought he could never work Yellow Hole again, but he wouldn't let go of it. Then Sean Manners showed up, wandering loco over the String. Everybody thought he'd died in Laramie. Must have been some rum pot they identified as him. We knew Sean would give us a hold over Ardis. Marval was a weak, sniveling little brat, and, if we could get Leo out of the way, Ardis would have a strong enough influence on the girl to make her deed us Medicine String. I wanted to eliminate Leo for good, but Ardis made us do it with that cattle deal."

"You went to a lot of trouble for a worthless hole in the ground," I said.

He set himself, raising his gun. "You're crazy. That mine's worth a million dollars. You know what it assayed before the water filled it up."

"Bibo put that assay in there," I said. "He salted it. Not ordinary salting. Not like you'd take a shotgun and blow dust into a rock. A ton of good ore. Packed in on mules and dumped down the hole. That's what you've done all this for."

"You're a damn' liar!" he shouted, and his first shot banged out above the slapping ties.

I pulled up my Bisley to fire, and then stopped. Beyond Wolffe, Ardis must have seen it. Maybe another woman wouldn't have had that much sense. Marval wouldn't. Ardis threw herself flat on the ties so I could shoot without fear of hitting her, and I let my first one go. It was a crazy way to shoot, jerking back and forth on those shifting ties and firing at another target jumping around as much as I was. He didn't back up. He just let me come on, taking time with each shot. I saw him jerk the second time I fired and thought for a moment I had hit him. But it must have clipped his coat or something because there was nothing unsteady about the way he answered my shot. It was his third or fourth that took my hand. I heard his gun cough and felt the shock almost instantly. I must have shouted with the pain, and I knew my Bisley was gone. I didn't even look at my hand. It felt wet and messy, and I hugged it in against my belly and caught myself from falling on the jumping ties, and started on forward again.

I saw Wolffe spread his legs and set himself, and I couldn't feel any fear especially. Maybe the wound made me a little dizzy. I was pretty close now. He leveled down on me, and then, just as he fired that last round, a sudden new shift of the ties unbalanced him. The slug whined by me somewhere above. He bent forward, lowering the gun, and began punching at the chambers. Then he must have realized I was too close for that. He quit trying to reload and stuffed the iron back into its holster, and bent forward a little.

"Running Iron." It was Ardis, and she was fighting her way toward us across the ties. "Running Iron. No. He used to be on the river. No . . ."

I knew what he used to be. I knew what he was now. And how it had to be. He was right that first time. A gun wouldn't be enough. Just taking a gun and shooting you wouldn't be enough. That's the way it was inside me as I took that last step and went for him. I didn't realize there was a grin on his face till I struck him. That was the way he met it. I guess he knew, too. Just a gun wouldn't be enough.

"Damn' fool," he grunted, and shifted his weight even as I hit him skillfully, the way a man used to riding timber on white water would shift it.

His right foot came out and caught me in the middle. The force of it bent me almost double across his knee, and my head rocked down to his blow behind my neck. I caught his ankle and pulled toward my head, jackknifing the leg beneath me. He spun on his other foot and kicked the leg straight, but it had caught him off balance long enough so he couldn't follow up that sock behind the neck, and I gave a heave on that straightening leg that threw me away from his arms. One of my feet went through the slippery bobbing ties up to the hip, and I was caught there, struggling with both hands to get out of the soggy wooden trap, the weight of all those other ties crushing my thigh as they jerked back and forth all around me. Wolffe was still grinning as he jumped toward me. He was as much at home here as I was on a bronco. I saw all his weight go to his right leg and dodged the kick of his left boot an instant before it reached my head.

Then, somehow, I had torn my leg free of the ties and was on one knee. He shifted in close till his Levi's jammed, harsh and wet, into my face, doubling over to give me an uppercut. It would have knocked me sprawling if I hadn't caught him around the knees. The blow left my head blind and spinning. I tried to fight up his body, feet seeking some sort of foothold on the treachery of those twirling, clattering, shifting ties. I felt like a dogie when it first tries to walk. He hit me again, and I thought he'd knocked my head off my body. I felt his weight jerk for the next blow and let go his legs to reach blindly for his arm.

I knew what side it would come from, and somehow I got my hands in the way. Wolffe's sleeve ripped through my fingers with the force of his blow, but I had his elbow, and I jerked down with all my weight. His feet made a desperate slipping, kicking sound as he tried to remain erect, but he lost the foothold and crashed down on top of me. I caught him with one hand in the hair, taking that moment while he was still off balance to straddle around on top of him, one of my legs going through the ties again into the icy water. But I was on top of him. I held him by the hair and hit him in the face. His hands clawed upward at my own face, my neck, my eyes, anything. He tried to put a knee in my groin, but I let my weight go down on him hard to block that, and hit him again. Still fighting blindly, I heard him shout something in a choked way, and that cut off with a gurgling sound. I hit him again, and my fist came back dripping water. Then my knees were in water on either side of him. I struck again and shouted with the pain of my knuckles beating into wood. Then my whole body was in the water, with the ties crashing in against me, trying so hard to knock me under they seemed alive. I had to let go Wolffe and grab at the wooden planks. My hands slipped off the wet, smooth surface of a pole tie. A slab tie knocked into my head, stunning me. The clattering sound rose about me and the slopping wash of the water. My legs slipped through the ties with a jerk, and I was in the freezing water up to my hips. I fought like a crazy man to get my legs out again, but the weight of the other ties pushed in, holding me tighter and tighter. Then I was down to my armpits. A quarter tie hit my elbow, stunning that arm so I couldn't flail with it. My forearms went beneath the ties, then up to my shoulder. Only my head and one arm were above it now. I was shouting something, or bawling, or cursing, I don't know which. I was beating blindly with my arm at the ties. Somehow, like the fear of a wild animal, away back in my mind I knew it would be through when my other arm went. The ties were like ice. Once under them there would be no getting above again. Then my other arm slipped through.

"Running Iron, Running Iron . . ."

166

I guess it must have been Ardis calling that. I guess it must have been her dragged me to the bank. I didn't know much between the time my arm went under and when I sat up with the feel of sand beneath me and looked dazedly out over the sea of clattering, bobbing ties.

"He's gone," she said, like she knew what I was looking for. "He was under the ties. I had all I could do to drag you out." Then she clutched at me with wet hands, and the smell of her hair in my face was damp, and her voice was intense. "I had to do it, Running Iron, they made me, they had Sean up there at the mine. They wouldn't even let me see him, but they had proof he was alive."

"How did Sean get the gun?" I asked her.

"The falling-block?" Her face was twisted. "The last time I was up at Yallow Hole to see Wolffe my gun disappeared from my saddle boot. Sean must have hooked it while I was with Cadaver and Wolffe. Cadaver brought it back to me when he came down to the A Bench to get Marval to sign that deed."

"And in between that time, your husband killed Bibo with the falling-block?"

Her face was against my chest. "Forgive him, Running Iron. Sean was just a poor crazy broken old man. He was weak to begin with, the way Marval's weak, and, when he lost everything in Yallow Hole, it broke him. He disappeared a few months afterward, and I thought he had died down in Laramie till Wolffe proved to me they had him up here. It was the hold they had over me. They could have done anything to Sean, up here. I couldn't let them do that."

"You still loved him?"

"No," she muttered. "How could I? How can you love a crazy man? He isn't the same person I married. But I couldn't let them hurt him. And then, when I'd thought him dead so long and found out he was alive again . . ."

"I guess I know," I said.

"They kept Sean in the mine," she said. "When you came, there was so much confusion Cadaver must have lost him. Sean followed me out that seep hole at the bottom of Number Two. Cadaver killed him when he tried to escape. When I saw that, there was nothing to hold me any longer. I wouldn't let them have Medicine String then."

"Why wouldn't you tell me what they were doing here?" I said.

"I thought you knew," she told me. "We all did. Leo never told Marval it was Bibo Adams who sold them Yellow Hole, but I knew, and I thought you'd come back with Bibo to cash in a second time when he heard Horse Creek was dry and knew the Hole would be empty."

"It was your idea to make it look like Leo had been rustling the stock?"

"I had to think of something to keep Wolffe from killing him," she said. "I never liked Leo. He was a stubborn, bitter, bigoted old fool, but I couldn't see him murdered. First Wolffe and I were going to brand a few Cut-and-Slash steers ourselves. With all the rustling around here, we knew it would mean jail for Leo. It's bad enough to send a man to jail, but it's the best I could do at the time, and it's better than being killed. Then we hooked onto your fresh trail that night you took a bunch of Newcastle's steers. Bibo was alone in the cabin when we reached it. I guess you'd gone on with the cattle."

"I'm glad to know all that," said a dry voice from behind us. When we had turned enough to see him sitting his sorrel there, it was Sheriff Monte Hale, chewing a hunk of plug like a cow on its cud. His rope-scarred old saddle creaked as he eased his weight forward a bit. "I'm glad to know it was Wolffe forcing you to do it, Ardis. Technically you're just as guilty as he is, no matter what means he used to gain your aid. But I never like technicalities, and, if that's the deed to Medicine String in the briefcase, you can hand it over and we'll forget what you was going to do with it." Then he was looking at me. "I'm glad to know it wasn't Leo doing the rustling, too . . . Running Iron Smith."

One of his hands had left the saddle horn, and there was a big six-gun in it. I stood up, feeling helpless as a dogie by his dead mama without my Bisley weighting my holster. Hale checked his tobacco.

"Marval hit for town as soon as you and Ardis left the A Bench. She told me who you was and who that old man was, and where you'd likely be heading for after you left the spread. Marval thought you'd come out here to kill Ardis, and that's the only way she knew to stop you. She's follering pretty close behind me with Newcastle and Farley French and some others. If they find out it was you doing the rustling, I don't know whether I can keep them from hanging you this second time or not."

"Here's the briefcase, Sheriff," said Ardis, and held it out toward him, and the rest happened so fast I didn't rightly see it. He made a move to grab it, automatically, but he was an old fox, and I saw the sly look slide through his eyes. But before he fully understood what Ardis was up to, she had taken a step toward him as if to hand over the case, and then made a slapping downward motion with it that knocked his gun toward the ground. The iron bellowed, and I saw the dirt the slug kicked up, and Ardis had jumped at Hale, hauling him from the saddle of his spooked sorrel. They rolled to the ground with Ardis on top. She spread out her legs and grunted, and got to her knees straddling Hale. Then she was on her feet, and I saw what had made her grunt. It's the way anybody would do when they give a jerk on something. She had jerked his gun from his hand while they were down there, and she had it now. He sat up, staring from Ardis to me.

"That's how it is, Sheriff," she said. "I'm sorry."

He didn't look as angry as he should have, and he didn't say anything I'd expected. "Then you'd better get a move on before Newcastle gets here, Ardis."

"Before we trail out, I'd like to ask you a favor," I said. "The horse I rode in is hitched up by Yellow Hole. It's got an old running iron beneath the saddle skirt. You might pick it up, and on your way back to Kemmerer put it on that grave by the old A Bench line shack. Bibo might like to have it as a marker."

Ardis turned to me. "Running Iron . . . ?"

"Yes," I told her. "I guess I'm through with the running iron. When me and Marval were out herding the A Bench beef that time, she told me something that struck home. She said I'd never stopped to think whether my trail was crooked or straight. She was right. I'd ridden with Bibo so long I accepted his way of life without ever stopping to question anything or ask myself whether it was right or wrong or good or bad. That night after Bibo was killed, I did stop to ask. I got some answers."

"Then you and Marval . . . ?"

"No," I said. "Bibo thought Marval was the one for me. Maybe I thought so, too, at one time. Maybe when I thought you were double-crossing me. Or when I thought you'd killed Bibo. But Marval ain't my kind. I'm not one to say whether she's weak or strong or big or little. All I know is she ain't my kind. And I ain't hers. Maybe I can throw away the running iron, but that won't change me completely. You can't ask a man to turn his horse smack the other way in the middle of a river."

"You're going to need a lot of help to keep you from finding another running iron," said Hale.

"I guess so," I said. "There's still a lot of crooked turns in my trail that'll take a sight of riding to straighten out, and my horse is still a wild bronc'. I sort of hoped I'd have someone to help me, like you say. A woman, maybe. Bibo told me that. He said a woman could give a man softness without making him weak. Maybe that's what I need. It'd take more of a woman

171

than Marval to ride my trail. It'd take a woman like you, Ardis."

"Then get on this horse," she said, "and let's go."

THE CURSE OF MONTEZUMA

Les Savage, Jr., narrated the adventures of Elgera Douglas, better known as *Señorita* Scorpion, in a series of seven short novels that originally appeared in *Action Stories*, published by Fiction House. She was, by far, the most popular literary series character to appear in this magazine in the nearly thirty years of its publication history. The fifth short novel in this series, "The Brand of Penasco", is included in *The Shadow in Renegade Basin: A Western Trio* (Five Star Westerns, 2000). The seventh, and last, story in the series, "The Sting of *Señorita* Scorpion", is collected in the eponymous *The Sting of Señorita Scorpion: A Western Trio* (Five Star Westerns, 2000). The short novel that began the series, "*Señorita* Scorpion", can be found in *The Devil's Corral: A Western Trio* (Five Star Westerns, 2003). This first story so pleased Malcolm Reiss, the general manager at Fiction House, that he wanted another story about her for the very next issue. The sequel, titled "The Brand of *Señorita* Scorpion", is collected in *The Beast in Cañada Diablo* (Five Star Westerns, 2004). "Secret of the Santiago", third in the series, is collected in *Trail of the Silver Saddle* (Five

Star Westerns, 2005). This is the fourth of the *Señorita* Scorpion stories and sixth to be collected in the Five Star Westerns.

In 1843 William H. Prescott completed his epic history, *The Conquest of Mexico*. The early chapters of this history recorded most of what was known of Aztec culture and the Aztec empire, and no historian since has been able to write of the Aztecs without referring to Prescott's monumental work. Les Savage, Jr., obviously availed himself of it when he came to write this short novel and united the milieu of the Aztec empire with his own legendary characters, *Señorita* Scorpion and her *compadres*, Chisos Owens and John Hagar. Savage's original title for this story was "Six-Gun Serpent God". The author was paid $365 by Fiction House on May 9, 1944. The title was changed to "The Curse of Montezuma" when it appeared in *Action Stories* (Spring, 45).

CHAPTER
ONE

Wave the parrot plumes again.
The *guachupin* now burns.
Quetzalcoatl comes to reign.
The Serpent God returns.

The three men sat hunched over in their saddles with backs to the wind that mourned down off the ridge like the plaint of a lost soul, fluttering the brim of Elder Fayette's hat against its crown with a constant, slapping sound.

"Can't you turn that hat around or something?" said Orville Beamont nervously. "Gets on a man's nerves."

Fayette's hard mouth curled at one corner contemptuously, and he didn't answer, and the hat brim kept on flapping.

"When's he coming, anyway?" muttered Beamont angrily. "He promised he'd be here before night."

"Don't say it like that," insisted Abilene, trying to light a cigarette for the third time. "He ain't a devil or something. He's human, just like you or me."

The wind rose to an unearthly shriek, whipping Fayette's hat brim into a mad tattoo for a moment, and then died to a soft whine again. Beamont suddenly stiffened. Fayette's mare whinnied and tried to bolt, and he caught it with a savage jerk on the reins.

"*Buenas noches, señores,*" said the man who had appeared so silently from the blackjack timber above them. "Have you been waiting long?"

Orville Beamont let out a gusty breath. "You! I thought it was him. Isn't he with you?"

The man was on foot, wearing a dark-blue, hooded cloak the Mexicans called a *capuz*. His shiny *mitaja* leggings gleamed dully as he came on down toward the three horsebackers, something serpentine in the lithe, sensuous movements of his slim body. He had a narrow, vulpine face beneath the hood of his cloak, and the slender, pale hands of a conspirator, and he kept rubbing his long forefinger against his thumb in an oily, habitual way, like a usurer who saw the promise of another gold piece.

"No, he is not with me," said the man. "We were all to arrive separately, if you recall. *Pues,* you have not prepared for him. A fire, *hombres,* a fire. After all, it is not every day you meet the reincarnation of Montezuma, returned to free his people from their servitude."

Fayette snorted. "Keep that tripe in your own duffel bag, Ortega. We didn't want to show any light with a fire."

"You are farther into the Guadalupes than any white man has ever been, *señores,* and there is no possible danger of anyone seeing you," said Luis Ortega urbanely, and turned to Abilene. "If you would be so kind as to get some wood?"

Abilene looked at Fayette. Fayette shrugged, then edged his mare over to an outcropping of rocks, and dismounted, kicking away the matted undergrowth until he had hollowed out a place for a fire. The dark-faced Ortega laughed softly and ran his slender hands up and down the gold-hilted cane he carried, looking up the cañon toward the sombrous peak, El Capitán.

Abilene came back with his dally rope hitched around his saddle horn, dragging a dead cottonwood log. It was rotten enough to split with a Bowie knife he took from his saddle roll. They banked kindling against the rock, out of the wind. The light flared under Abilene's match, catching redly across the impatient line of Elder Fayette's hard mouth. Beamont had been standing nervously by his horse. He jerked around suddenly.

"Whassat?"

The Indians had appeared without sound. They stood like silent ghosts, just outside the circle of firelight.

"All right, all right," said Fayette. "Come on in."

"*Señor* Fayette," hissed Luis Ortega, "you do not speak to the Lord Montezuma in that fashion. I warned you . . ." He turned to the pair of Indians, and Fayette thought a mocking note had entered his suave voice. "We thank Quetzalcoatl for your safety, *Tlatoani* Montezuma. Please accept our humble companionship and join us."

Fayette's eyes narrowed, studying the Indian who stepped into the light. He was a huge man, well over six feet tall in his rawhide *huiraches*, his tremendous shoulders and great, broad chest swelling a mantle that hung to below his knees. At first Fayette thought the cloak was of vari-colored cloth, then he realized it was feathers, feathers of a dozen different hues, catching the firelight in a bizarre pattern. The second inscrutable Indian spread out a gold cloth, and Montezuma seated himself cross-legged without a word. He held up his great head, the haughty beak of his nose throwing a deep shadow over the curl of his arrogant mouth.

Luis Ortega picked up a handful of earth, kissed it, threw it into the flames. "Xiuchtecutli, the Fire God. May he consume the *guáchupin*."

Beamont's thin head jerked toward him. "*¿Guáchupin?*"

"The *guáchupines* are descendants of the upper-class Spaniards who have been ruling Mexico since Cortés conquered the Aztecs." Ortega smiled softly. "The *guáchupines* are the tyrants who will be annihilated in the all-consuming fire of Xiuchtecutli, now that our Lord Montezuma has returned."

"All right," said Fayette. "All right. How about the business? Does he speak English?"

Montezuma had been sitting silently, heavy-lidded eyes staring blankly into the fire, as if he were lost in reverie. His voice startled Elder Fayette, deep and hollow.

"I speak all languages. I am *Tlatoani*. I am a supreme ruler. I am Montezuma."

Standing out in the darkness by the horses, Abilene spat. Fayette glanced his way a moment. He couldn't see him very well, but he knew how the supple hands would be hitched into the cartridge belt of that Beale-Remington Abilene wore. Orville Beamont spoke in his nervous, spiteful way.

"We didn't come here to discuss Aztec mythology. Let's get down to business."

Ortega turned toward him. "*Señor* . . ."

Montezuma stopped Ortega with a wave of his bronzed hand, looking at Beamont. The Indian's eyes seemed focused for the first time. They held a strange, glittering intensity. Beamont flushed angrily. He wiped the back of his hand across his mouth in a jerky gesture, eyes shifting before Montezuma's black glare.

"You do not believe Montezuma has returned?" asked the Indian.

"I didn't say that . . ."

"You do not believe Montezuma has returned." It was a statement this time, and it held something final. "You are an unbeliever."

"*Señores*," said Ortega swiftly, "we did not come here to quarrel. It would be wise of you, *Señor* Beamont, to watch what you say. *Tlatoani* Montezuma, forgive the *Americanos*. They are ignorant."

"Their ignorance is no excuse."

"Look," said Fayette, "let's scrape the fur off and get down to the hide. You're going to do a job for us, and we're going to pay you. That's simple enough. You want to hear what the job is, or shall we call it a sour deal?"

Ortega's words slipped from his flannel-mouth, as sly and furtive as his eyes, and he rubbed his forefinger against his thumb in that way. "*Pues*, of course, you shall not call it a sour deal. Who else could do the job? You have tried, and failed. *Por supuesto*, if you will use a certain amount of tact, we shall come to an amicable agreement." He turned obsequiously to Montezuma.

179

"It is this, my lord. For a long time now, *Señores* Fayette and Beamont, and certain of their constituents, have had ... ah ... shall we say ... ambitions concerning the Big Bend. Unfortunately there are those in Brewster County who do not sympathize with these ambitions. Elgera Douglas, for one, the heiress to the Santiago Mine. Chisos Owens, who is the friend of every *peón* this side of the Río."

"Peons," spat Orville Beamont. "That's just it. A whole bunch of small-time peon *rancheros* holding little spreads and controlling all the water. What chance has a big operator?"

"Your cattle don't seem to be dying," said Ortega slyly.

Beamont jerked his hand in a nervous gesture. "That's not the idea. Fayette and I haven't got enough cattle now to put in your left saddlebag. And it won't do us any good to get more if we don't have the water for them."

"Ah, yes." Ortega's voice was insinuating. "You wish to expand. What a laudable ambition."

Fayette squatted there without speaking, letting Beamont go on, watching him with a faint contempt in the curl of his lip. Perhaps Orville Beamont sensed the sly mockery in Ortega's voice. He rubbed the back of his hand across his mouth, speaking jerkily.

"Yeah, yeah. We've tried to put through legislation for a fair division of the water. But the Douglas girl and Chisos Owens have Brewster County sewed up. Sheriff Hagar's their man. Alpine's the county seat, and whatever legal measures we've tried to take there, Hagar's stopped."

Montezuma looked up. "Legal measures?"

Beamont wiped his mouth. "Yeah ... uh ... the legal measures we ..."

"I don't think you know what legal measures are, *Señor* Beamont," said Montezuma. "Are you a hypocrite as well as a thief?"

Beamont's voice was shrill. "Listen ..."

"Why not speak the truth?" interrupted Montezuma, staring blankly back into the fire. "Alpine is the county seat for Brewster. It is the shipping center for all the Big Bend. A lucrative plum for any political machine that could break the hold that the Douglas-Owens faction has on the county. In a cattle country, the man with the most cattle can invariably gain political control. And in a dry cattle country, such as the Big Bend, the man who wants the most cattle must have the most water. As long as the Douglas-Owens faction is in power, the small *rancheros* will be protected, and the water rights will be equally divided so that no one man, or group of men, can get the upper hand."

Fayette's laugh was harsh. "How well you put it."

Montezuma didn't seem to hear him. "Whatever political measures you have tried were certainly not legal, *Señor* Beamont. And the other measures? Terrorism? You thought you could drive the *rancheros* away from their water with your raids. I understand Elgera Douglas can handle a gun. Was it she who put a stop to that? But not before several small *ranchcros* had been murdered, eh? Pablo Otero's two sons. Sheriff

181

Johnny Hagar is still looking for their murderer. Wouldn't he be surprised to know you are the man he wants, Orville Beamont?"

Beamont jumped to his feet, watery eyes wide. "You're lying. How did you know? You're a lying son-of-a . . ."

Montezuma's gaze swung to him, focusing suddenly in that strange, glittering intensity. "I am a *Tlatoani, Señor* Beamont. A supreme ruler. I know all. You led those raids on the *peónes.* It was your guns that killed Otero's two sons!"

"You're a liar!" screamed Beamont. "You're no *Tlatoani.* You're just a damn', greasy Indian, lying in your filthy teeth . . ."

The gunshot deafened Fayette. He saw Beamont stiffen. He saw Beamont claw at his skinny chest. He saw Beamont fall over onto his face in the fire.

For a long moment, nobody moved. The mahogany color left Elder Fayette's heavy-boned face until it was dead white beneath his soft-brimmed hat. He hadn't seen Montezuma draw the gun. He couldn't see it now. The Indian sat in that utter composure, his eyes looking into the flames without seeming to be focused on anything. His hands lay on his knees, empty. The only man with a gun out was Abilene, standing back there in the darkness by the horses, the Beale-Remington gleaming fitfully in his hand. But he hadn't fired. Fayette had caught the movement of his draw an instant after the shot. Finally Fayette spoke between his teeth.

182

"Why did you have to do that?" he asked Montezuma.

Ortega took a sibilant breath. "The life of any man is *Tlatoani* Montezuma's sovereign right to take, or save."

The two Indians came from the darkness like wraiths. Fayette wasn't aware of them till they stood over the body, tall and stalwart in gilt-edged loin cloths and plumed bonnets, as alike as two barrels of a scatter-gun. Without a word, they lifted Beamont and carried him out into the darkness.

"Now," said Ortega smoothly, "shall we go on?"

Fayette looked toward him. Luis Ortega smiled, shrugging his shoulders, and his words were oily.

"Come now, *Señor* Fayette, you cannot tell me Beamont's death bothers you so much. He was a contemptible *borrachín*, of small value to either you or us. I have no doubt you planned to eliminate him."

Fayette lowered himself to a squatting position again with a slow, deliberate control over his weight that was surprising in such a heavy man. He looked into Montezuma's blank eyes.

"Sort of up to date, isn't it, for the reincarnation of Montezuma to carry a hide-out?" he said thinly. "All right. All right. Just don't try it on me, *compadre*. You haven't got enough lead in that cutter to stop me before I'd kill you so dead you'd never reincarnate."

"*Señor* . . . ," Ortega began.

"Shut up," said Fayette. "I'm talking to Montezuma. You claim you can get rid of Chisos Owens and *Señorita* Scorpion? All right. I don't think you can, but I'll give you a crack at it. Elgera Douglas's Santiago

183

spread is down in the Dead Horse Mountains. The only way in or out of the Santiago Valley is through a mine shaft. Beamont tried to get in three times when he was raiding down there, and couldn't do it. I've paid to have the girl nailed on the outside, more than once, but she can handle a gun better than any man in Texas, and she's a wildcat, and she still wears her boots sticking straight up."

"You have the payment?" asked Montezuma.

"You'll get your payment," said Fayette, "when you prove you can do the job."

"Getting rid of the girl and Chisos will pave the way to your control of the Big Bend," said Montezuma. "But you'll not be through fighting when they're dead. Johnny Hagar is as dangerous as either of them. This Chisos Owens, is he really as strong a man as you claim?"

Fayette nodded his head toward the lean, silent man standing out by the horses. "Abilene's been with me a long time. I never thought I'd see the man he couldn't take care of. He couldn't take care of Chisos Owens."

Montezuma stared into the fire. "I have been hunting a man such as that for a long time. I shall need him in the days to come. It would be a crime to waste him by killing him. Why not turn his strength into our strength?"

"I'd give anything to have Chisos Owens riding in my wagon," said Fayette. "But you can't buy him."

"I did not mean that," said Montezuma, and his voice held a brooding portent, and he was looking into

184

some infinity beyond the fire, his eyes blank and glazed. "There are other ways, *Señor* Fayette, other ways."

Surprise crossed the harsh planes of Elder Fayette's face for the first time. "What do you mean?"

Montezuma began to speak.

CHAPTER
TWO

As Mictlantecutl in Hades rules
So I will rule above.
And turn strong men to traitor-fools
Who betray the ones they love.

The norther that had been building for a week now
swept into the Santiago Valley with all its fury, howling
dismally outside the sprawling adobe ranch house, bending
the willows in the small *placeta* behind the building
until they brushed against the earthen roof top with a
mournful, scraping insistence, as if seeking the safety
inside. Elgera Douglas sat in the huge oak armchair by
the roaring fire at one end of the long parlor. Her
blonde hair fell, shimmering and unruly, along the
curve of her cheek, flushed from the heat of the blaze.
There was something wild in the arch of her eyebrow, a
tempestuousness in the piquant curve of her pouting
lower lip. She sprawled in the chair like a boy, the length
of her slim legs accentuated by the tight-fitting *charro*
trousers, gaudy with red roses down their seams.

She stiffened suddenly as the man entered the room
from the hallway, her blue eyes flashing in a startled
way, like a doe surprised at a pool.

"Were you thinking, *Señorita* Scorpion?" said Lobos
Delcazar, his white teeth gleaming in a grin. "About
Chisos Owens, perhaps?"

186

She tossed her head. "Never mind. Have you looked at the guards at the mine?"

"Not yet," said Lobos. "But you have nothing to worry about. Nobody can get into this valley. Two men in that mine could hold off an army."

Since the mysterious raids had been sweeping the Big Bend and Pablo Otero's two sons had been murdered, Elgera had hired extra men to guard her spread. Lobos Delcazar had been recommended by Johnny Hagar, and deputized for the job. He was the cousin of Ramón Delcazar, who was Chisos Owens's best friend. He was a big, swaggering man, Lobos, wearing a Mexican dragoon's coat with red cuffs and collar over his white silk shirt. To show off a waist as slim as a girl's, he wore a broad, red sash, tied on the right side and hanging down his leg so that the fringed edge touched the top of his right polished Blucher boot. There was something ceremonious in the way he slipped a reddish bean from his pocket, passing it to his mouth.

"What are you eating all the time, Lobos?" asked Elgera. "¿Frijoles?"

Lobos laughed, brushing his finger across his mustache affectedly. "No, señorita, not beans. Peyote."

"¿Raíz diabólica?"

"Ah, señorita, some may call it the devil weed," he said, and his red sash twitched as he moved toward her. "But, in truth, it is a boon to mankind. It makes life a gorgeous dream." He bowed low to her. "Many of the Mexicans use it. Perhaps you would let me inculcate you into its sacred mysteries."

187

He was almost leering, and she caught the slight dilation of his black pupils, and then the faint glaze that passed across his eyes following the dilation. She had seen it before, and somehow it made her feel that beneath all his affected ostentation Lobos Delcazar was not quite so colorful or gallant as he seemed, or so harmless.

"You'd better go out and see about changing the guards," she said, and rose from the chair.

He pressed a brown hand to his heart, and she thought his voice sounded mocking. "You would send me away so soon, *carisma!* All the *hombres* in Alpine talk about the wild girl of the Santiago, and now, when I finally see her, she sends me out into the storm."

Señorita Scorpion hitched her gun around. "Lobos."

He straightened slowly, and took a step backward. His eyes were on the gun, and his grin was suddenly forced. It was a big Army Model Colt with black, rubber grips, and it hung against her slim thigh heavily.

"*Perdóneme*," he said. "I did not realize it was that way. Would you really use that gun on me like they say, *señorita?*"

"What do you think?"

He had recovered his composure, and he brushed his mustache with a finger, grinning broadly. "*Dios*, I think you would. *Sí*. I think you would. I'm going, *señorita*, I'm going right now. I hope you will forgive me. I am an impetuous fool. *Adiós, señorita*. It breaks my heart. *Adiós* . . ."

Laughing, he turned and swaggered to the door. The fire was almost swept out by the gale as he opened the portal. He had to turn and lean his weight against it to close it.

Elgera turned back to the chair angrily. Yet, as she sank into it again, she couldn't help comparing Lobos with Chisos Owens. Lobos was the kind of man who should appeal to her, really, the handsome swagger, the dash, the wildness. But, somehow, it was always Chisos, big and slow and stubborn, patiently waiting for her. The blue of her eyes deepened, staring into the fire. If she could only be sure how she felt for Chisos. She knew she loved him, yet there was something wild and untamed in her that rebelled at the thought of settling down.

She was still sitting there when the wind once more almost extinguished the fire. Elgera turned in the chair to see her brother bursting into the room. He was tall and lanky, Natividad Douglas, with jet black hair and blue eyes, long legs bowed slightly in greasy *chivarras*. He ran to the chair without shutting the door behind him, grabbing Elgera by the arm.

"You've got to get out!" he shouted above the screaming norther. "Something's gone wrong! They've gotten through!"

She was out of the chair, jerking loose from him. "Who's gotten through?"

"I don't know!" he yelled. "I was coming from the bunk-house down by the river and saw them riding out of the mine!"

Above the wind, she heard the first, faint shots, then the dull tattoo of hoof beats. Someone yelled from far away, the sound warped by the storm. Elgera pushed by Natividad, breaking into a run for the hall door.

"Not that way!" he called. "You'll be caught . . ."

She ran down the hall to the right wing of the house, boots pounding the hard-packed, earthen floor. The wind struck her like a wall when she tore open the rear door, driving her against the outside of the house. She bent almost double, long hair streaming behind her as she struggled away from the building. The slope rose behind the *hacienda* into the Sierra del Caballo Muerto — the desolate Mountains of the Dead Horse, lifting their jagged, red peaks up to surround the Santiago completely. The only way in or out of the valley was through the shaft of the ancient Santiago Mine that opened out above the house. Elgera could hear the shouts and gunfire more clearly now. A ridden horse passed her far to the right, racing down the hill toward the river below. Other riders clattered by on her other side, missing her in the darkness.

Two of them hauled up on sliding haunches by the corral above, and one man jumped off his mount to unlash the let-down bars. Elgera ran toward them, drawing her Army Colt. The one still mounted caught sight of her. He wore some sort of long cloak that whipped about him as he whirled in his saddle to fire.

She began shooting now. The one on foot turned from the bars, trying to get a rifle from the boot on his rig. Elgera's second shot caught him, and he fell back against the cottonwood post. His horse bolted, spooked by the gunfire. The mounted man had to stop shooting

190

and fight his own frenzied horse, wheeling and plunging on up the hill, trying to turn it back.

The slope shook as more horsemen passed Elgera, farther out, whooping savagely, going on down toward the bottom of the valley. A red light flared up behind her. They had set fire to the house.

She reached the corral before the man above had gotten his horse turned around. She ran past the one sagging against the bars, thinking her shot had finished him. She was tearing at the top bars when he threw himself on her from behind.

"*¡Miquistli!*" he screamed, and she caught the flash of his huge knife coming down on her.

Elgera whirled, throwing up her gun. The blade clanged off the Colt's barrel. The gun dropped from her stunned fingers, and the man's sweaty, fetid weight was against her, streaked with ochre and vermilion, black teeth showing beneath lips peeled back in a snarl. Gasping with the pain it must have caused him, he struck at her again. She jerked to one side beneath him. The cottonwood bar shuddered as the huge knife struck it near her shoulder.

Elgera threw herself forward, grabbing the man about his legs. They rolled into the grama grass. The girl fought savagely, clawing, biting, kicking. She came on top of him and rammed a vicious knee into his stomach. He choked and doubled up, trying to jab upward with the big knife he still held. But it was too long a weapon for close work, and she caught his wrist.

"*¡Miquistli!*" he bawled again, jerking away from beneath her.

191

She was thrown off balance. He rolled over on her. She held his wrist in a desperate grip. He tried to jerk the knife from between them before his full weight descended on her. But he didn't quite make it, and he came down on her heavily, and his body stiffened suddenly. He sprawled out on her, his gasp hot in her face. She struggled from beneath him, seeing that he had plunged the strange knife into his own body by rolling onto it.

The wind caught at Elgera as she ran toward the corral again, scooping up her gun where she had dropped it, jamming in fresh loads. Other horsemen had spotted the corral, and a bunch of them was wheeling toward it. But Elgera knew she could do nothing on foot, and she ran in among the squealing, kicking remuda of *Circulo* S horses, seeking her own palomino. There was no time to stop for saddle or reins. Reaching the big, golden stallion, she ripped off her long bandanna and grabbed the horse's creamy forelock, jerking its head down to knot the handkerchief around its jaw in a hackamore.

The riders were wheeling outside and shooting into the corral. A big mare screamed and reared and went down beneath the other frenzied horses. Elgera jumped aboard her palomino, cutting around to the rear of the corral where it was clear. She pulled the animal about and began firing her gun into the air. The thunder of shots behind them drove the remuda forward out the gate. The press of their hurtling bodies smashed against a section of the fence nearest the opening, taking it with them. And riding their tails like an Indian was *Señorita Scorpion*.

She had one long leg hooked across the palomino's broad, bare back and was bent forward, lying along its left side, as she pounded out. The riders had to break away from the point of the herd, and they were still milling around on either flank as the girl passed them. One wild-eyed horsebacker tried to follow her, gun stabbing the darkness. She turned, fired, and saw his horse stumble and fall, pitching the rider over its head.

Elgera rode with the stampede into the junipers on the slope above the house, then cut down through the trees, skirting the burning building. The majority of the raiders had gone on down into the bottom of the Santiago where the *Circulo* S cattle were. Already a greater thunder than that of the stampeding horses was beginning to roll up to the girl.

She passed one of her own men, sprawled out where he had been caught running across the ford of the river, his face and torso lying on the sandy bank, his feet sunk in the water.

She splashed to the other side and raced past the bunk-house. It was a blazing holocaust, a few remaining timbers reaching up through the flames like blackened bones. A riderless horse passed her going the other way. Then she crossed the bed ground of the cattle, and saw the tail of the stampede ahead. She couldn't understand why they were driving the herd northeast. The way out of the valley was to the west, behind her. The only thing ahead of her . . .

A strange, feral look crossed her face as she realized what did lie ahead of her. She bent forward on her horse, screaming at it in the wind. The stallion stretched out beneath her, lathered flanks heaving as it poured on the speed. A motte of poplars swept by it in a shadowy pattern, and she broke into the open sachaguasca flats beyond. Then she saw the first of the riders ahead. Some of her own men were still going, their guns spitting redly, now and then.

Elgera passed another body, sprawled on the ground, catching the impression of a paint-streaked face staring blankly upward. She fought her horse around the flank of the herd, bent low. The singular golden color of the animal was lost in the darkness and billowing dust, and the riders must have taken her for one of their own. She passed half a dozen of them, and they didn't look twice. Then ahead, on the swing, she saw her brother riding a big black. He was firing across the sea of horns at a dim rider far to the front.

"Natividad!" screamed the girl. "Get up to the point! They're stampeding them toward the cut! Can't you see? They'll go over the cliffs!"

Natividad turned in his saddle, waving his gun. They were charging up the steepening slope through crackling sagebrush, and it looked like one smooth incline forming a flank of the jagged range that towered ahead, but there was a big cut that ran transversely across the shoulder of the mountain, not a quarter mile in front of the herd, a cut deep enough to finish every animal running, if they went into it.

Elgera's palomino passed Natividad's black, and she dropped over to hang on one side as she brought up with the next man. He glanced back at her, twisted around to fire. Over the humping withers of her palomino, she shot the rider from his saddle.

Four more horsebackers had been galloping farther out on the flank, and they quartered in through the dust as they saw their man go down. Elgera shifted her gun across the palomino's back, throwing down on the man leading the quartet.

Then she stopped her Colt there, with her thumb holding the hammer back, and her mouth opened in a soundless cry. The man across her sights wore a strange, gaudy cloak that flapped away from shoulders like a range bull's. His sun-bleached eyebrows and stubble beard gleamed pale-blond against the face colored like old saddle leather from the sun. He was close enough by now for her to see the fiendish grin that drew his lips back against teeth stained black. There was something savagely eager about the way he raised his six-shooter to fire at her.

"No!" she called helplessly. "No . . ."

The man's gun flamed again and again. She didn't know which bullet struck her shoulder. It was as if a giant hand had torn her from the palomino. Screaming agony blotted out most of her consciousness when she hit. Through the awful pain, she was aware that she bounced and rolled, with the cattle thundering all about her, the ground shaking and rumbling beneath her.

Someone wheeled a horse above Elgera, jumping off. She felt hands lifting her up. She tried to aid as she was dragged out of the path of the running animals. A pair of steers shook the ground in front of her. The man dragged her toward an uplift of sandstone. A big heifer charged by behind. Then she was laid gently down, sobbing and shaking with pain and reaction. It was her brother, bending over her, breathing heavily, tearing her ripped, bloody shirt away from the bullet wound in her shoulder.

The sound of running cattle gradually died, and the dust settled softly back to earth, and it was ominously silent. In a little while, a cavalcade of horsemen passed them below, picking up the black horse Natividad had left behind, then going on back toward the burning house.

"Did you see who was leading them?" she queried. "Did you see who shot me?"

Natividad shook his head. "No, Elgera, all I cared about was getting you out of there."

She put her face against her brother's chest and began to cry again, and it wasn't because of the pain, now, and her voice had a dull, hopeless sound.

"It was Chisos Owens," she said. "Chisos Owens."

CHAPTER
THREE

The Gods of Night are from Atzalan.
The *Señores de la Noche* are nine.
Their sacred sword is the *macapan,*
Their powers of darkness mine.

The norther had blown itself out, leaving a sombrous pall of yellow dust above Alpine. The hitch racks of the county seat were full of horses, huddled together as if they sensed the strange foreboding that seemed to have settled over the town, their tails fluttering in the last vagrant gusts of biting wind that mourned across Second Street.

Elgera had gotten her wound tended by Dr. Farris. Now she stood in the sheriff's office down Second Street from Main, watching Johnny Hagar apprehensively.

It was said, in the Big Bend, that Sheriff Johnny Hagar would be grinning when he came face to face with the devil himself. He wasn't grinning now. He stood in front of the girl, turning the strange sword over and over in his hands. It was made of some tough wood, about three feet long, with sharpened pieces of obsidian attached to the flat blade for cutting edges.

A man walked past the open door, head bent into the wind. His boots made a hollow sound on the plank walk.

197

"Crazy knife, isn't it?" said Elgera nervously. "The Indian who attacked me at the corral used it. You know most of the tribes, Johnny. I thought maybe you could tell me where it comes from."

Johnny Hagar studied the knife silently. He was a well-proportioned man for his six feet four, broad shoulders filling out his flannel shirt, twin, ivory-handled Peace-makers riding slim hips in an arrogant, reckless way. He kept his curly, black hair cropped close, accentuating the youth of his clean-shaven jaw and straight, frank mouth. The only thing that might have indicated his true sophistication was his eyes. The faint wind wrinkles at their corners gave them an older, worldly wise look. Or perhaps that look emanated from the eyes themselves. He had been around.

"You were wiped out?" he said finally.

"I'd sunk most of my cash in the herds," she said, "and improvements on the spread. They ran every cow I owned off the cliff. Whatever else I had was burned in the house and outbuildings. My uncle and brother were guarding the mine. You know how the lay of that land is. They could have held it against all the cavalry from Fort Leaton. Only somebody coming in from behind could have gotten past them, or someone they trusted enough to allow close in. Chisos Owens . . ."

She broke off, turning toward the window so Hagar wouldn't see the tears welling in her eyes. *Yes, they would have trusted Chisos Owens with their very lives. It must have been pitifully simple for him.* She shook her blonde head angrily, seeing that most of the huddled mounts at the hitch rack in front of this office bore the Teacup brand. Across the street in front of the Alamo Saddlery a little knot of dusty cowhands stood talking in low tones. On the corner of Main and Second, by the Alpine Lodge, were others.

"I see Fayette's in town with his whole army," she said. "Is that how we stand?"

"Our position isn't so good," said Hagar, "and he knows it. I think he's getting ready to push something. If it was just a matter of stacking my guns against Fayette, I wouldn't worry. But you know it's never been that. As long as Chisos and you were the strong hand in this county, and backed me, whatever play I made was all right with the county commissioners. But with Chisos out from under now, and you financially wiped out, Fayette will pump the first wrong move I make, and start putting pressure on the county board, and the courthouse gang, and I'll be out of office."

She nodded dismally. "I'm afraid we've got too many people in this county who blow with the wind. Mayor Cabell. Judge Sewell. More than one county supervisor I could name . . ."

"Sí," said Ramón Delcazar. "And right now, it looks like the wind has shifted to Elder Fayette. It looks like he will get his water from us small *rancheros* without any more trouble, eh? It used to be Chisos who protected us. And now, with him doing this, what chance have we? I still can't believe it. My best friend. Chisos Owens. Burning the very house he helped me build. Butchering my *pobre* cattle. Leading the attack on you, Elgera."

He shook his head morosely, sitting on the desk with his bare feet on Hagar's swivel chair. He was Lobos Delcazar's cousin, a slim young Mexican with the tails of his white cotton shirt slapping outside his cotton trousers, and a pair of black-butted .45s strapped around outside of that.

"Montez came in yesterday from Persimmon Gap," said Hagar. "Same story. Five hundred of his cattle run off. Spread ruined."

"Lobos?" said Ramón. "You say you couldn't find his body?"

"No," said Elgera. "The last time I saw your cousin was just before he went out to change the guards at the mine. We found several of my own hands dead, and three of those raiders. Natividad and I hid in the rocks until they left. He's still down at the Santiago with the wounded. All I brought north with me was that knife, Johnny."

"I'm sorry to see it," the sheriff said, looking at the sword. "I heard they were rising again, somewhere up in New Mexico. I didn't think it had to do with the raids that have been sweeping the Big Bend. I sort of thought Fayette and Beamont were behind them. Do you know what a *macapán* is, Elgera?"

"*Dios*," said Ramón, jumping off the desk. "Is that a *macapán*?"

"Who's rising again?" asked *Señorita* Scorpion. "A *macapán*? What are you talking about?"

"The Montezuma cult," said Hagar somberly. "Not many people know about it. In Eighteen Forty-Six, when the United States went to war with Mexico, the

Mexican government wasn't very sure just how loyal their northern province of New Mexico was. In order to strengthen that loyalty, the officials in Mexico City sent to New Mexico a manuscript claiming that, when Cortés had conquered the Aztecs of Mexico in Fifteen Twenty-One, he had married an Indian princess named Malinche. According to this manuscript, Malinche was the daughter of the Indian emperor named Montezuma, who ruled the land to the north. Thus, as part of her dowry, she brought to Cortés the province of what is now New Mexico. The whole story was a fabrication, of course, designed to prove to the Indians of New Mexico how much they owed allegiance to Mexico. In reality, Malinche was Cortés's mistress, hated by the Aztecs."

Ramón was watching Hagar with a strange intensity. "How can you be sure of that, Juanito?"

"It's a historical fact," said Hagar. "Also, there was no northern emperor named Montezuma. Montezuma II was in reality the ruler of the Aztecs at that time, and his death was brought about by Hernando Cortés. The Mexican government twisted these facts for their own use. The upperclass Spaniards who ruled Mexico after Cortés were known as *guáchupines*. These tyrants have been hated bitterly and traditionally by the Indians of New Spain for the last four centuries. Cortés was the first *guáchupin*, and, when he caused Montezuma to be killed, it made Montezuma a martyr, and his name became the symbol for all *guáchupin* tyranny. The Mexican officials in Eighteen Forty-Six knew how much sympathy the Indians had for the symbol, and

201

used it in their document, not only to prove how conclusively New Mexico belonged to Mexico, but in a hope that the name would sway the Indians."

"It swayed them all right," said Ramón. "But not the way the Mexican government had planned. The manuscript had no effect as propaganda. You will remember that the Americanos took New Mexico with hardly a shot fired."

"What this manuscript really did," said Hagar, "was to start a strange, new religion almost overnight, known as the Montezuma cult. The Papagos applied the name Montezuma to their Elder Brother, a god that had existed long before Hernando Cortés was born. The Pecos Indians claimed Montezuma had been born in their village . . . was supposed to have worn golden shoes and walked to Mexico City, where the guáchupines confiscated them so he couldn't walk back. The Pecosenos kept a sacred fire burning night and day in their kiva, awaiting the return of Montezuma."

"And they use this sword . . . this macapán?" asked Elgera.

"A macapán is the sword of the ancient Aztecs," replied Hagar. "I found out a lot of this from Waco Warren. You know him, Elgera. One of my deputies. Half-breed Comanche boy. He claims there's something going on in the Guadalupes. The Indians know a lot more about those things than we do. I'd take his word. If they are rising again, it's too bad. No telling who belongs to them and who doesn't. Could be all around us, and we wouldn't even know it. Most of the peons down here have Indian blood in 'em. Get them soaked in red-eye and thinking they're descended from the Aztecs, and you have a Montezuma on your hands. I don't like it. Fanatics have tried to use the symbol of Montezuma before to unite the Indians against the white man down this way. You can understand how dangerous it would be, used by the wrong man . . ." He broke off, and his eyes darkened as he looked past Elgera, and his voice was suddenly brittle. "Oh, hello, *Señor* Ortega."

Ortega carried a gold-handled cane over one arm, and rubbed his hands together in an oily way when he spoke. He was the kind of man whose words hid from each other.

"*Buenos días, Señor* Hagar," he said sibilantly. "My . . . ah . . . consignment was not on the afternoon train. We thought perhaps that you could throw some light on the matter."

"Hell, Ortega," said Elder Fayette, shoving past him. "You beat around the bush too much. Say it straight. The rifles have disappeared, Hagar. By your order, it seems."

Fayette reminded *Señorita* Scorpion of Chisos Owens in that moment, standing with a stubborn, inexorable look to the forward thrust of his bulky shoulders. Teacup riders filled the doorway behind their boss, and spilled out across the sidewalk into the street, and Mayor Cabell had difficulty getting through them. He was a dowdy little man in a rumpled Prince Albert, his gray hair fringing a baldpate. He cleared his throat.

203

"Yes, Sheriff," he said pompously. "Disappeared. *Señor* Luis Ortega is the Army contractor, as you know. Or do you? Yes. Five hundred Henry repeaters, Hagar, consigned to Fort Leaton. That's a lot of guns to disappear. Yes, a lot of guns."

Hagar suddenly grinned. "Isn't it, Mayor? You must be mistaken. Those guns were never under civil jurisdiction till the Army picked them up here at Alpine. I'm the only one with authority to issue any order releasing them. And I certainly didn't do that. There was an armed guard aboard the train, and I had two deputies down at the station, waiting to hold the rifles till a troop from Fort Leaton came after them with the wagons. Nothing short of the U.S. Army could have gotten away with those guns."

"The sheriff of Terrel County," said Fayette heavily, "got a wire, ordering him to unload the guns at Sanderson and hold them there for the troop from Fort Leaton. The wire was sent from here, under your authority, Hagar. Soldiers arrived at Sanderson, with the wagons, accompanied by one of your deputies, and took the guns."

"Yes." Mayor Cabell cleared his throat. "Yes. Took the guns. And now, a Captain Maryvaille is here with his Army wagons, and a troop of cavalry, expecting to find the Henrys waiting. He says Fort Leaton did not send any troop to Sanderson, and they have not received the guns."

"Perhaps," said Luis Ortega urbanely, "you can enlighten us, *Señor* Hagar."

The Teacup riders shoved in farther, and Elgera suddenly felt a strange suffocation. She turned from Fayette to Hagar, fists closing. A tall, young captain pushed his way through the crowd, slipping off a white glove. His forage cap sat on his clipped blond hair jauntily, his arrogant face was flushed.

"Is this your sheriff, Mayor Cabell?" he asked in a loud voice. "I demand you put him under arrest immediately."

"Ah, *Capitán*," interposed Ortega. "Surely we can settle this unfortunate error without such . . . ah . . . drastic measures. After all, if Sheriff Hagar made a mistake . . ."

"Diverting government supplies *is* a mistake," said the captain, fixing Ortega with his cold, blue eyes. "You're the contractor? I should think you'd be the first to want the culprit attended to. And you, Sheriff. What in thunder did you plan to do with that many guns? I can't understand it."

Hagar turned calmly and took a big ring of keys off a peg on the wall, then chose one carefully, and inserted it in the lock on the barred door that opened into the corridor between the cells at the rear. At the other end of the corridor was the back door leading into an alley. Elgera began to edge between Hagar and Fayette. If Hagar wanted it that way, all right.

"What are you doing, Sheriff?" demanded Cabell.

"I'm unlocking the door." said Hagar, watching them. "Is this your frame, Fayette?"

Fayette glanced imperceptibly at the Teacup riders behind him. "Frame?"

205

"Frame-up," said Hagar, opening the door unhurriedly. "I never sent any wire to unload the guns at Sanderson. The only way it could have come from this office was that one of my deputies sent it without my authority. Who did you reach, Fayette? Waco Warren? I don't think you could buy him. Nevada Wallace?"

Hagar had moved so calmly, so obviously, that none of them had realized his intention at first. Suddenly Fayette sensed it. He jumped forward.

"Don't let him get through that door. The back way . . ."

The sudden scuffling surge of men stopped as soon as it had begun. Fayette stood where he had taken the leap toward Hagar, a dull flush creeping into his heavy face. Elgera hadn't actually seen the movement of Hagar's hands. Somehow he held his guns now, and he was grinning easily, and backing through the door.

"I don't know what this is about," he said. "I'm not going to take any frame-up sitting down. Don't try to follow me."

"Drop your iron, Johnny!"

As if jerked by a string, Johnny Hagar whirled and fired at the huge, yellow-haired man in the rear door before he had finished shouting. It was Nevada Wallace, and his gun went off at the roof as he staggered backward into the alley, grabbing at the hand Hagar's slug had smashed.

Elgera threw herself at Fayette, tripping him over onto her own body as he jumped for Hagar again. The others swarmed past as she fell beneath Fayette's great weight. Desperately she caught at the captain's boot.

206

He stumbled and kicked her hand free, and threw himself into the hallway as Hagar swung back. Elgera struggled to get out from under Fayette, a sea of kicking, shuffling boots surrounding her.

"Get those guns!" the captain shouted.

A Peacemaker boomed, and someone grunted sickly. Fayette got to his hands and knees above Elgera. She clawed at him, trying to kick his legs from beneath him again. He hit her in the face. Then he was off her, throwing himself into the struggling mass of men. She could see dimly that all but two were in the hallway fighting Hagar now. Mayor Cabell still stood between her and the door.

"Please." He cleared his throat. "Please. Johnny was the best sheriff this town ever had. Be careful. Yes."

The light from the front door was blocked off then, by the second man's body. He seemed to bend over Elgera from behind as she struggled to her hands and knees, dazed from Fayette's blow. She realized suddenly that the man had placed himself so as to hide her from the mayor, and she tried to jump erect. She caught a blurred view of *mitaja* leggings, and heard his voice soft in her ear.

"I . . . ah . . . regret this exceedingly, *señorita*."

There was a sudden, shocking pain. There was nothing.

"I am glad to see you are regaining consciousness," the cultivated voice was saying. "It was an execrable thing to do, but necessary, you must agree. They would have put you away with Hagar, I think. Perhaps for aiding and abetting his escape, or trying to. The charge wouldn't have mattered. They just wanted their paws on you."

Into her vision swam the narrow, vulpine face of Luis Ortega. The hood of his cloak was thrown back, and his queued, black hair lay like a slick skullcap over the top of his thin head, gleaming in the light of an oil lamp on the marble-topped table.

"You are in the Alpine Lodge," he said. "The Teacup riders Fayette left out in Second Street were very solicitous when I told them you had been . . . ah . . . incapacitated in the struggle. They even offered to accompany me to the doctor's office with you. A whole lot of them. They said they would wait outside. I did not know the doctor was such a good *amigo* of yours. It simplified matters . . . and that alley his back door opens onto. *Gracias a Dios, señorita,* you are now hidden from them right under their very noses."

"Why?" said Elgera, and the springs squeaked as she swung her legs to the floor.

"Why?" he repeated. "Perhaps *you* will elucidate."

"Why did you get me out of it?" she asked. "What do you want?"

"Aha." He laughed softly, tilting his head back. "You are a singular judge of character, *señorita.*"

She moved unsteadily to the window. The two-story Alpine Lodge stood on the northwest corner of Second and Main. She was on the second story of the side facing across Second to the Mescal Saloon on the southwest corner of Main and Second, and the sheriff's office farther down Second. A couple of Fayette's Teacup hands stood in the door of the sheriff's office.

Another came out of a building farther down the street, looking toward them and shaking his head.

Elgera's eyes were caught by movement on Main. Two more Teacup men had come out of Si Samson's livery stable on the other side of the street, and stood looking up toward the brick depot at the north end of town. Luis Ortega's oily voice startled her, coming from directly behind.

"*Sí*, they are looking for you, *señorita*. Perhaps it was Fayette's meaning to get you and Hagar both out of the way at one blow, eh?"

She turned angrily. "Fayette was connected with that business about the guns then?"

Ortega shrugged his shoulders, and his words slid unctuously through a secretive smile. "You ask me? Perhaps many men are connected with it, *señorita*, who you would never suspect were connected with it, and then, again, perhaps many men who you would suspect were connected with it were not connected with it at all."

"I would suspect you were connected with it," she said, "in more ways than just that of the government contractor who doesn't seem at all worried about the money he stands to lose by the theft of his guns."

A mock hurt look tilted his brows; he held out his slim hand, opening his mouth as if to protest. Then his mobile lips slipped into that sly smile, and he began to chuckle sibilantly.

"*Sí, señorita, sí, sí.* Perhaps you are *correcto*. Let us say that I am an *hombre* who is not averse to making a few *pesos* on the side. And it is a fact that the more

209

sides an *hombre* looks on, the more *pesos* he is likely to find."

"Saving me was one of those sides?"

"Ah, *señorita*, you do me an injustice," he said. "What *caballero* wouldn't throw his life at the feet of such a *carissima?* You can have that free of charge. But, shall we say, there are other . . . ah . . . services I could render you . . ."

She turned away from the window. "I was ruined in that raid on my spread. I couldn't pay you for anything, and, if I could, I wouldn't."

He held up an ingratiating finger. "Ah, perhaps your cattle were killed and your home destroyed. But you have some . . . ah . . . liquid securities left. Not enough to do much against Fayette, perhaps, but enough, I'm sure, to propitiate the sordid god of gold that I have the unfortunate weakness of worshipping."

She started for the door. "Thanks for helping me. I'm sure there's nothing I could want from you."

"Before you throw yourself to Fayette's dogs," he said, and it stopped her, and he began rubbing his thumb against his forefinger. "I see I must come to the point. How much would you give to find *Señor* Chisos Owens?"

Elgera felt the blood drain from her face. *Chisos?* A wild look flashed in her eyes. She moved toward Ortega in a swift, tense way, like a cat about to leap.

"You know where Chisos is?"

Ortega took a step backward, holding up a hand. "I have certain connections, shall we say, that would assist you immeasurably in finding him. I am sure the Alpine

National Bank would honor your check for . . . ah . . . ten thousand, yes, ten thousand dollars, made out in my name, if you would care to have access to those connections."

The shot outside was flat and muffled. There was another one. Someone yelled downstairs, then the *thud* of feet came from the hall. Elgera had started for the door again when in burst Waco Warren, one of Hagar's deputies, the half-breed Comanche with his buckskin leggings tucked inside old cavalry boots. He must have been falling when he thrust the door open. He hung onto the knob, and the portal swung in with his weight, carrying him on around with it till the door smashed against the wall. He went to his knees there, with his head against the panels and his back toward Elgera, his fist still closed desperately on the knob.

"Elgera," he gasped, trying to rise. "They're taking Hagar away. Nevada. Fayette's men. Said they're taking him to Terrel County because the crime was committed there. You know that's a lie. They won't take him to Sanderson . . ."

She hadn't yet reached the deputy when someone else ran in the doorway. A gun bellowed. Waco grunted in a sick, hollow way. He jerked on around, and his shoulder brushed Elgera's outstretched hand as he fell on his face with his legs all twisted up under him.

Elgera didn't know just when she had drawn her gun. It must have been the reaction to the shot. She stood there with the big Army Colt leveled at the man in the doorway, and she had gotten it out soon enough, she realized, to have him covered before he even began

211

to raise his own .45s from where they had been pointed at Waco Warren.

"Don't lift them any higher, Ramón," she said, and she was turned now so she could see Luis Ortega. "In fact, you'd better just drop them."

Ramón Delcazar's mouth opened slightly. Then his .45s made a metallic *thud* on the floor, one after the other. Ortega was bent forward with his gold-handled cane gripped in both hands, as if he had started to do something with it. He straightened with an effort. His chuckle was weak.

"*Por Dios, señorita*, my eyes must be going bad in my old age. I did not see you draw that gun. How did it get in your hand?"

"Why," asked Elgera whitely, "did you have to do that?"

Ramón looked surprised. "I thought Waco was after you . . ."

Elgera didn't look at the dead man, lying on the floor. She was trying to keep from feeling the horror of it. She was remembering how Hagar had said they would be everywhere, now, if the cult was rising again, and that there would be no telling who belonged, and who didn't.

"Oh," she said, "you thought Waco was after me. Are you part Quill, Ramón?"

Ramón nodded. "*Sí*, my grandmother was a Quill. A pure-blood Indian of Mexico. And that makes me . . ."

He stopped suddenly, a strange look crossing his face. Elgera backed across the room and shoved up the window overlooking a shed roof that slanted down into the alley behind the Alpine Lodge.

"*Señorita*," said Ortega, "what about our . . . ah . . . arrangement?"

The girl threw a slim leg over the sill. "I don't think I want your connections to help me locate Chisos, Ortega. I have some connections of my own, and they only play one side of the game at a time. Don't follow me for a while. I'd very much like an excuse to kill you, either of you!"

CHAPTER
FOUR

In *Tonalamente*, the *Book of Fate*,
All things are decreed and written.
For Chisos Owens it is now too late.
John Hagar shall next be smitten.

The campfire winked, small and lonely, in the malignant darkness that cloaked the Barrillas, and that pressed in on Hagar with a frightening intensity as he sat cross-legged before the softly snapping flames, trying not to look at the circle of faces surrounding him, silent, inscrutable, waiting. Farther out, he could see the circle of wagons with U.S. Army showing vaguely on their blurred white tilts.

"You were the deputy with that troop of cavalry who got the rifles at Sanderson?" said Hagar thinly.

Lobos Delcazar was dumping coffee grounds from a paper sack into a tin coffee pot. He still wore his blue dragoon's coat with the red cuffs and collar, and his fringed sash twitched at his Blucher boot with each movement. He showed his white teeth in a grin.

"Sure, Hagar, that was me. I didn't have any trouble, as your deputy. We timed it nicely, no? I fixed the guards down there at the Santiago so Chisos Owens could get through without any trouble, and left even before he got there, on my way to Sanderson to meet my troop of cavalry and pick up the guns."

214

"Oh," said Hagar. "It was you who fixed the guards at the Santiago? We sort of had Chisos pegged for that one. Why didn't you just shoot the girl in the back, too, while you were about it?"

"Do you think I am the kind who shoots women, Johnny?" said Lobos, looking hurt, and then he grinned. "Besides, Elgera is too good with an iron. I don't think even you could edge her out. Why should I take chances with a wildcat like that when it wasn't necessary? Chisos Owens was supposed to have taken care of her. Nevada tells me he slipped up, though."

Nevada Wallace stood uncomfortably to one side, the firelight glinting on his curly yellow hair. The Peacemakers didn't have their rakish threat, somehow, on his thick hips; they looked ponderous and ineffectual. He must have coveted them for a long time. They were the first things he took from Hagar. He had taken the sheriff east, toward Sanderson, until they were out of sight of Alpine, then turned north into these mountains. The hand Hagar had wounded in the jail was bandaged. Nevada kept moving it around as if it hurt him, and his mouth took an ugly twist whenever he looked at Hagar.

"The girl hit town this morning," he said sullenly. "Fayette tried to get her when we hooked Johnny, here. She got away somehow. I think that Ortega had a hand in it."

Lobos poured water from a five-gallon Army canteen into the coffee pot, sighing. "*Sí*, I suppose Ortega did have a hand in it. He has a hand in 'most everything, it seems. Like that gun deal. Ortega found out Elder Fayette would pay him twice as much for those Henry repeaters as the Army would. The Army had already given him his payment, however . . . an outrageous price, by the way . . . and he didn't want to lose that. They could hardly demand a refund, though, if the guns were diverted by a party who could not possibly be identified with Ortega, could they? He was quite willing to sell the guns again, under those conditions."

"What did Fayette want with the guns?" asked Hagar thinly.

"He wanted to give them to us," said Lobos, and laughed. "I see you are confused. We wouldn't have fooled with Ortega or Fayette, understand, but we wanted those five hundred Henry repeaters, and were in no position to take them by force. Thus, we contracted to do a little job for Fayette, in return for his getting us the rifles. Ortega, as a government supply contractor, had access to a number of uniforms. Thus Fayette's riders became a troop of cavalry. I couldn't use my own boys there, could I? Even that short-sighted Sanderson sheriff would have smelled some bad beans if I'd showed up with a bunch of Indians in U.S. cavalry uniforms. Nevada was the one who wired to unload the guns at Sanderson. There you have the whole little conspiracy. Fayette gets his job of work done. Ortega gets two prices for his guns. We get the guns. We even get you, as sort of a bonus. Nevada gets to be sheriff. Ah, how happy everybody is."

Very clever, thought Hagar, and he could feel the frustrated anger building up in him again. He had tried to control it all the way from Alpine. It was boiling near the surface now. He wondered how much longer he could hold it in. Very clever. So they had it all sewed up. Him all sewed up. Everything all sewed up. He put his manacled hands in his lap suddenly and knotted them together till his fingers hurt.

Outside the circle of wooden-faced Indians, a dozen white men were stripping off yellow-striped cavalry trousers and blue coats. Abilene came walking over, Elder Fayette's right bower, a lean, taciturn man who had ridden with Nevada and Hagar from Alpine. He was constantly rolling wheat straws, and Hagar guessed it was as good a way as any to keep his fingers supple for the big Beale-Remington he wore. Abilene studied the cigarette he was building, speaking in a toneless, impersonal voice.

"I'll take the Teacup boys back now. Coming, Nevada?"

Hagar looked up sharply. "Yeah. Go ahead, Nevada. You should make a good sheriff. I guess you've been with me long enough to learn all the little tricks. Tell Cabell hello for me. Tell all my friends hello. I must have a lot of friends in Alpine."

"Shut up," said Nevada sullenly.

"I thought you were my friend, Nevada," said Hagar. "That's funny, isn't it? I thought all of you were my friends. Lobos and Cabell and Ramón Delcazar and Waco Warren and you, Nevada . . ."

The yellow-haired man dropped his good hand to the white butt of a Peacemaker. "I said . . . shut up."

"Your trust is childish." Lobos laughed. "Fayette reached Nevada a long time ago. Promised him a spot in his set-up. Nevada's always had his eye on your job, and your guns. You should never trust anyone, Hagar. Look what Chisos Owens did to *Señorita* Scorpion. The girl will be the next one to turn on you . . ."

"Don't talk about her," said Hagar between his teeth.

"Why not?" said Lobos. "Women are the ones you should trust the least. I would rather turn my back on a sidewinder than a woman. And that wild girl. *¡Caracoles!* She is the worst of all. She is just a little . . ."

Hagar's face twisted, and he grunted with the effort of coming up off the ground and throwing himself across the fire at Lobos. He slammed his manacled wrists into Lobos's face. Straddling the man's body as it went down, he beat at him again. Over Lobos's yell, Hagar caught the scuffle of feet behind him. A blow on the head drove his face into Lobos's chest. He sprawled helplessly on the man beneath him. Lobos struggled out from under, scrambling to his feet. Hagar tried to rise to his hands and knees, but another savage blow put him flat again.

"That's enough, Nevada!" shouted Lobos hoarsely.

Hagar rolled over spasmodically, throwing his arms up to guard his head. He could see the giant, yellow-haired man bent over him, heavy face stamped with a brutal hatred.

"That's enough, I said!" screamed Lobos in a rage.

218

Nevada grunted as he struck again. Hagar caught the blow on his shoulder, crying out with the stunning pain. The gunshot drowned his voice. He heard the *thud* of a six-shooter dropped by his head. Nevada's tremendous body crashed down, knocking the breath from Hagar. He was rolled toward Lobos, and he lay helplessly beneath Nevada, staring at the tall man in the blue dragoon's coat. Still holding his smoking Colt, Lobos Delcazar moved toward Hagar. His face was livid with rage, and bleeding where Hagar had smashed him with the handcuffs.

He stooped to roll Nevada off the sheriff. Hagar felt his body grow rigid. He lay there, stunned and sickened, knowing whatever he did now was no good, and his eyes opened, wide and clear, as he stared up at Lobos, because that was the way he would take it whenever it came.

Lobos's body was trembling perceptibly, and his gusty breathing had a harsh, uncontrollable sound. His black eyes glittered, the pupils dilating and contracting, and his lips writhed across his white teeth without any sound. He held his Colt pointed at Hagar's head. Hagar could see his finger quivering on the trigger.

Suddenly Lobos took a ragged breath and straightened with a jerk, turning away as if to find control, and his voice shook. "All right. All right, Hagar. If it was up to me, I'd kill you for that. But it isn't up to me. Maybe this way is better. Killing a man finishes it off so quick, anyhow. You'll pay, Hagar, more than you can imagine, you'll pay."

The men around the fire had all risen, and were just settling back now, watching Lobos or Hagar. Lobos untied his gaudy neckerchief and stooped to the big Army canteen. He wet the silk cloth and began to wipe his bleeding face. Squatting there, still holding his gun in one hand, he looked up at Abilene.

"You tell Fayette, if he doesn't like what happened, he can send another one of his sheriffs out, and I'll do the same with him," said Lobos. "Tell him to send you, Abilene. Yeah. Tell Fayette to send you."

Abilene's opaque eyes were as impersonal as his toneless voice. "Never mind. We didn't figure on using Nevada. He was too dumb to make the kind of tin badge Fayette wants. You saved us a piece of business, that's all."

He turned and rounded up the Teacup riders who had posed as troopers, and they filtered silently out through the wagons toward the horses. Still dabbing at his face, Lobos took the boiling coffee off the rocks and began to pour it into tin cups. Hagar rolled over on his belly, shaking his head dazedly. The men around the fire were all watching him now, faces unreadable. There wasn't a white man among them.

Lobos held out a cup of coffee. "Go ahead, Johnny. It's all over now. You'll need something. We've got a long trip ahead."

Hagar took the cup, holding it tentatively in his hand. Lobos unbuckled his own gun belt and turned to take Hagar's ivory-handled weapons off Nevada. He caressed one of the white butts.

"You know," he said, "I'm sort of glad it happened this way. I always thought these guns would look nice on me."

He laughed suddenly, and shoved the holsters down snugly against his legs. Hagar stared at Nevada's body. He turned away, sickened. Lobos jerked his head toward the dead man. Two of the Indians rose and dragged Nevada away.

"Go ahead," he said. "Drink it, Hagar. Make you feel better, eh? Everything's over now. Drink it."

Hagar took a sip, grimaced. "Tastes like alkali."

Lobos looked into the fire, a peculiar lack of focus to his eyes, and he grinned inanely. "*Sí*, it sometimes does. You will get used to it after a while."

Hagar took another drink. "What do you mean? What's your cut in this, Lobos? Did Fayette promise you a soft spot in his county? Or cash on the barrel head?"

Lobos looked at Hagar without seeming to see him. "Neither, Hagar. I do not care to have a job with Fayette's bunch when he climbs into Brewster County's saddle, because he won't sit there very long. And whatever we do is not for money."

"We?" said Hagar, and looked around at the silent group again. They were drinking coffee, too, watching him over the rims of their cups. He suddenly felt dizzy. Then his head seemed to expand like a balloon. The tin cup *clinked* against a rock as he dropped it. "We?" he said again, and giggled drunkenly.

Lobos laughed, too. "Yes, we. Not these men specifically, though they belong to us."

"Us?" said Hagar, wondering what the hell was wrong with him. "What kind of coffee was that, Lobos? Us?"

Lobos took several reddish beans from his pocket and popped one into his mouth, chewing it slowly. "It was partly coffee. *Sí*. Sometimes we take it like this" — he put another bean in his mouth — "the traditional way."

Hagar giggled foolishly, swaying forward suddenly. "Whaddaya mean? Whaddaya talking about?"

"You will find out, *Señor* Hagar, and, when you do, believe me, you will wish you hadn't."

She was an old woman with a furrowed face the color of worn saddle leather, sitting cross-legged in the smoky wickiup somewhere north of Horse Thief Crossing on the Pecos. She was a Comanche, with her stringy gray hair braided over her right shoulder and falling down in front of her greasy, buckskin shift. She was Waco Warren's mother.

"So they killed my son," she said dully, and her utter grief shone in her eyes. "I know Ramón Delcazar. I didn't think he was the kind to shoot his friends in the back. But they are rising again, and how can we know who are our enemies any more, and who are our friends?"

She rocked slowly back and forth over the fire, hugging skinny arms tightly against her chest. Elgera Douglas sat across from the old woman. The shimmering beauty of her long blonde hair was filmed with dust, and a burning, feverish look marked her face. Finally the hag spoke again.

"How did you escape from them, *muchachita?*"

Señorita Scorpion shrugged wearily, forced to admire the woman's effort at self-control. "The alley behind the Alpine Lodge runs between Second and First. The Alamo Saddlery fronts on Second, a storeroom behind that opens onto the alley. I hid in there till night. Fayette's men had all the streets out of town blocked and were stopping all the riders, coming or going. They couldn't guard every inch. I slipped by them on foot and hiked to Marathon where I got this horse."

Little by little the Indian's grief began to seep through, and her voice shook now, although she tried to control it. "You found Hagar in Sanderson?"

Elgera shook her head. "They didn't take him there."

The first hoarse sob escaped the old woman. Then she began to hum under her breath, a monotonous, choked sound, with her seamed face appearing from the smoke as she swayed forward, and disappearing again as she swayed back. Her hollow intonation grew louder, and Elgera realized it was the death chant for Waco Warren.

"He was a good boy," muttered the old woman in a stifled sing-song voice. "It didn't matter if he was a half-breed. John Warren was a good man, and Waco Warren is gone to our old gods. And Johnny Hagar is gone, too. First it was Chisos Owens. Now Johnny Hagar. You would follow them of your own free will?"

"They didn't take Hagar to Sanderson," said Elgera tensely. "Where did they take him? What are they doing

223

to him? I've got to go after him. Maybe it's too late for Chisos. But Hagar . . ."

"You don't realize what you say." The old woman's voice was a hollow chant. "You don't realize what it means to go after them. They have many powers that you or I do not understand. They are all around us. We cannot say who belongs to them, and who doesn't. Chisos Owens has lost his soul to them. Johnny Hagar is now in their hands. You do not know what you are doing."

Elgera's voice sounded desperate. "I do. I can't sit by and see this happen to them. They're my friends."

"You will avenge my son's death?"

"If I can. How?"

"The only way you can help Hagar, the only way you can stop all this, is to reach the one who thinks he is the reincarnation of Montezuma, and kill him," the old woman said in a sudden burst of viciousness. Then she resumed her chanting. "That would avenge my son's death. But only those who pay homage to the gods of ancient Atzalán know where Montezuma reigns. I do not worship Quetzalcoatl, but I am an Indian, and know many things the white man does not know. I can tell you that somewhere in the Guadalupes the Montezumans are gathering."

"I didn't think even the Indians knew what was in those mountains," said Elgera.

The old woman nodded, swaying back and forth more swiftly. "The Guadalupes are inaccessible in many places, and my people have never penetrated them. But the Montezumans are gathering. From as far south as

Mexico City come Quills, and from the Sierra Madres come Yaquis, and from Chihuahua and Durango come Mexicans who claim to be descended from the ancient Aztecs. Each month on the first night of the full moon, the new ones gather at the deserted Apache Mine south of Pecos, and one of Montezuma's *techutlis* comes to get them."

"*¿Techutlis?*"

"The *techutlis* are a knightly order of the Aztecs," muttered the hag. "This *techutli* leads the newcomers westward from the Apache Mine, traveling only at night, and no white man knows of their coming or going. But the Comanches do, and the Apaches. Yet, even my people have only been able to trail them as far as the outer slopes of the Guadalupes. Those warriors, who followed them in, never came back. Do you still wish to go, *muchachita?*"

"I told you," said Elgera grimly.

Waco Warren's mother began to nod her head in a sharper rhythm now, and tears were streaming from her eyes, and it cost her more of an effort to go on talking. "Very well. In two days the moon will be full again. A new group will be meeting at the mine, and the *techutlis* will come for them. You will be one of their number. *Pues*, the Montezumans know you are looking for them. Your blonde hair would mark you as quickly as the gold color of your palomino marks it as your horse. You will not go as Elgera Douglas."

Elgera felt her breathing become heavier, and she licked nervous lips, watching the old woman sway toward her through the smoke, and sway away from

225

her, and unconsciously she began to sway slightly, too, and the smoke rose up to envelope her, thick and choking and black, and funereal in its portent.

CHAPTER
FIVE

This portal's guard is Tlaloc
The God of Evil and Sin.
Death is the key to its lock.
Doomed are who enter herein.

The two men sat hunched over in their saddles. Elder Fayette's heavy Mackinaw was torn and burned down one side, and the granite planes of his face were covered with dark smudges, and there was a livid scar across one weathered cheek that might have been made by a bullet. His big-knuckled hands were gripped tightly on the saddle horn. The hard line of his mouth was twisted with the rage that shook him whenever he thought of what had happened.

"I might've known this is what I'd get, doing business with a loco Indian like that," he muttered through locked teeth. "All he helped me get Chisos and Hagar for was so I'd get those guns for him. It isn't just *guáchupines* he wants to burn . . . it's every white man in Texas, with me in the same war sack as the rest!"

Abilene was rolling a cigarette. "Five thousand cows. That's a lot of beef to mill in the river till they drown. Nobody else but Chisos Owens could've gotten through our boys to do it. I guess Montezuma knew what he was doing when he hitched Chisos to his team instead of killing him."

Elder Fayette's voice trembled slightly. "Maybe he thinks I won't come after him. Maybe he thinks wiping out my spread finished me like it did the others. I won't be finished till I find him. I swear to God, Abilene, I'll find him and tear his heart out with my bare hands."

He stopped, breathing heavily. The round glow of Abilene's cigarette bobbed in the darkness. Fayette looked downslope in the direction Abilene had indicated. The first of the cavalcade was hardly visible, winding down the bottom of the narrow cañon, mere shadows against the darker rise of the opposite ridge. Fayette kept his voice down with an effort.

"For once, Ortega was telling the truth. The Apache Mine on the first night of the full moon. This cañon on the third. That's about right for the distance, if they don't do any daytime riding."

"That isn't like Ortega, telling the truth," said Abilene. "Maybe he'd just as soon have you out of the way as Montezuma."

"And maybe I'll kill him, too, when I find him," grunted Fayette. "You coming?"

Abilene flipped his wheat straw away. "As long as you pay me on the first of every month, I'll follow any trail you put your horse to."

Fayette took a heavy breath and turned his Choppo horse down through the timber toward the cavalcade. Near the edge of the trees, Abilene gigged his mount up suddenly and grabbed Fayette's arm. They halted and waited there in a thick stand of somber aspen, while a pair of ghost-like riders padded through the timber just below them, some distance up from the main party in the bottom of the cañon. Fayette held his mare there for an interval, and another pair of flankers rode by. Then he nodded, sidling down the slope toward the tail of the cavalcade. He and Abilene had almost reached it when, above them, they heard the faint sound of a third pair of outriders passing through the timber they had left.

One of the last riders in the main line turned toward them as they trotted in. All Fayette could see was the dim flash of eyes from beneath a *rebozo* that served as both hood and veil. They might have been dark eyes, but the night gave them a strange, bluish gleam. A woman?

"You shouldn't fall behind like that, *señores*," said someone from farther ahead. "The *techutlis* will kill you if you lag."

"*Sí*," muttered Fayette, and saw the woman turn away.

Dawn lit the morning sky from the east, and ground fog wreathed up around Fayette's legs, chilling him. He could see how high they really were now. The terrain dropped away behind him in a dim dawn glow for what must have been 100 miles. Out of the bluish-gray fog rose the peaks they had passed, and beyond that a vast expanse of salt flats he knew to exist somewhere south of the Guadalupes.

Fayette glanced sharply to his right. A pair of riders who had been flanking the cavalcade all night sat over there, dim, haunting shapes on vague shadow horses.

There was another pair on the other side. And two more were closing in silently from behind.

An indurate look crossed Fayette's dusty, smudged face, and he hunched bulky shoulders down into his Mackinaw and gave his Choppo the boot, following the others down the slope ahead.

Nothing would stop him from reaching Montezuma. It was what he had come here to do. He would do it. In his utterly single-purposed mind it was as simple as that. And the rage that had been building in him ever since his spread had been burned was a hot, writhing, living thing that swept all doubt or questioning from his thoughts, leaving only the savage, driving desire to get his hands on the Indian.

They turned into a valley that soon became a narrow cañon, and then a knife-blade cut, with walls so steep that the pinkish morning light faded into a darkness as cold as the night they had left behind. Finally the cavalcade was halted, and the riders began to dismount. Fayette saw that a file of Montezuma's *techutlis* had been waiting for them in the cut here, tall, hawk-beaked men with exotic plumed headdresses, gleaming bronze bodies, naked but for the gilt-edged loin cloth Fayette had heard Ortega call a *maxtli*. Striking a discordant note in their barbaric appearance was the bandoleer of cartridges each man wore slung over his shoulder, and the bright, new Henry repeater crooked in his arm. Sight of that brought a thin rage into Fayette's red-rimmed eyes.

They began gathering up the horses, and leading them toward another cañon that opened into this one from the side, and Fayette was turned away when the *techutli* came to take the reins of his jaded Choppo. Past the dismounted crowd, Fayette had seen what he first took to be the box end of the cañon. Now he realized that huge square blocks of granite had been set into the knife-blade cut, forming a wall some fifty feet high that closed the cañon off completely. One of the blocks had been swung out at the base of the wall, leaving a dark tunnel that must lead on through it, but Fayette couldn't see the other side.

The woman in the *rebozo* turned to him, and there was something about the lithe movement of her body that he seemed to remember. She was tall, even in flat-heeled, rawhide *huiraches*, and a lock of thick black hair curled from beneath her shawl. She wore a split buckskin skirt, dirty and greasy now, belted around her slim waist by a string of hammered silver bosses.

Fayette bent forward. "Don't we know each other?"

"I am Lola Salazar," she said. "I danced in the Alamo Saloon at San Antone."

"I've been there," he said. "I don't remember you."

"I remember you," she said, and nodded her head toward the rock wall. "That is Tlaloc's Door. They will inspect each one of us as we go through. They'll see you're an *Americano*, *Señor*."

"Will they?" he said, and reached up for her *rebozo*, saying: "Lola Salazar?"

She struck his hand down, whirled, and ran toward the crowd. A pair of armed *techutlis* were standing by the door, stopping each man or woman as they passed through. Fayette took a step after the girl, then shrugged, turning to Abilene. The lean, impersonal man nodded, taking a drag on his wheat straw.

"You know what to do when we reach the door?" said Fayette.

"Go through it," said Abilene. "You take care of the two boys there. I'll cover your tail. We'll make it."

Four *techutlis* were coming up behind Abilene, and one of them looked intently at Fayette's face, and began to come forward faster. There were only three of the crowd left to go through the door. One was passed by the guards, then the next. The girl was last. She said something in Spanish. The guard nodded. She disappeared into the dark tunnel.

"*Un momento, señores,*" the man behind Abilene said. "*¿Eres Americanos?*"

"*¿Americanos?*" said the guard at the door, and whirled around.

Fayette took three leaps to him and smashed him back against the wall, wrenching the Henry from his surprised grasp. The second *techutli* there spun around and pulled his rifle into his belly for a snap shot. Fayette whirled, swinging his weapon around in a vicious arc that caught the man in the face. The *techutli*'s Henry exploded into the air as he crashed back into the rocks and slumped to the ground.

Fayette tried to whirl around again to the man he had taken the rifle from, and dodge at the same time. But the Indian was already on him, grappling for the gun. Abilene's Beale-Remington boomed, and someone screamed, and it boomed again. Then another *techutli* threw himself on Fayette, and the big man went down

232

beneath the two struggling Indians, still holding the rifle in both hands and jerking it back and forth savagely.

A rawhide *huirache* slammed him in the face. Spitting blood, he butted his head upward and caught a man in the belly, carrying him back to the wall. He let go the rifle and got his hands in the *techutli*'s long, black hair and beat his head against the stones once. He dropped the dead weight of the man and whirled.

The other Indian had gotten the rifle. He had it above his head, and, even as Fayette came around, he saw that whatever he did would be futile, and that kind of a blow would finish it.

With the rifle coming down, the *techutli* suddenly gave a spasmodic grunt. Instead of putting his full weight into the blow, the Indian let go the rifle and fell forward against Fayette. The Henry bounced off Fayette's shoulder. He stepped back and let the man fall to the ground on his face.

The girl still stood in the bent-over position she had reached after striking the man. The rifle she had scooped off the ground was held in both hands, still a little off the ground. She dropped it, and straightened. Abilene jumped over one of the men he had shot behind her, holding his smoking Beale-Remington in one hand, and his cigarette in the other. Farther back, more *techutlis* were returning from the cañon to which they had taken the horses.

"You came back to do that?" asked Fayette, looking at the girl with surprise still in his face, and then glancing at the man lying at his feet.

"Do you know what it means to be captured by them?" she panted. "I couldn't let that happen even to you . . . Elder Fayette!"

She turned and ran into the tunnel. Fayette's mouth opened slightly, then he turned and followed her. Abilene came behind him, and the black shadows swallowed them greedily.

CHAPTER
SIX

Dance upon my coffin, *hombres*
Naught but death can be my goal.
Make the darkness ring with *tombes*
The red peyote has my soul.

Sometimes he had a dim memory of another life, far away from this one, and sometimes it seemed to him that he had been known by another name. They called him Quauhtl now, which meant Eagle, and was a good name, they said, for the war lord of Atzalán. Often he would sit cross-legged like this on the first terrace of the House of the Sun, trying to remember that other life, that other name.

He was a big man, Quauhtl, with shoulders that revealed their singular size even under the mantle of brilliant, egret feathers he wore. His heavily muscled torso had a ruddy look, as if freshly exposed to the sun, and his square, solid flanks were covered meagerly by a *maxtli* fringed with fur.

From where he sat on this giant pyramid, he could look across the broad valley to where the mountains rose in purple haze many miles away. He could follow with his eye the winding Road of Death that led to the narrow cañon in those mountains that contained Tlaloc's Door, the only entrance or exit from this City

235

of the Sun People. Absently he took a reddish bean from a pouch at his waist and popped it skillfully into his mouth, chewing it slowly. His eyes seemed hard to focus, and he smiled inanely. It always affected him that way. Peyote. His religion now. The beans were mild compared with the ritual performed every month, five days after the first full moon, in the sacred fire chamber where the eternal blaze was kept aglow for Montezuma, and for the gods of Atzalán. There, for five days and five nights, with the *tombes* beating out their monotonous rhythm and the fires burning red, the *techutlis* made peyote anew. For many days after that Quauhtl lived in a wild haze. He could recall only vaguely the rides to the outer world where he fought the *guáchupines*, pillaging and burning and looting. Then, in about three weeks, the effects of peyote began to wear off, and, instead of remembering battles and war, he would begin to recall that other life, and that other name. But before anything became clear, he was taken to the fire chamber again and treated once more to peyote.

All around him were gigantic pyramids such as the House of the Sun. Most of them had been built by people from Atzalán many centuries before, and were in ruins. Only recently had *Tlatoani* Montezuma set out to rebuild them. Every month a new party of workers arrived, and new warriors, and new slaves, and just this morning another group of them had come marching down the Road of Death from Tlaloc's Door.

They were in the courtyard below Quauhtl now, and soon, he knew, they would begin their revelry, as they always did the night after their arrival. They had to be

236

inculcated into peyote, too, for it was their religion. They would do it in the courtyards, however, for only the knightly order of the *techutlis* were ever allowed in the sacred kivas. He was a *techutli;* he was a great warrior, so they told him. He sighed heavily, popping another bean into his mouth. He didn't know. Sometimes he could remember being a warrior. Sometimes he couldn't remember anything. Just now, he couldn't think.

Quauhtl felt the first throbbing of the *tombe*. He could see one of the ceremonial drummers beating his huge skin drum on the first terrace of the House of the Moon across the courtyard. Another *tombe* took up the rhythm, slowly at first, an interval of perhaps half a minute between each echoing thump.

The gaudy, feathered mantle swirled around Quauhtl's great frame as he rose and moved toward the steps leading from the House of the Sun down to the courtyard. His heavy Bisley .44 sagged against his bare leg, and he shifted the cartridge belt with a hairy hand. Already fires had been lighted in the braziers. He stopped by one, finding the huge Guadalajara jars of mescal, pouring a drink into a smaller clay *olla*. He drank deeply, leaving only a few drops to toss over his shoulder for the God of Revelry.

"Tezteotl," he muttered, "may you be drunk forever," and then laughed thickly and turned to watch the dancers.

The *tombes* were beating faster now, and more drums had joined in, and the high notes of a flute added their eerie call, rising and falling on the last, red light of a dying afternoon. Some of the men and women kicked off their *huiraches* and began the *Matachine*, the dance of Malinche, their bare feet slapping against the checkered, marble floor in time with the *tombes*. Quauhtl saw one swarthy half-breed in rawhide *chivarras* pulling a woman into the dance. She was trying to break free from his greasy hands, looking around her wildly.

"*¡Pelada!*" the man shouted at her, tearing off her *rebozo*.

Her hair had been piled up beneath the shawl, and it fell in a blue-black cascade about the shoulders of her silk blouse. Quauhtl felt his huge, rope-scarred fists close slowly. *Where had he seen that girl before?* She was no *charra* girl, brought in to marry one of the slaves. The half-breed stood there a moment, holding the *rebozo* in one hand, staring stupidly at the woman. Perhaps he had never seen one so beautiful before. Her rich lips curled around something she spat at him. The half-breed flushed, then made a lunge at her.

"*¡Dios*," he shouted, "*que una bella . . .* "

She whirled from him, trying to run, but the crowd got in her way. The half-breed caught her arm, pulling her toward him. The others were laughing and calling to them now, and the woman looked around like some wild animal caught in a trap. There was something about the flushed look of her face, the stormy flash of her eyes that drew Quauhtl irresistibly. He started shoving his way through the crowd, grabbing a man's shoulder to thrust him aside.

238

"*¡Bribón!*" the Indian yelled, turning to grab at a Bowie in his belt. Then he saw who it was, and stumbled backward. "Quauhtl," he muttered. "*Techutli* Quauhtl . . ."

Quauhtl shoved on, hardly hearing it. The half-breed had the struggling girl in his arms and was laughing drunkenly, trying to kiss her as he jerked her out onto the dance floor. Quauhtl reached out a heavy hand and caught the half-breed's arm, squeezing as he pulled.

The man's face twisted, and he jerked around, releasing the girl as he tried to pull free. Quauhtl spun him on around almost indifferently, and then gave him a shove. The half-breed stumbled backward, tripped, fell.

"*¡Borrachón!*" he said hoarsely, grabbing for his gun as he rolled over and started to get up. "*¡Cabrón!*"

Then he stopped cursing, and stopped trying to get up. His mouth stayed open a little, and a fascinated look came into his eyes as he stared at Quauhtl. There was an ineffable menace to the big man, standing there with his great shoulders thrust forward slightly, settling his weight a little into his square hips. His craggy face didn't hold much expression, and his dull eyes hardly seemed to be looking at the half-breed. The wailing flute had died, and the drums were slowing down. The half-breed licked his lips and began moving away in a crawl, and then stopped again.

"*Dios,*" he almost whispered. "You want her? Go ahead, take her. Go ahead."

Quauhtl waited a moment longer. Then he grinned inanely, and turned his back on the man. The flute rose

239

shrilly, and the drums thundered into life again. The half-breed scrambled to his feet and disappeared into the crowd, casting a last, pale look over his shoulder. Quauhtl caught at the woman, not surprised that she didn't resist this time. He was their war lord, wasn't he?

He began to spin her, slapping his feet against the floor in the traditional steps of the *Matachine* that they had taught him. The sweat broke out on his forehead, and the peyote heated his blood, and he threw his head back and roared, spinning faster and faster. The girl tossed her head wildly, a strange look on her face. She seemed to abandon herself to the mad beat of the drums, whirling with him till her skirt whipped up about her bare legs, her hair swirling in a perfumed curtain about his face. The other dancers began to pull away from them, watching.

"*¿Quién es?*" shouted someone.

"She is Lola Salazar," answered a man. "She was a dancer in San Antone, she said. *Por Dios*, I believe it."

"No," shrilled a woman from farther away. "She is no Lola Salazar. You wanted Malinche? There she is. The daughter of Montezuma. The bride of Cortés. Come back to rule beside our *Tlatoani*."

"Malinche!" howled a Yaqui, and the others took it up in a crazy chant that kept time to the *tombes*. "Malinche . . . Malinche . . . Malinche . . ."

Quauhtl saw the look in her eyes, then, and realized she had been watching him all the time that way, and now, as if she had waited for the swelling roar of the sound to drown out what she said, he saw her red lips part in a word, and didn't know whether he actually heard it, or read it in the shape of her mouth.

"Chisos," she almost sobbed. "Chisos . . ."

"What?" he shouted. "Chisos? I am Quauhtl."

"Don't you know me, Chisos?" she panted, whirling in close to him. "Elgera. Don't you remember? What have they done to Hagar? Please, Chisos . . ."

The echoing crash of a great cymbal drowned her voice. Quauhtl spun to a stop with his feathered cloak settling about his bare legs, and the intense silence hurt his eardrums. The flute had stopped; the drums had stopped; everything had stopped. He was still holding the slim, lithe woman when the voice came from above. It wasn't a loud voice. It was sibilant and cultivated. Quauhtl saw the flush drain from the woman's face, leaving it suddenly pale.

"The Lord Montezuma would see this woman, Quauhtl. Bring her to the House of the Sun at once. It is his command!"

Elgera Douglas followed Chisos Owens through the silent crowd of men and women, feeling their eyes on her all the way. She had lost Fayette at Tlaloc's Door. They had gone through it and gained the inside before they had seen more techutlis coming toward them on the Road of Death, drawn by the gunfire. Abilene and Fayette had disappeared into the timber on the slopes inside the door, but Elgera had caught up with the rest of the newcomers who had already gotten through, and lost herself among them. Waco Warren's mother had dyed Elgera's hair and brows black, and given her the clothes, and she was tanned deeply by the sun, and up to now had passed for the dancer from San Antone.

Chisos guided her up the stairway with a heavy hand on her elbow, and kept looking at her in a strange, puzzled way, his eyes clouded and dull. Behind, the *tombes* had begun to beat again, and the flute wailed. On the first level of the terraced pyramid stood a large screen of parrot feathers, hiding a statue from the profane eyes of the commoners below. The idol was carved from shining black obsidian, representing a man, ears bright with earrings of gold and silver, lips painted with gilt. Upon its head was a golden miter, and in its right hand a sickle, and over the shoulders was thrown a magnificent, white robe.

"You like the *itzli, señorita?*" said a soft voice from behind them. "It is a statue of Quetzalcoatl, the Serpent God."

She turned slowly, hiding her surprise well enough. It was the same voice that had ordered her brought to the House of the Sun, and she had recognized it below, and she recognized it now. There was something puzzled in Luis Ortega's dark, vulpine face as he bent forward to study her.

"Lola Salazar? Is that what they said your name was? Have we met?"

"I danced in San Antone," said Elgera huskily.

He tilted his head toward the stairs, ascending to the second terrace, and allowed Chisos to lead the way. "Ah, *sí*, San Antone. I have been there. *Pues*, no, *señorita*, the *techutli* who brought you newcomers here has already told *Tlatoani* Montezuma of your singular

242

beauty. And now the people have begun to think you are Malinche. It has been written in *Tonalamente*, the *Book of Fate*, that she should be reincarnated along with Montezuma. And if our lord thinks you are Malinche, you will be empress of all Texas, *señorita*."

They passed a pair of wooden-faced guards at the third terrace. Ortega caught Elgera's elbow, slowing her so that Chisos pulled ahead of them on the next stairway up. Elgera shook Ortega's hand off.

"You mean Montezuma wants me to . . . ?"

Ortega nodded his head vigorously. "*Sí, sí*, he has been waiting for Malinche's return. And, as I say, if he thinks you are Malinche, you will marry him and rule with him. *Así*, you will need someone to help you along here, someone to smooth the bumps that will inevitably arise among such strange people. I know their ways, their rituals, their gods. A personal advisor, shall we say? *Sí*, a personal advisor."

"What do you get out of it?"

He raised his eyebrows in that hurt look. "Ah, *señorita*, not what I get out of it, but rather what you get . . ."

"I know you, Ortega."

"*Dios*," he said, and then chuckled. "It would seem my reputation has spread farther than I thought. All right, *señorita*. Montezuma means to wipe the white man from Texas. He is loco, but that is beside the point. As empress, you will have access to . . . ah . . . certain things that would benefit me to some extent."

She couldn't help smiling faintly. "Anything that could be converted into cash, you mean."

243

He grinned slyly. "You *do* know me, don't you?"

"And you'd rather Montezuma wasn't aware of this little arrangement," she said.

"*Señorita*," he chuckled, "how well we understand one another."

At each of the seven terraces there was another pair of guards, all with Henry repeaters, not seeming to be aware of the girl as she passed. With the *tombes* pulsing behind them, they reached the top. In the center of the final level was a building built of the same blocks of porphyry that formed the pyramid and covered with a polished coat of lime that shone weirdly in the red afternoon sunlight. Ortega muttered something to the guard at the entrance. The tremendous oak doors stood open, with curtains shutting off the entrance, embroidered heavily with silver and gold. They clanged metallically as the guard pulled them aside.

Ortega and Elgera walked down a huge, colonnaded hall with fires burning in stone braziers along the walls faced with gleaming alabaster. Their footsteps echoed dismally on the smooth floors, coated with ochre and polished till they shone dully. The girl was ushered through a portico decorated with grotesque carvings of serpents, and into a great audience chamber. She stopped short, with her first look at Montezuma.

He sat on a dais across the floor of checkered black and white marble. His majestic head was crowned by a *copilli*, a golden miter that rose to a point above his forehead and fell down behind his neck. There were three other corridors leading from the room, one on either side of the highbacked throne, and one directly behind it.

Ortega led *Señorita* Scorpion across the great hall. Her glance was fixed on Montezuma's darkly ascetic face, and there was something about the peculiar lack of focus in his eyes that reminded her of Lobos Delcazar.

"This is the woman?" said Montezuma, and the hollow rumble of his voice startled Elgera. "Did you do business with her, Ortega?"

Luis Ortega's lithe body seemed to stiffen. "*¿Qué?*"

"Like you tried to do business with Elgera Douglas?" said Montezuma. "Ramón Delcazar has come from Alpine. He tells me it was you who helped the blonde girl escape from the sheriff's office there."

Ortega's voice was suddenly obsequious. "Ah, *Tlatoani* Montezuma, only to better serve your interests. I was leading her to you."

"Better to serve *your* interests, you mean," said Montezuma. "If you had left her alone to be taken along with John Hagar, she would have been handed over to Lobos Delcazar, and would have been in my hands now. You have been talking with a forked tongue long enough, Luis Ortega. I am glad to see you brought me this woman promptly. You have, at least, carried out your last duty without a mishap."

Ortega's eyes darted around the room in a sudden, fearful way. "My . . . last duty, *Tlatoani?*"

Montezuma waved his hand imperiously. A pair of stalwart guards stepped from the squad standing to one side of the throne, moving with a swift, measured tread toward Ortega. He took a step backward.

"No," he almost whispered, and then his voice began to rise. "*Tlatoani* Montezuma, I swear I am your slave. My life is yours. I would never do anything against your interests. *No, no, no . . .* "

The last was a scream, and he turned and darted toward the curtained doorway of the corridor to the right of the throne. Two guards appeared through the hangings. Ortega whirled back. The other pair of guards came up from behind him. He struck at one with his cane, stumbled backward, then they had him, wrenching his arms behind his back.

"No!" he screamed. "*Señorita*, don't let them do this to me. They will sacrifice me to Quetzalcoatl. No. *Tlatoani. Señorita.* Empress Malinche . . ."

Writhing and screaming, the two husky *techutlis* carried him through the door at the rear of the throne. Montezuma waited till his howls had died away down the corridor. Then he bent forward, and his eyes were suddenly glittering intensely at Elgera, and she felt herself swept with a strange dizziness.

"Malinche," he intoned, and there was a fanatical sincerity in his voice. "They were right. You are Malinche. We shall wed before Quetzalcoatl and rule all of Texas. The white man shall burn with the *guáchupines*, for they are all tyrants, and my people shall have the land that belonged to their ancestors."

The sound hadn't been audible at first, above the throbbing background of *tombes*. But now Elgera saw

Montezuma's great head tilt upward, as if he were listening. She heard the gunshots, too.

From the corridor leading off to the right, a guard burst through the curtains and dropped them from behind him with a *clang*. He stumbled toward the throne, holding bloody hands across his belly.

"*Tlatoani* Montezuma," he gasped, and fell to his knees. "*Está ese borrachón*, Elder Fayette. *Está* Fayette!"

He fell over on his face, and didn't say anything else, and wouldn't be saying anything else again, ever. Elgera saw the faint rise of Montezuma's great, bronze chest beneath his feathered mantle. It was the only sign he gave. He raised his hand, about to say something. Before he could speak, a guard ran into the chamber from the corridor that led out to the front of the pyramid.

"*Ésta* Abilene!" he shouted. "*El Americano . . .*"

Another volley of shots behind cut off the rest. Someone yelled outside. The *tombes* had ceased now.

"Quauhtl," said Montezuma composedly.

Chisos Owens bowed, called something to the guards by the throne as he whirled, and ran toward the corridor from which the second guard had come, pulling the Bisley he wore. Four of the *techutlis* followed him from the squad by the dais, and Elgera heard the echo of their feet down the corridor, and then a sporadic series of shots. She looked around swiftly.

"You are afraid, *señorita?*" said Montezuma. "They will never reach me. I am invincible. I am immortal."

"Are you?" said Elder Fayette, stepping through the doorway to the right of the throne.

There were only two guards left by the throne. They turned, jerking Henrys around. The sound of Fayette's sixgun rocked the room. The first guard went down without firing. The second got a bullet out, but it went into the floor as he fell forward on his face. The hammer snapped on Fayette's gun as he pulled the trigger a third time. He tossed the weapon aside, still coming forward, stepping across the body of the guard who had first come from that doorway. He didn't seem to see Elgera. His burning eyes were fixed on Montezuma. From outside there was another rattle of shots.

"That's Abilene," said Fayette through his teeth. "He came up one stairway. I took the other. I guess he won't get by Chisos, will he? That's why we split up. I knew one of us would have to meet Chisos, and I knew that one wouldn't get through. The other one reached you, though, didn't he, Montezuma?"

Montezuma rose, nostrils flaring like some wild stallion in a rage. Yet he seemed held there for that moment by the sight of that big, inexorable man, coming steadily toward him in a heavy, unhurried walk. Elgera could understand that. Few others would have gotten this far. Perhaps only one other. The one Fayette had recognized for being that kind. Chisos Owens.

Fayette took a step across the first guard he had shot and stumbled, and Elgera realized he was wounded. But his voice was steady, and he kept going toward Montezuma.

"Did you think you could play the game both ways to the middle like Ortega?" he said heavily. "Let me get those guns for you and then wipe out my spread? Did you think that would finish me like it did the others? I won't be finished till I get you, Montezuma. I don't care much what happens after that. Nobody's crossed me yet and stayed around to tell about it. You won't be the first. I've come to get you."

Montezuma leaned forward, all his fanaticism suddenly bursting through his austerity with a hissing venom. "And did you think I wouldn't wipe you out with all the other *guáchupines* in Texas. Oppressors. Tyrants. You are one of them, Fayette. You can't harm me."

Fayette staggered and began to move forward faster, his voice gasping. "Go ahead, pull that hide-out. Remember what I told you? You haven't got enough lead in that cutter to stop me before I get you. Go ahead . . ."

His words were cut off by the blast of the first shot. Fayette grunted sickly, bent over, and stepped across the body of the second *techutli* he had killed. The next shot thundered. Elgera saw Fayette jerk and bend farther forward with his hands outstretched now in a blind, groping way. As the third shot filled the room, Elgera ran to the side of the throne, reaching for something beneath her shirt.

Montezuma bent forward for the last shot. His face twisted as he squeezed the trigger on his Krider Derringer. It took Fayette squarely. With a terrible, animal scream of pain, Fayette threw himself forward,

249

his indomitable will carrying his heavy body two more stumbling paces to crash into Montezuma.

For a moment they struggled there, Fayette's head buried in Montezuma's chest, blocky hands clawing off the feathered robe. Montezuma took a step back and almost fell from the raised dais, trying to pull free. Fayette smashed him in the face. Montezuma took another step, striving desperately to tear the relentless man off. Then the Indian quit struggling and looked down at the head buried against his chest, and a strange look crossed his dark face. He reached up and pried Fayette's hand from around his neck as if he were releasing himself from something vile. The marks of the fingers showed white on his bronze skin. He pried Fayette's other hand off the smooth muscle of his shoulder. He took another step back, and let the dead man fall to the floor.

Chisos Owens came through the curtain of the front hall. "We got Abilene. Fayette . . ."

He stopped as he saw Fayette, and his eyes raised to Montezuma, and they widened as they saw *Señorita* Scorpion.

"This is a nopal thorn I have pressed against your back," the girl told Montezuma. "It's been soaked a year in the venom of a hundred diamondbacks. An old woman down by the Pecos gave it to me. She didn't think you were immortal. Make the wrong move, and we'll find out."

While he had been struggling with Fayette, Elgera had gotten around behind Montezuma. She stood with one hand caught in the golden belt around his

250

muscular middle, the other pressing the sharp point of the nopal thorn into his flesh. She felt the slow stiffening of his tremendous body.

"*Tlazteotl*," he hissed.

"What's that?" she said.

"*Tlazteotl*," Chisos Owens answered. "Queen of witches!"

CHAPTER
SEVEN

The Book of Fate was begun
In the sacred Temple of War.
It ends in the House of the Sun.
Read *Tonalamente* no more.

Small fires burned in stone braziers along the corridor, and their sibilant hiss haunted the ghostly passage, and the gleaming walls seemed to eddy and writhe with a thousand flickering serpents of garish, red-shadowed light thrown upon them by the flames. Chisos Owens led, glancing back over his shoulder with that confused look on his face. He was completely under Montezuma's domination, and he knew a wrong move from him would mean his lord's death. Elgera still walked behind the Indian, one hand in his belt, the other pressing the poison thorn against his back.

It was the same corridor into which Ortega had been taken by the two guards, and its gradual decline was leading them down into the bowels of the pyramid. Elgera spoke thinly. "This had better take us to Hagar."

"We are going to the sacred fire chamber," said Montezuma, having recovered some of his composure again. "The kiva. These temples were erected many centuries ago by a branch of the Aztecs who migrated this far north. I was born of Yaqui parents in the Sierra

Madres and discovered these ruins when I was a young man. I knew then that it didn't matter who my parents had been. In *Tonalamente*, it is decreed that Montezuma should be reincarnated and find his old gods in the ancient city north of Tenochtitlán, which you know as Mexico. You cannot desecrate those gods, *señorita*. You are a fool to try."

The corridor opened abruptly into a square room with a statue of Quetzalcoatl in the center. Lashed to the sacrificial altar of jasper at the idol's feet was Luis Ortega, writhing and panting, his face bathed in sweat. There was a guard on either side of him, and an old, bearded *nualli* in a long, black robe.

"*Tlatoani* Montezuma," quavered the ancient medicine man, bowing low, and then he seemed to see the strained expression on Montezuma's face, and how close Elgera stood to the Indian. A guard made a motion with his rifle.

"Tell them how it is," snapped Elgera. "Tell them to drop their hardware and go ahead of us."

Montezuma obeyed, and the guards slowly let their Henrys clatter to the floor, watching Montezuma with puzzled eyes. Ortega's babbling voice rose shrilly.

"*Señorita, en el nombre de Dios*, free me. They are going to sacrifice me to the Serpent God. They are going to cut my heart out with a *macapán*."

For a moment she was moved to pity. Then she remembered what Ortega was, and she realized, if she let go of Montezuma to cut the Spaniard loose, it would be her last mistake. Her face hardened. She shoved Montezuma on, the guards and the old man preceding them into the corridor on the other side.

"¡Madre de Dios!" screamed Ortega, writhing on the altar. "¡Señorita . . . cut me loose . . . señorita . . . Dios, Dios . . ."

His scream broke into a crazed sobbing, and then even that faded and died behind them, and the only sound was the serpentine hiss and snap of the small fires lighting the way. Finally, from ahead, Elgera heard the first dim, monotonous chanting.

"They are inculcating the unbeliever, Hagar, into peyote," said Montezuma hollowly. "In two days he will no longer doubt our gods. He will be a *techutli* as great as Quauhtl, and with two men like that I can rule the world if I choose."

They twisted and turned through the maze of corridors that honeycombed the great pyramid, the strange chanting becoming louder. Then, from ahead, Elgera saw the outline of yellow light around a curtained doorway. The guards before the portal bowed to Montezuma till their parrot plumes scraped the ochred floor.

"Tell them to go inside ahead of you," said Elgera. "And no slips."

She felt the magnificent muscles of his back tense against her knuckles as he took a breath before he spoke. The guards bowed again, sweeping aside the curtain. Chisos followed them in, then the bearded *nualli*. Elgera shoved Montezuma after them.

The first man she saw was Johnny Hagar, the manacles on his wrists and ankles attached to chains socketed in the floor, spread-eagling him on the cold cement. His only garment was the gilt-edged *maxtli*, clinging wet with perspiration to his flat belly and lean shanks. His dark eyes had a strange glaze, but there was recognition in them as he jerked his head to one side and saw her.

"Elgera!" he gasped.

"Oh," said one of the men who had been bending over him, and straightened. "Elgera."

"Don't do it, Lobos," snapped the girl. "You'll be killing Montezuma."

Lobos Delcazar stopped his dark fingers before they touched the ivory butts of Johnny Hagar's Peacemakers. The ceremonial drummers at one side of the room sat with their hands suspended over the skin *tombes*. Montezuma drew himself up, and his hands were around in front of him. Elgera tightened her grip on his golden belt.

"Unlock Hagar, Lobos," she said. "The rest of you move over to the wall. You, too, Chisos."

"Chisos?" said the big man. "I am Quauhtl."

The guards moved slowly to the wall, smoke from the blazing fires shredding across in front of them and hiding their tense faces for a moment. Lobos unlocked the manacles, and Hagar had trouble rising. He put his hand to his head and shook it dazedly. He almost fell when he reached out to unbuckle the cartridge belts of his Peacemakers from around Lobos's red sash. Elgera sensed the movement of Montezuma's hands, hidden from her in front of his body.

"What are you doing?" she snapped. "Stop it!"

The first shouts came from outside, and the sound of running feet. She had expected pursuit as soon as someone found their emperor gone from the audience chamber and all those dead guards there. She couldn't help the turn of her head toward the sound.

Montezuma took that moment to lunge away from her. She yanked backward on his belt, throwing her whole weight against it. She crashed on back to the wall, belt flapping free in her hands. The sudden release caused Montezuma to stagger forward and almost go on his face. He had unbuckled the belt.

One of the guards yelled and knocked the fire out of the brazier, throwing the small kiva into semidarkness. A *tombe* thumped hollowly as one of the drummers upset it, scrambling erect. Elgera had made Chisos give her his Bisley upstairs. She wrenched the .44 from her waistband, struggling away from the wall.

"Get out the door!" shouted Hagar.

His guns boomed, and someone screamed. The body must have fallen into the other brazier, for there was a hissing sound, and the room was plunged into intense darkness. The Peacemakers boomed again, and a man went through the door, taking the curtain with him, and fell in the corridor outside.

A man crashed into Elgera, and she struck viciously. He grunted and went down. Hagar's guns drowned the other sounds after that, racketing hideously. Then she was caught by the elbow, and the sheriff's voice was harsh in her ear.

"Out the door, I told you."

"Think I'd leave you?" she cried, and was carried across the body in the doorway by Hagar's rush. He yanked her down the corridor in the opposite direction from which she had come, for there were other guards running toward them down there. A man ran through the doorway, shouting. It was Montezuma. Hagar pulled her around a corner, and they were plunged into the darkness of an unlit corridor.

"Chisos," she panted. "We can't leave him."

"What could you do with him?" asked Hagar, running beside her. "He's filled with peyote. It's sort of a dope, like marijuana. Regular religion with the Indians for centuries. Takes about five days to get you completely. I've only had two days of it, but I'm in a daze already. Crazy with it. Feel like I'm drunk or swimming or something."

"How did they get you to take it in the first place? How did they get Chisos to take it?"

"Ramón Delcazar spent the night on Chisos's spread," said Hagar. "Must've mixed peyote beans in with his coffee, like they did with me. Can't tell the difference. I thought I was drinking coffee till it was too late. Devotees of the stuff eat the beans raw, like Lobos. In that fire chamber they force it down you in liquid form. Can't keep your mouth closed, tied down like that. They hold your nose so you have to drink it or choke to death."

"Isn't there any hope?" she said.

"For Chisos?" he panted. "Yeah. If we could get to him, there would be. The effect of the beans eaten raw is milder and lasts only a few hours. But these *nualli*

257

mix something they call *teopatl* in with the liquid peyote, made from the roots of *vinigrilla* or something. Takes a man's soul, Elgera. Robs him of any will of his own. Makes him forget everything. It lasts about a month. At the end of that time they have to take him back to the kiva and dope him up again for five days. Chisos has been out about a month, from what Lobos told me. He must be about ready to come out of the haze. If we could only get him to recognize us, to remember who he really is . . ."

They must have been running through a section of the pyramid not yet rebuilt by Montezuma's slaves. The corridor was littered with rubble, and Elgera kept stumbling in the utter darkness. From behind, the shouts and other sounds of pursuit drowned her gasp as she tripped over a rock and fell flat. She could hear Hagar, running on ahead. Then he stopped, and his voice sounded muffled.

"Elgera?"

"Here," she said, standing up and groping her way down the wall. She reached a corner. *Was that why his voice had sounded muffled?* Light glowed dimly behind her as the first man appeared, carrying a torch. Behind him were others, stumbling and tripping across the débris.

"Elgera!" called Hagar sharply.

It seemed to come from ahead. She fumbled around the corner, and it was dark again, and she ran forward, feeling her way. She was quite far down this corridor when she saw the man with the torch pass its end and go on down the other corridor, and the others followed him. The silence that fell after they went by struck at her ominously. She drew a sharp breath to call.

"Hagar?"

There was no answer. She went back the way she had come, and turned out into the other corridor in the pitch blackness. Driven by a growing panic that she couldn't suppress, she began to run, and the sound of her footsteps rolled ahead of her and came back multiplied, and engulfed her with a thousand sibilant echoes, like the hollow shackles of some malignant giant.

She ran blindly through a maze of corridors, stumbling, falling, hesitant to call Hagar now for fear the others would hear her, Bisley clutched in a palm sticky with cold sweat. Then she began to see faint light from ahead, and finally burst through one of the silver-embroidered curtains into a square room where a man lay bound on a block of jasper in front of the idol of Quetzalcoatl.

"*Señorita*," moaned Luis Ortega weakly. "Please. I beg of you. Mercy. Cut me loose."

She sagged against the wall, brushing damp hair back off her forehead, unable to believe she had found her way back here. Then, still gasping from the run, she tore the *macapán* out of the idol's hand and sawed the rawhide lashings binding Ortega. He rolled off and lay on the floor a moment, panting. His gold-handled cane and blue cape were beside the statue. He got to his hands and knees and crawled to them, mumbling, then he rose and turned toward Elgera, eyes furtive.

"I know who you are now," he panted. "*Sí. Señorita* Douglas. Montezuma didn't realize what he was doing when he crossed your trail, did he? *Pues*, neither did I. But it was I who helped you. Remember? *Sí*, twice I helped you. I will help you again, *señorita*, and this time I won't ask a *peso* for my services. You can have them *gratis*."

He began to rub his forefinger with his thumb, and came on toward her, his voice growing stronger, more oily. She took a step backward, watching his face.

"There are secret doors leading out onto each terrace," he said. "*Sí*, we will not have to go back through the throne room. I think we're about finished here anyway, eh? It was a loco idea of Montezuma's. I don't think he could have ruled *Tejas*, even with Chisos Owens. There will be other empires to rule. We could do a lot together, you and I . . ."

She took another step back, and tripped on the altar. While she was off balance like that, she saw him whip the blade from his cane, and lunge.

"*¡Degüello!*" He screamed Santa Anna's cry of no quarter.

She threw herself backward over the altar. Ortega's blade flashed through the soft collar of her shirt. She twisted as she fell, catching the sword for that moment. As she struggled to rise, Ortega lunged away, trying to tear his steel free. She gained her hands and knees and threw herself at him from there. Her weight carried him back against the far wall. She heard the blade tear from her shirt.

"*Bruja*," gasped Ortega, whipping the sword free.

She caught the blade in her bare hands, twisting it sideways away from her as he struck. It went past her body, and he tried to pull it back again. Steel sliced through her fingers with searing pain, covering them with blood. Ortega's whiplash body was like a writhing snake beneath her.

She rose on one knee and came down with her other in his belly. He gasped and collapsed back against the stone, face twisted. She caught the sword again. His grip on it was relaxed for that moment, and she tore it free, twisting it to grasp the gold-encrusted hilt in a bloody fist. She was straddling him with the sword turned, when he gathered himself and lunged blindly up beneath her. She didn't even see the blade go in. She only heard him gasp.

"*Madre de Dios . . .*"

He sagged back against the lime-coated stones. She let go of the sword and rose, looking blankly down at the dead man. Suddenly she turned and picked up the gun she had dropped and ran across the room to the hall leading above. Secret doors? How could she find them? She burst through a curtained aperture into the next corridor, running on an upward slant. Her movements were sluggish and painful. She was breathing in short, agonizing gasps. She stumbled through another curtained doorway and came abruptly to a halt, realizing too late that it had led her into the throne room.

Guards were running back and forth across the great hall, and two slaves were carrying one of the men Fayette had shot out the door on the other side. A squad of *techutlis* was drawn up in front of the dais, and half a dozen robed old men were fluttering around Montezuma. He was giving an order to a runner and, from the height of his throne, was the first to see Elgera. He stood up suddenly, and the direction of his glance caused the others to look that way. Chisos Owens turned toward Elgera where he stood at one side of the dais.

"It is the woman, Quauhtl!" thundered Montezuma. "Kill her!"

Johnny Hagar's hands were bleeding from feeling his way along the jagged, broken surface of the walls. He didn't know how long ago he had lost Elgera. Now he was lost. He had reached a dead end. He stumbled over the rubble-strewn floor, trying to find the corner of the hall to get his bearings. His breathing sounded harsh in the eerie silence. His feet made small, scraping sounds across the stone.

Once he felt himself swaying and knew that it was the peyote in him, and another time he was startled by his own drunken giggle. Then his bloody fingers slipped into a deep crack above his head.

"*¿Cuánto nos venderá?*" said someone in Spanish, and it sounded as if it came from the wall itself.

Suddenly the stone heaved outward, throwing him backward, and the next voice burst on him loud and clear: "Shut your mouth, or I'll show you what he will pay us. If we don't find them, Montezuma will have our heads."

The man stopped, and stood there in the opening left by the huge rock that had swung inward on a pivot.

He was silhouetted by the smoky red light of a torch held by a *techutli* behind him. Hagar had been smashed back against the opposite wall and was too dazed to go for his guns in that first moment when there might have been a chance, and now he didn't go for them, because he saw how it was.

"Hello, Ramón," he said, and took a step away from the wall to get his elbows free for when it came. "I guess having your spread wiped out didn't hit you as hard as it might. Or did you burn it yourself to make everything look right?"

Ramón Delcazar had changed his white pants and shirt for a feathered cloak, but he still packed his black-butted .45s belted around his gilt-edged *maxtli*, and he shoved the cloak back, and kept his hands far enough above his guns, because he saw how it was, too.

"*Sí*," he said, moving carefully in through the door. "I burned my spread. It would have looked funny if mine was spared when all the others were raided, wouldn't it?"

"Give me some elbow room, cousin," said Lobos Delcazar, and swaggered in behind Ramón. He, too, saw that whoever made the first move now would start the thing, and he kept the curl of his fingers off the gold-chased butt of the Colt he had strapped back on. "It looks like I'll get those Peacemakers, after all."

"We'll toss for them," said Ramón.

The *techutli* behind Lobos stuck his torch into a brazier on the wall. There were two others following him, carrying Henrys, but up to now the two cousins had filled the narrow doorway and blocked Hagar off from the guards, and the *techutlis* were waiting for them to start it.

The echoes of Ramón's words diminished down the corridor and died reluctantly, and then the only sound was the harsh scrape of feet across the stone and the almost inaudible sibilance of the men's breathing. The scrape of feet stopped, and it was only the breathing, and then Hagar took a last breath and held it, and Lobos did the same, the way an experienced gunman will when he senses the moment at hand. Ramón and the utter silence held them all there for that last instant with the red light flickering across their strained faces and catching the waiting glitter of their eyes.

"*¡Carape!*" shouted Lobos, and started it.

Hagar was still grinning when his guns bellowed. Lobos staggered backward, and his Colt went off at the roof, and the *techutlis* jumped away from his body as it fell in their midst. Ramón spun up against the wall with a scream, dropping one of his .45s, desperately trying to throw down with the other one to hit Hagar as his hammer dropped.

The *techutlis* burst through the door over Lobos's body, Henrys bellowing. With the first .56 slug knocking him backward, Hagar thumbed out two more shots. Ramón grunted, dropped his other gun, and doubled over. A guard stumbled and went to his knees, and then on his face, sliding almost to Hagar's feet before he stopped.

"Come on, you damned *borrachónes!*" brayed Hagar, laughing crazily. "Come on, come on, come on . . ."

264

Drunk on peyote, inflamed with the roar of battle, he swayed there in that last moment, screaming at them, Peacemakers filling the hall with an unearthly racket as they bucked up and down in his bloody hands. The last two *techutlis* threw themselves on him with demented howls, shooting their Henrys from the waist. Hagar thumbed his right-hand gun, and then his left, and saw one man jerk to both bullets. Then another Henry slug caught the sheriff, and the man he had shot came hurtling into him, and Hagar crashed to the floor beneath the body.

He struck the stones with his right-hand gun pinned between his belly and the *techutli*'s. He tore his left-hand weapon free, firing at the last man from where he lay on his back beneath the dying *techutli*. It was all a haze, a twisted, screaming face, the stabbing flame of a levered Henry blinding him, the rocking bellow of his own Peacemaker deafening him, and the jarring pain of Henry lead tearing through the body above him and driving down into his own.

"*Kill her!*" The order still rang in Chisos Owens's ears. He stood there, looking at the girl, aware that the throne room had become silent, that all the *techutlis* were waiting for him to carry out Montezuma's order. But there was something in the girl's eyes. She held out her hand.

"Chisos," she said faintly. "Chisos . . ."

"Quauhtl!" roared Montezuma. "I command you. Kill her!"

Chisos? She kept calling him that. He couldn't take his eyes away from hers. They were deep blue, and he seemed to be sinking into them, and suddenly he could remember the other name. *Chisos Owens.* With that single memory, others began to come, crowding in, flooding his brain. Names he had tried to recall without success, people he had remembered only as nebulous entities that would never quite come through the fog of peyote. *Alpine. Johnny Hagar. Ramón Delcazar. The Santiago. Señorita Scorpion. Yes, Elgera Douglas.* He had loved her. Why did this girl bring back those memories? And what was he doing here in this great hall, with all these strange men in feathered cloaks around him, and that wild-eyed loco standing on some kind of a throne? *Elgera Douglas?*

"Quauhtl," thundered Montezuma. "I command you . . ."

With an animal roar of rage, Chisos Owens whirled and threw himself toward the throne. The surprised guards didn't try to stop him till he was almost there. He crashed through their ranks like a bull through bee brush.

Without stopping or slowing down or even seeming to see the men who had tried to get in his way, he caught the first one's rifle and, using it as a lever, spun him away into the others. He smashed through two more farther on, knocking them to either side. He caught a fourth with a backhand swing that sent him rolling across the floor.

266

Elgera Douglas? He had loved her. And this Montezuma had sent him out to kill her. He remembered it now.

"Quauhtl . . ."

Chisos crashed into Montezuma before he had finished shouting, huge frame knocking the Indian off the throne. They struck the floor, rolling over and over like a pair of fighting cats. Montezuma got his hands and knees beneath him finally, and tried to rise.

Chisos slugged him behind the neck with a blow that would have killed another man. Montezuma quivered, set himself, and heaved upward. Chisos struck him again, riding his gigantic torso. Montezuma took that one, too, and kept on rising, the muscles in his legs standing out in great, trembling ridges. He shot one of his legs out suddenly, catching Chisos behind the knees.

Chisos staggered backward to keep from falling. He hung onto Montezuma, and the two of them went stumbling and lurching out through the doorway that led to the terrace, both trying vainly to keep erect. Chisos's feathered robe caught on the angle of the opening, and it was torn from his great shoulders. Then they went down again, and rolled on across the terrace, fighting, grunting, slugging. Chisos sensed they were coming to the edge, and sprawled out to stop their momentum.

There was a terrible, animal vitality in Montezuma's writhing, swelling, surging body. Chisos got one arm hooked around the Indian's neck and struck him again and again, and any one of those blows might have

267

finished it, but Montezuma's huge frame shook to each one, and he grunted sickly while he grimly fought to rise again.

Suddenly he shifted his weight and caught Chisos's wrist. Levered away from the man, Chisos couldn't hang on with his other arm around Montezuma's neck. The Indian released the arm and jumped up and backward. Chisos rolled like a cat, and was on his feet when the Indian threw himself in again.

The two men met with a fleshy slapping sound there on the very edge of the terrace, bathed in the blood-red light of the late-afternoon sun. Montezuma's magnificent torso was wet with perspiration, and the straining muscles writhed beneath the smooth, bronze skin like fat snakes. Raging with peyote, Chisos fought like some savage animal, snarling and roaring, great calves knotting and rippling as he braced his feet widely on the ochred stone. They were locked inextricably together on the edge of the terrace, and a single wrong move from either man would have sent them hurtling over the edge. It was a contest of sheer brute strength, with each man straining desperately to turn the other one outward and force him off. Finally Montezuma brought his greater height and weight to bear, levering Chisos around with his back to the empty space that reeled beneath them. Chisos could hear the strange sigh that rose from the multitude of slaves and workers gathered in the courtyard below.

Slowly, inexorably Montezuma was forcing him to yield, bending him outward, backward, downward. The Indian's right arm was locked around the small of

Chisos's back, and his other hand was in Chisos's face, shoving relentlessly. Chisos had his forearm around Montezuma's neck, and he could feel the man's muscles swell and bulge, and his grip there was gradually slipping. His ribs began to make popping sounds. Stabbing pain shot through his chest. He was bent like a bow, and the only thing that held him from falling was his arm around Montezuma's neck. He could feel his wrist slipping across the slippery skin. Then, from far away, he heard the girl's call.

"Chisos! Chisos!"

He drew in a great, last, desperate breath. His lips flattened against his teeth stained black with cochineal. The muscles across his tremendous shoulders humped into a bulging, obstinate line. Montezuma gasped hotly in his face, trying to force him on down. Face twisting with the effort, Chisos Owens began to straighten again.

Montezuma braced his feet anew and gripped Chisos tighter, trying to stop him. He threw his weight against Chisos. He strained to halt that huge, straightening frame. Chisos came on up.

In final desperation, Montezuma shifted his feet farther back for more leverage. With the Indian's right foot sliding back, Chisos surged on up and twisted sharply in Montezuma's grasp. He caught the Indian's arm and slipped under it, his chest slamming into Montezuma's hip. The Indian tried to throw his weight over onto Chisos. It put him off balance. With his own legs in front of Montezuma and the bulk of his torso bent down to one side, Chisos heaved. The Indian

269

screamed as he went up and out and down, down, down.

Chisos fell to his hands and knees to keep from following Montezuma. Gasping and quivering there, he saw what had held the *techutlis* in a little knot just outside the door. Hagar must have found his way up from below. He sat against the wall, holding both guns in his lap, his face set in a bloody, grinning mask. Still on his hands and knees, Chisos turned to look over the edge.

A guard on the next level had run to the sprawled body of Montezuma. Another came up, and they turned Montezuma over. One of them looked upward.

"*Es muerto,*" he said. "He is dead."

Supporting the wounded Hagar between them, Chisos and Elgera moved through the great, silent audience chamber, down the corridor, out onto the terrace, and down the steps. Abilene had taken these front stairs up, while Fayette had taken the rear. On the stairs between the third and fourth levels, they passed Abilene. He lay across the body of a guard he had killed. His Beale-Remington was gripped in one supple hand. A cigarette was in the other.

At each following level on the way down, two guards lay dead where Abilene had passed, going up. Elgera and Chisos half carried Hagar through the silent, stunned crowd, still staring, wide-eyed, up to that ledge where Montezuma lay. The whole incredible edifice of the cult had been built on the premise that Montezuma himself was invincible and immortal. His death utterly smashed that edifice. As if they were ghosts, Elgera and the two men moved out of the city. Once in a while someone turned to look blankly at them, and his mouth moved in some soundless word, and he turned back to look at the House of the Sun.

Elgera was watching Chisos intently. He kept shaking his head, blinking his eyes.

"All those ranches I raided," he said, "all those people I fought. They were my friends. I tried to kill you. I burned your Santiago and ran off your herds. I . . ."

"No," she almost sobbed. "You didn't know what you were doing. You weren't responsible. Don't you think your friends will forgive you? I forgave you a long time ago."

"As for your real friends, Elgera's right," gasped Hagar, "they'll forgive anything you did, Chisos."

The Indian guards still accepted Chisos as Quauhtl, their war lord, and got three horses at his order. The three remained there a moment, looking back through Tlaloc's Door to the doomed city.

"With Montezuma dead, they'll all drift back to their own tribes," said Chisos dully. "It's hard to think that's all finished. Seems like I never knew any other life."

They had to help Hagar onto his horse, but he was grinning, and he looked at Elgera when he spoke. "Yeah, that's finished. But there are other things. I'm going to buy me a new, white Stetson and a pair of Mexican spurs with wheels as big as the wheels on a Murphy wagon, and the first Saturday night after we get back, Elgera, you'll find me on your doorstep, a-courting."

Chisos looked up, and it was the first time since Elgera had found him here that *Señorita* Scorpion had seen him grin.

"You're wrong, Hagar," he said. "She'll find *us* on her doorstep, a-courting."

ABOUT THE AUTHOR

Les Savage, Jr. was born in Alhambra, California and grew up in Los Angeles. His first published story was "Bullets and Bullwhips" accepted by the prestigious magazine, Street & Smith's *Western Story*. Almost ninety more magazine stories followed, all set on the American frontier, many of them published in Fiction House magazines such as *Frontier Stories* and *Lariat Story Magazine* where Savage became a superstar with his name on many covers. His first novel, *Treasure of the Brasada*, appeared from Simon & Schuster in 1947. Due to his preference for historical accuracy, Savage often ran into problems with book editors in the 1950s who were concerned about marriages between his protagonists and women of different races — a commonplace on the real frontier but not in much Western fiction in that decade. Savage died young, at thirty-five, from complications arising out of hereditary diabetes and elevated cholesterol. However, as a result of the censorship imposed on many of his works, only now are they being fully restored by returning to the author's original manuscripts. Among Savage's finest Western stories are *Fire Dance at Spider Rock* (Five Star Westerns, 1995), *Medicine Wheel* (Five Star

Westerns, 1996), *Coffin Gap* (Five Star Westerns, 1997), *Phantoms in the Night* (Five Star Westerns, 1998), *The Bloody Quarter* (Five Star Westerns, 1999), *In The Land of Little Sticks* (Five Star Westerns, 2000), *The Cavan Breed* (Five Star Westerns, 2001), and *Danger Rides the River* (Five Star Westerns, 2002). Much as Stephen Crane before him, while he wrote, the shadow of his imminent death grew longer and longer across his young life, and he knew that, if he was going to do it at all, he would have to do it quickly. He did it well, and, now that his novels and stories are being restored to what he had intended them to be, his achievement irradiated by his powerful and profoundly sensitive imagination will be with us always, as he had wanted it to be, as he had so rushed against time and mortality that it might be.